CHARLIE AND THE CHRISTMAS FACTORY

AND OTHER STORIES

PUFFIN

PUFFIN BOOKS

UK | USA | Canada | Ireland | Australia
India | New Zealand | South Africa

Puffin Books is part of the Penguin Random House group of companies
whose addresses can be found at global.penguinrandomhouse.com.

www.penguin.co.uk www.puffin.co.uk www.ladybird.co.uk

Penguin Random House UK

First published 2024
001

Illustrations by Rikin Parekh

Printed in Great Britain by Clays Ltd, Elcograf S.p.A.

The authorized representative in the EEA is Penguin Random House Ireland,
Morrison Chambers, 32 Nassau Street, Dublin D02 YH68

A CIP catalogue record for this book is available from the British Library

ISBN: HB 978-0-241-61877-6
ISBN: TPB 978-0-241-61878-3

All correspondence to:
Puffin Books
Penguin Random House Children's
One Embassy Gardens, 8 Viaduct Gardens, London SW11 7BW

MIX
Paper | Supporting responsible forestry
FSC www.fsc.org FSC® C018179

Penguin Random House is committed to a sustainable future for our business, our readers and our planet. This book is made from Forest Stewardship Council® certified paper.

About the Authors

Adam Hills is an internationally recognized comedian and host of award-winning Channel 4 show *The Last Leg*. His collection of stories from a life in comedy, *Best Foot Forward*, was a *The Times* bestseller. He is also the author of the hilarious children's book series Rockstar Detectives.

Adam Kay is an award-winning writer and non-award-winning doctor. He has sold over five million books in 37 languages, including one million children's books, making him one of the UK's bestselling children's authors. He lives in Oxfordshire with his dog, husband, two children and beloved BAFTA.

Ben Bailey Smith is a British actor, rapper, comedian and screenwriter, and creator of the BAFTA-winning CBBC comedy *4 O'Clock Club*. His first children's picture book, *I Am Bear*, was an instant hit with critics and readers alike, and he has since written two early-reader favourites for Bloomsbury, *Get A Move On!* and *Crumbs!* His middle-grade debut, *Something I Said*, published in 2021.

Elle McNicoll is a bestselling and award-winning novelist and screenwriter. Her debut, *A Kind of Spark*, won the Blue Peter Book Award and the Overall Waterstones Children's Book Prize, and she has been nominated four times for the Carnegie Medal for Writing. She is an advocate for better representation of neurodiversity in publishing, and currently lives in North London.

Greg James and Chris Smith are the multi-award-winning and bestselling authors of *The Great Dream Robbery*, *Super Ghost*, *The Twits Next Door* and the Kid Normal series. Outside of their writing partnership, Greg James is a radio and television broadcaster, and Chris Smith a solo author of acclaimed children's books *Frankie Best Hates Quests* and *Clarity Jones and the Magical Detective Agency.*

Hannah Gold is the multi-award-winning author of the internationally bestselling *The Last Bear*, *The Lost Whale*, *Finding Bear* and *Turtle Moon*. She grew up in a family where books, animals and the beauty of the outside world were ever present, and is passionate about writing stories that share her love of the planet. She lives in the UK and is an ambassador for Whale and Dolphin Conservation.

Konnie Huq is a well-loved broadcaster, writer and speaker, who was a familiar face for over a decade as the longest-serving female presenter on legendary children's TV programme *Blue Peter*. She is also a King's Trust and British Asian Trust ambassador. Konnie became a bestselling children's author after releasing *Cookie and the Most Annoying Boy in the World*.

Nadia Shireen is a bestselling children's author and illustrator. As well as the hugely successful Grimwood series, she has also created several picture books, including *Barbara Throws a Wobbler*, *The Bumblebear* and *Billy and the Beast*.

She co-hosts children's book podcast *The Island of Brilliant* alongside Children's Laureate Frank Cottrell-Boyce. Nadia has been shortlisted for several awards, including the Roald Dahl Funny Prize, Brandford Boase Award, The Lollies and the Waterstones Children's Book Prize. She lives in Brighton.

Nathan Bryon is an actor, a BAFTA nominated screenwriter and a *Sunday Times* bestselling author, who grew up eating as much Uxbridge Road Caribbean food as his bank balance would allow. His first picture book, *Look Up!*, was the number one picture book from a debut author and illustrator in 2019, and won the Overall Waterstones Children's book prize in 2020.

Pamela Butchart is a teacher and the writer of many award-winning books, including *The Spy Who Loved School Dinners* and *My Head Teacher is a Vampire Rat*. She is also author of the bestselling picture books *Never Tickle a Tiger*, *Yikes, Stinkysaurus!* and the hugely successful Baby Aliens series.

Sally Rippin is the Australian Children's Laureate for 2024–2025 and has written over a hundred books for children and young adults, many of them award-winning. Sally loves to write stories with heart and characters that resonate with children, parents and teachers alike.

Sibéal Pounder is the number one *New York Times* bestselling author of the much-loved children's fiction series Witch Wars, the Bad Mermaids series, *Neon's Secret Universe*, and the Christmas hit *Tinsel*. She has also written *Beyond Platform 13*, the sequel to *The Secret of Platform 13* by Eva Ibbotson, and the novelization of the film *Wonka*. Her World Book Day book, *Bad Mermaids Meet the Witches*, was a *Sunday Times* bestseller, and her debut, *Witch Wars*, was shortlisted for the Waterstones Children's Book Prize and the Sainsbury's Children's Book Award.

CONTENTS

Sibéal Pounder

In the early hours of Christmas morning, a girl arrived at the gates of Mr Willy Wonka's Chocolate Factory.

A purple girl.

She had a purple forehead and a purple nose and purple cheeks and a purple neck. When she removed her woolly gloves it was plain to see that there was not an inch of her that wasn't purple – every finger was purple, even her nails. She gripped the icy gate so tightly that the deep dark purple on her knuckles drained to violet.

At her feet sat a large wriggling sack.

Inside the factory, while everyone else was still asleep, Charlie Bucket was busy preparing for **CHRISTMAS DAY.**

He had transformed the grand Chocolate Room overnight – its edible grass was now covered in sparkling white chocolate that **CRUNCHED** underfoot like crisp snow. Candy baubles hung from yule-log trees made of scrumptious chocolate sponge and the whippiest whipped cream. Gingerbread men sprouted from flowers painted in red, green and gold along pathways paved with warm mince pies. A cinnamon mist filled the air, making the whole place smell **DELICIOUSLY** festive, while on the bubbling chocolate river, Mr Wonka's pink boiled-sweet of a boat was decorated with twinkling edible tinsel.

Charlie eyed the tinsel hungrily – especially the bits trailing in the melted chocolate. But he had promised himself he wouldn't eat a thing.

Not until the children arrived.

Because this year, Christmas Day would include three very special guests: the lucky winners of three foil tickets striped in red, green and gold. For the first time, Charlie Bucket was opening up his factory for a day, just like Mr Wonka had done years before. It was all anyone in the world was talking about.

Charlie had been so busy since Mr Wonka retired that he hadn't had time to invite anyone into the factory. Everyone knew special things were happening inside, of course, from the loud **CLANGS** and **BANGS** and strange-coloured smoke rising from the chimneys. Some new products had been filtering into the shops, like the best-selling, tongue-tingling, impossibly gloopy, Charlie's Chocolate Toothpaste. It was exactly what it sounds like – toothpaste made of chocolate. It cleaned teeth better than actual toothpaste, so no adult could object. Children up and down the country had smiles so bright, teachers were resorting to wearing sunglasses, and dentists were going out of business. So, with such fun new additions to the Wonka chocolate line, it stood to reason that what was *inside* the factory, the things yet to be seen or tasted, were going to be very special indeed. Charlie was determined to live up to the rumours and to give the three winners an unforgettable day, just like the one he'd had. All he hoped was that they'd be nice children, not children like Veruca or Mike or Vi–

'VIOLET!' came a shout, and Mr Willy Wonka clattered into the room, wearing a dressing gown made of purple velvet – just like his signature coat. Although he was older now, his eyes were as bright and as sparkly as ever.

'Violet Beauregarde is at the gates!' He turned to an Oompa-Loompa and said, 'Still *very* purple.'

(Years ago, when Mr Wonka's finest gum creation was in its development stage, Violet had chewed it and turned purple. Permanently, it now seemed.)

The Oompa-Loompa studiously whipped out a clipboard and made a note under the NOVELTY GUM LONG-TERM SIDE EFFECTS section.

Charlie stood frozen to the spot, unable to believe what he was hearing. It was – he checked his watch – six o'clock in the morning! What could Violet Beauregarde want? He hadn't seen her in years, not since they'd both found **GOLDEN TICKETS** in their chocolate bars and been among the first children to see inside Mr Wonka's factory. He charged down the hall, tightening his dressing-gown belt as he went. Mr Wonka galloped behind him, his gold-topped cane rapidly striking the ground as he tried to keep up.

'What do you think she wants, dear boy?' he asked Charlie.

'I have no idea,' Charlie said as he unbolted the door and stepped out into the cold. Through the flurry of snow he could see Violet standing there, in all her purple glory – and at once, every second of his first trip to the factory came flooding back. A huge grin spread across his face.

'Well, hurry up and open up! It's an emergency!' Violet shouted.

Charlie glanced up at a lit window at the very top of the factory and gave a nod. There was a click and a little whirr, and the gate swung open.

As soon as it did, he could see the squirming sack at Violet's feet.

'It's a long story, Charlie,' she said, her words squished between the gum she was chewing. She began dragging the sack towards him, struggling to move it more than an inch at a time.

'What's in –' Charlie began.

'LET ME WALK AT LEAST!' came a shout from inside the sack.

Violet stopped and sighed, and then began to untie the strings.

'Violet . . .' Charlie said slowly. 'Who's in there?'

Mr Wonka stood behind the door, shielded from view. He rarely stepped outside the factory – it was a long-standing habit. 'What's happening?' he whispered. but Charlie couldn't hear him through the whistle of the icy wind.

'So, I wanted to prove he was real,' Violet said as she struggled with the strings.

Charlie's stomach lurched. It couldn't be. She couldn't have . . .

'I chewed *a lot* of Wonka gum over the last year,' Violet explained. 'Enough to line a chimney.'

'Oh no,' Charlie whimpered.

'Charlie, my boy, what is she saying?' Mr Wonka hissed, but Charlie still didn't hear him.

'Got jaw cramp and everything from all the chewing,' Violet went on. 'Lined every inch of the flue, then he came down and –'

'Oh no!' Charlie cried.

'Exactly. But it gets worse,' Violet said.

'Worse?!' Charlie said.

'Is this about the purpling?' Mr Wonka pressed.

'I didn't realize I'd caught him, for a while,' she said. 'And he was there for hours before I checked . . . Um, how many hours was it?' She looked down at the wriggling sack, just as a bearded old man popped out.

'Four hours!' he cried indignantly, rising to his feet.

'Four whole hours,' Violet confirmed with a nod. 'Enough to throw the whole present-delivery timings out of whack. Plus, in those four hours, the reindeer flew off with the sleigh and all the presents.'

Charlie stood in shocked silence, feeling as SMALL as a speck at the feet of the great man himself. He was exactly how Charlie had imagined him: PUFFED up with pure magic, with his shiny red suit, glossy white beard and big black boots shedding soot on to the snow. The chewing gum stuck all over him and the furious face were, however, a bit of a surprise.

'Anyway, to cut a long story short,' Violet continued, 'he said Christmas could be saved if I brought him to his old friend – the only person in the world who might be able to help.'

'Kringle, you old chimney sweep!' came a delighted shout, and Charlie turned to see Mr Wonka standing in the doorway, gesturing for Santa to come inside.

Violet leaned into Charlie and whispered, 'Apparently they go way back.'

❄

Charlie watched, unable to believe his eyes, as Mr Wonka and Santa Claus sat sipping mugs of melted chocolate by the chocolate river. They were deep in conversation, their faces serious.

He supposed it made sense that they would know each other. Maybe everyone who made the world **MAGICAL** for children knew each other. Perhaps there was a club.

He glanced at Violet and saw she was watching the pair of them too. Charlie knew she must be thinking the same thing he was: how magical and impossible the whole thing seemed.

Charlie checked his watch. It was almost seven o'clock! The competition winners would be arriving at any second.

'That's settled then!' Charlie heard Mr Wonka say. 'I'll take my glass elevator and track down the reindeer and presents. There's still time to save Christmas. And I know just the thing to get that gum out of your beard. Or that beard out of my gum! You sit back and relax, put your feet up and enjoy the chocolate.'

'Actually,' Charlie said nervously, 'that might not be possible. You see, we have three children arriving soon to tour the factory.'

'Oh, well,' Santa said, 'in that case, I should probably hide!'

'We'll hide you deep in the factory,' Mr Wonka said, as two Oompa-Loompas appeared at Santa's side and grabbed an arm each. 'They'll escort you to somewhere suitably secret . . . and delicious.'

Charlie breathed a sigh of relief. But it was short-lived, because almost immediately he felt a tremble underfoot. He watched, confused, as baubles fell from the trees and gingerbread men flopped face first into the snow. The whole place was shaking now!

Charlie's parents appeared in the doorway, and his grandparents too.

'Charlie,' Grandpa Joe said. 'What is that rumbling?'

'My false teeth are jumping!' Grandma Georgina cried.

Charlie looked to the Oompa-Loompas for an answer, but they seemed as confused as everyone else.

The rumbling grew stronger, so strong that the

chocolate river began to quiver like jelly.

'Hold on to your hats!' Mr Wonka cried. 'Because if the whole place blows . . . we'll at least save our hats!'

'If it blows?!' Charlie cried, his voice barely rising above the deafening sound around them.

The thought of an explosion was enough to send Santa into a panic. 'It's Christmas Day!' he roared. 'I can't *die* on *Christmas Day*!' And with that, he dived face first into the chocolate river.

'Santa's in the soup!' Grandpa Joe cried as Santa sank from sight.

'Oh . . .' Mr Wonka said, pausing to consider what had happened. 'Normally I'd be furious about someone tainting the chocolate river, but a nice dash of Santa's magic might actually do it some good. And the children will never see him in there, which is a neat solution, don't you agree, Charlie?'

But before Charlie could answer, an almighty **CRASH** sounded from the ceiling.

Everyone looked up.

There came a peculiar scraping and scratching sound

and soon tiny chunks of roof were pouring down on them like hailstones.

'I thought this was meant to be the best chocolate factory in the world!' Violet scoffed. 'Look at the state of that roof.'

Charlie ducked under a tree for shelter and watched with amazement as the little holes that had appeared in the roof were filled again . . . by minuscule boots. One pair, then two, then thousands of them, with bells on their curled toes.

'This isn't one of your new inventions, is it?' Violet groaned.

'No,' Charlie whispered, just as the boots popped through the roof. But they weren't just boots – they were attached to little **CREATURES,** hundreds of them, who were now dropping down into the factory.

'Those are ELVES!' Violet cried in amazement.

'Yes, we are elves!' one of them

squeaked. 'Fearsome ones, here to save Santa!'

'We've got candy canes and we're not afraid to use them!' said another.

'Mind the perfect chocolate-snow floor!' Charlie winced as he darted about trying to catch them before they hit the ground. But it was no good. Elf after elf landed with a thud and a puff of powdery white chocolate and soon the whole room was engulfed in white-chocolatey smoke.

Charlie coughed his way towards the clump of elves gathering in the middle of the room. When the smoke finally cleared, he took a proper look at them.

Their hair was red, their clothes green. Their tights were striped like candy canes.

He couldn't believe it.

'Welcome, elves!' Mr Wonka said, his arms open wide in greeting. 'Let me first assure you, Santa is safe and well.'

'Then where is he?' an elf demanded.

An awkward silence fell.

'He's gone for a quick swim,' Charlie said tentatively. 'In the, um, chocolate river.'

All eyes shifted to the bubbling river.

'We'll fish him out and he'll be as good as new,' Mr Wonka said casually. 'Better than new actually, because he will be very chocolatey.'

The elves huddled together and descended into a chattering frenzy. Charlie checked his watch. Lovely as it was to have the existence of elves confirmed, he didn't have time for this.

'We heard a rumour that he ended up here against his will, that *someone* captured him,' an elf said, breaking from the group and marching towards Charlie. 'So who did it? We heard it might've been done with some gum?'

'*Some gum?*' Violet scoffed. 'The *best* gum. And not just some, *a lot* of it. Probably record-breaking amounts, actually.'

At that, the elves all raised their candy canes.

'There's no need to get upset. Please, let me get you

some chocolate,' Charlie said, flashing them a big smile. 'And we can discuss –'

BONG! . . . *BONG!*

'Charlie!' Grandpa Joe cried. 'It's seven o'clock! The competition winners are here!'

❄

Felicity Custard had been the first person to find a Red, Green and Gold Ticket, hidden inside the wrapper of the very first Wonka chocolate bar she'd bought. She had always been incredibly **LUCKY** – and if there was something to be won by chance, then she would always win it. It did make life a bit boring sometimes, though. It was hard to appreciate things when they fell into your lap. So she stood outside the gates with a somewhat sullen expression, wearing a large headband covered in Brussels sprouts (a vegetable she had been lucky enough never to have to eat). Her mother stood at her side, eyeing the factory nervously. Although her daughter was very lucky, the factory was notorious – she'd heard those stories about the purple girl.

'I wonder what the twist will be?' said the boy standing next to them. He was Jim Roarman, the second child to find a Red, Green and Gold Ticket. He had wild wiry hair and wore an unseasonable pair of sunglasses. He'd found his ticket by inventing the special specs, which could see through the outer wrapper of any chocolate bar. After that, finding a ticket was a simple matter of travelling round the world and visiting every shop that sold Wonka bars until he found a winning one. With his gran's help, he'd found one after a mere two weeks of searching. His gran stood proudly next to him now, her matching glasses dangling precariously on the tip of her spindly nose.

'What do you mean, *the twist*?' Felicity Custard asked, fixing Jim with a bemused stare. 'And why are you wearing sunglasses?'

'These are actually Wonka Bar Imaging Glasses,' he said proudly. 'Last time they hid Golden Tickets in Wonka bars, a scientist called Professor Foulbody tried to make a machine that could see through the wrappers, but he failed. I cracked it! I'm going to show Charlie my incredible Imaging Glasses, so he can improve his ticket system in the future.'

'You should say nothing,' the girl said with a sly smile. 'And then when they do the tickets again, sell the glasses. You'd be very rich indeed.'

The boy considered it for a moment. 'Anyway,' he went on, 'the twist I was talking about is – well, you know the story, right? I've read everything about it. Years ago, children went into the factory for a tour, but Mr Willy Wonka ended up giving the whole factory to Charlie. There's got to be a twist again this time. Maybe one of us gets a chocolate factory for Christmas!'

The girl laughed. 'Charlie's only been in charge for about seven years. He's not much older than us! He's not handing over the factory any time soon.'

'I wonder if the twist is that we become best friends with the Oompa-Loompas and then they come to our house to play!' shouted someone behind them.

They turned to see the third child holding a Red, Green and Gold Ticket. His name was Winston Little and he was the youngest of the winners. Despite what his name suggested, Winston was not very little, just bang on average height for his age. One of his large front teeth was missing, and he wore a T-shirt that read: *I love Oompa-Loompas.*

'I'm just here for the Oompa-Loompas,' he said.

He had brought his father with him, who was looking rather green in the face. He'd helped Winston find the ticket by eating as much chocolate as possible – a new world record of ten thousand bars in a month. He was understandably feeling sick at the thought of seeing a whole factory full of the stuff.

'An Oompa-Loompa wouldn't be interested in going to your house to play,' Felicity Custard said matter-of-factly. 'They only spend time in the chocolate factory, or in Loompaland. Both are incredibly **MAGICAL** places, I'm afraid.'

'I have some really great swings in my garden,' the boy protested. 'So great they'll knock your teeth out. And a dog called Doompety . . .'

A large crowd of onlookers had also gathered in front of the gates to the factory, keen to see if they could peek inside. Some were still in their pyjamas, others were playing with their new Christmas presents. Some children were complaining that Santa had forgotten to visit them at all. There were film crews and reporters and people eager to get a photo of Charlie the great chocolatier – and maybe a sighting of Mr Willy Wonka too. There was great excitement in the air, an electric anticipation as the clock chimed ten.

BONG! . . . *BONG!*

Everyone held their breath and watched in wonder as, right on time, the gates began to open. Effortlessly, they pushed aside the thick snow and came to a halt with a *click* just as the clock stopped chiming.

Everything and everyone fell silent.

For a moment nothing happened, no one breathed; the world stood perfectly still. And then suddenly, a light! A small purple light flicked on above the entrance. The crowd gasped and then the door to the factory inched open.

Instantly, a chocolatey smell engulfed the street and everyone began taking great big sniffs of the delicious scent.

Then a young man stepped out from inside – and the crowd went wild. He wore a big grin and a JOLLY Christmas jumper covered in knitted Wonka bars. He opened his arms wide and said, 'Merry Christmas to you all! Ticket holders, please come in!'

The winners didn't waste a second. They rushed forward, their feet slipping and sliding under them as they went.

But then, much to the astonishment of the crowd, *another* figure stepped out of the factory, and everyone fell silent once again.

'Is that . . .? No, it can't be . . . I think it's Violet Beauregarde!' someone whispered, sending a ripple of excitement through the crowd.

'It's really her!'

'The gum girl!' someone else shouted.

'I always thought she should've won. She was so passionate about gum!'

'See what can happen if you try eating *anything* inside the factory,' Felicity Custard's mum whispered in her daughter's ear.

'COOL!' said Felicity Custard, looking Violet up and down with admiration.

Charlie smiled at the children. 'Are you ready for a Christmas you'll never forget?'

❄

Charlie stood outside the doors to the Chocolate Room and took a deep breath. He'd left the elf problem for his family, Mr Wonka and the Oompa-Loompas to deal with . . . So there was a chance he was about to open the door to find a spectacular mess.

The three children looked up at him expectantly.

'An important room, this,' Charlie said, trying to buy every extra second of time that he could. He pulled a key from his pocket and turned it in the lock, and though he was worried about what lay beyond, he was fizzing with excitement. It was as thrilling to share the factory with others as it was to be a child touring it. 'This is the nerve centre of the whole factory,' he went on, his heart bursting at the thought that maybe the children were feeling just as **EXCITED** as he had once, and still did every time he unlocked the doors to the Chocolate Room. He turned to them and beamed. 'I've given it a festive revamp, just for you!'

He tentatively pushed the doors open.

The children gasped!

The adults gasped!

Charlie gasped!

The place was elf-free. There wasn't a single footprint in the edible snow – it had been smoothed to perfection. The holes in the ceiling were still there, but no one seemed to notice those.

'It's all for you,' Charlie said kindly. 'Please help yourself to anything in here – it's all edible.'

The children stood with their jaws dropping to the floor, staring at the chocolate river. Everyone had heard about it, but to see the river with your own eyes was really something special.

'Here,' Charlie said, handing everyone a Christmas mug. 'Taste it.'

They all eagerly plunged their mugs into the

BUBBLING liquid and drank, their faces instantly lighting up with pure sugary JOY. Then they snapped the handles off the mugs and ate those too!

Charlie unravelled some tinsel from the boat and handed pieces of it to them, and they wrapped it round their necks like scarves, dropping their chins to taste the chewy strands. Soon the children, and the adults as well, were tearing around the room, taking a bite out of everything in sight. There were people scaling chocolate trees and people face down on the mince-pie path. Gingerbread men were thrown through the air along with gooey baubles and puffs of white-chocolate snow. The room was alive with munching and crunching and sighs of pure delight.

'This room will host our Christmas feast,' Charlie said excitedly. 'The Oompa-Loompas will set the table while we are on our grand tour of the factory!'

At the mention of Oompa-Loompas, Winston Little burst into life, spinning in circles and squealing.

'He's an Oompa-Loompa superfan,' Felicity Custard explained.

'Will we see them soon?' Winston asked eagerly.

'Oh, absolutely!' Charlie said, as he glided through the winter wonderland. 'We'll meet them all soon. Now, you must remember to follow me and keep close behind – we have so much to see! We will visit some special *Christmas* rooms. Not all of the factory, though – it's far too big to see in one visit.'

Without warning, Mr Wonka materialized beside Charlie. Everyone dropped what they were eating and gawped at the great man.

'It's Mr Willy Wonka!' Jim's gran wheezed.

Mr Wonka bowed.

'I'm going now,' he announced, tipping his hat. 'I'm off to find the presents in my glass elevator and save Christmas.'

Everyone looked confused.

'You just worry about your guests, Charlie, and leave the rest to me. I'll be back before you know it.' And with that, he charged off.

Charlie smiled at the group. 'As eccentric as ever,' he said, laughing nervously.

'What did he mean by *saving Christmas*?' Jim Roarman asked.

'Um . . .' Charlie said awkwardly.

'Can we see another room now?' Winston begged. 'One with an Oompa-Loompa in it?'

'Yes, of course,' Charlie said, relieved the subject had been changed. 'Come on, follow me and jump aboard!' And with that, he slid down a chocolate-covered hill and leaped on to the pink boiled-sweet boat. It rocked, splashing a spray of liquid chocolate up at the children on the banks, who opened their mouths to catch it on their tongues.

'It looks a little unsafe,' Felicity Custard's mum said. 'Are you sure it can carry all of us, Charlie? Do you have insurance?'

'Oh, please do not worry,' Charlie assured her. 'This boat is chiselled out of pure boiled sweet. There is nothing safer than that!'

Felicity Custard's mum raised an eyebrow, but the children didn't need reassuring – they leaped quickly into the boat and sat behind Charlie in a neat little row. In the seats behind them sat their adults and Violet.

'Hold on tight!' Charlie instructed, and with a wobble and a ***WHOOSH*** they set off. Charlie stood tall on the bow, navigating the choppy chocolate river as they bumped under a bridge and round a bend. They travelled through a warren of dark underground tunnels, each smelling more delicious than the last. Finally, they took one last turn before coming to a halt at a door marked: *HO! HO! HO!*

'A little Oompa-Loompa humour there,' Charlie said. 'It's actually a very important Christmas treats tasting-room. In here we are developing some of our most ambitious Christmas eatables. Including *this*.' He held up a lollipop that looked like a Christmas pudding. 'Inspired by the famous Wonka gum that turned Violet . . . er, violet.'

Everyone turned to gawp at Violet and she stared right back at them.

'This lollipop takes you through an entire Christmas meal,' Charlie explained.

'Oooh,' Jim said. 'This is exactly like my invention – the toe-nut. It's a doughnut but one you can wear on your toe.'

'That sounds delightful, Jim,' Charlie said kindly.

'Let me see that lollipop!' Jim said, grabbing it.

'Oh, I wouldn't eat it,' Charlie said. 'The recipe hasn't been perfected yet.'

'Don't do it, Jim,' Violet whispered, her usual coolness suddenly gone.

But it was no good. Jim took a bite. 'Ooh,' he said straight away. 'It tastes like turkey and potatoes and Brussels sprouts and –'

'He's turned green!' Jim's gran screamed.

'Oh dear. Um, please don't worry,' Charlie said, as he desperately searched for something comforting to say. 'You . . . actually really suit green.'

'Change him back!' his gran yelled. 'I don't want my grandson to be green. He's the colour of vomit!'

'Or,' Charlie said, 'a beautiful plant. A pile of peas. A friendly frog . . .'

'You will pay for this!'

'They won't,' Violet said, with a knowing look.

'I promise, by the end of the day we'll reverse any side effects,' Charlie said with a smile. 'We've advanced a lot in our remedy department. Now, let's go inside the Christmas tasting-room – if you think that lollipop was DELICIOUS, Jim, just you wait!'

Charlie climbed off the boat and made for the tasting-room door, rambling as he went. 'There are many treasures in here. Jelly stockings, knitted with delicious strawberry and liquorice laces. Completely usable, as long as you don't eat them first. Oh, and my favourite: Mistletoe Soda. We're still working on the freezing effect – it sticks the drinker's lips in a permanent pucker, which is a bit unfortunate . . .'

But his guests weren't paying any attention; they were whispering among themselves, distracted by their new green friend.

'Welcome,' Charlie announced grandly, 'to the Christmas –' He cracked the door open and froze. Inside, he could see almost every Oompa-Loompa in the factory smooshed against the walls and the ceiling and each other, trying to control what looked like at least a thousand wriggling elves!

He quickly slammed the door shut.

Everyone stopped whispering and looked up at him.

'That room is actually not the best one to see right now,' Charlie mumbled.

'Why?' Winston Little asked, and Charlie felt slightly relieved – they obviously hadn't glimpsed what was inside.

He leaped back on to the boat, and hastily navigated it further down the tunnel. 'I've thought of something better,' he exclaimed, as the boat shuddered to a halt next to a small row of vending machines designed to look like gingerbread houses.

'Here we have our North Pole Gobstoppers! Now, these are really special.' Charlie placed a chocolate coin in the slot of the vending machine and twisted the handle. There was a *click* and out rolled a red-and-gold-striped gobstopper.

He held it carefully between his fingers and lifted it up for the children to see.

'This,' he whispered, 'tastes like elf food.'

'Elf food?' all the children said at once. 'What does elf food taste like?'

'Mostly **MAGIC,'** Charlie said. 'But with a hint of marshmallow.' He waved his hand about. 'Would anyone like to try it?'

'ME!' cried Winston Little.

Violet placed a hand on his shoulder. 'You know,' she whispered, 'tasting things in this factory when you have a descriptive name, like *Violet* or *Little,* never ends well.'

'Huh?' Winston said. 'But my name is Little and I'm trying a prototype elf-food-flavoured gobstopper – what could go wrong?'

And with that he popped one into his mouth.

'Isn't it delicious?' Charlie said with a grin.

Smoke began to billow from Winston's ears.

'It tastes nice!' Winston shouted. 'But my ears feel funny!'

'Huh,' Charlie said, bending down to inspect his ears. They seemed to be warping, stretching . . .

When the smoke cleared, Winston's dad screamed.

'Your ears, Winston! You have pointy elf ears!'

'Huh,' Violet said. 'I really thought it was going to . . .'

'Ah, a minor side effect,' Charlie said, eager not to let the malfunction affect the trip.

'Minor?!' Winston's dad screeched. 'They look pretty major to me – look, this one is as big as my foot!'

'Don't worry,' Charlie said as they jumped back in the boat and he steered them further into the depths of the factory. 'All temporary – you have my word.' He guided the boat downstream, all the way to a large steel door with a big frosted handle.

'Now this really is the very best bit,' Charlie said. 'Behold, the Scrumptious Snow Room!'

❄

Inside, the Scrumptious Snow Room held exactly what it said on the door – pure scrumptious snow, thick underfoot, with extra snow piled high in every corner. Snow fell from above, swirling past flying candy canes that were kept aloft with little wings.

'ANGEL CANES!' Charlie said, plucking one from the air. 'Not quite ready, but by next Christmas we're hopeful one of these will make you fly with a single lick!'

Felicity Custard grabbed one and held it in front of her face, examining its little white wings.

'Oh, but I wouldn't lick it now,' Charlie warned. 'It's not perfected yet. We haven't tested the side effects.'

'As someone who's been there, done that, got the purple T-shirt, I'd say you want to listen to him,' Violet said.

'Exactly,' said Felicity Custard's mother with a hint of panic in her voice. 'Listen to Violet. She's purple!'

But Felicity Custard just shrugged. 'I'm *lucky*, remember.' Then she gave the candy cane a huge lick.

Everyone fell silent.

A good minute passed and nothing happened.

'Do you feel . . . all right?' Charlie dared to ask.

'My feet feel funny,' Felicity Custard said, and a second later she rose up off the floor! But she didn't move far, just an inch or so. She wobbled a little, but that was it.

'You *are* lucky,' Violet said.

Charlie beamed. 'Oh, this is great news. Perhaps they really will be ready for the shops soon.'

'I'm FLOATING!' Felicity Custard cried with delight. She flopped forward and picked up some edible snow, formed it into a ball, then threw it at Winston.

He tore across the room, his earlobes scraping the floor, and grabbed some snow too. He took a bite, then rolled the rest into a ball and lobbed one back. 'It's delicious!' he cried.

'SNOWBALL FIGHT!' Jim Roarman roared. **'EDIBLE SNOWBALL FIGHT!'**

Charlie raced across the room and pressed a button. Huge mechanical snowflakes emerged from the walls, with a snowball-shaped hole at their centre. They whirred and spun like great wheels, whipping the snow up from the ground into scoops, churning them round and dropping them down a funnel before firing them out of the middle of the snowflake like cannon balls.

'Snowballs everywhere!' Charlie cried. 'These are my snowball-fight machines! The snowballs are edible, and if you hit one of the snowflake cannons, the snowballs it's making will change flavour!'

The children went wild, ducking and diving and army-crawling through the snow. Jim hit the target on the snowflake cannon and suddenly –

'It has changed from white chocolate to berry flavour!' Winston said in amazement as he licked the snowball. 'It tastes like delicious berry ice cream!'

Felicity Custard hit a cannon this time.

'Cinnamon!' Winston cried. 'And marzipan!'

Again and again they hit the machines and snowballs flew through the air in every delicious flavour you could imagine – and a couple of awful ones too.

'Ew! SOOT!' Jim said, gagging.

'Christmas cake! Figgy pudding! Advent-calendar chocolate!'

The children were catapulting themselves across the room, mouths open, catching the snowballs in mid-air. The adults joined in too and soon everyone was so full of flavoured snowballs that all they could do was lie on the ground, sweeping their arms up and down by their sides as they made **DELICIOUS** snow angels.

Charlie joined them and looked up at the snowy ceiling, the flapping Angel Canes and the last of the shooting snowballs. It was as magical as he had imagined. It was the best Christmas ev–

BOOM!

'What was that?' cried Winston Little's dad as he wrapped his arms round Charlie's ankles in fear.

The whole place shook and shook again. Then somewhere in the distance there was an almighty ***CRUNCH.***

The door flew open and a thick cloud of smoke filled the room, making them all cough. When it cleared, Charlie could see Mr Wonka in the doorway, his tall hat completely squashed and singed at the edges and the top sprinkled with little shards of glass.

'Oh no,' Charlie whispered.

The children gasped at the sight of the great chocolatier, charred like a roasted marshmallow.

'The launch was unsuccessful. The glass elevator is now out of action,' Mr Wonka explained. 'I do believe all those holes in the ceiling the elves made –'

'ELVES?!' the children cried in unison.

'Yes, elves,' Mr Wonka said before continuing. 'The holes they left in the roof earlier confused the navigation beams, and we crashed sideways on take-off.'

Charlie slapped a hand to his forehead, unable to find the right words.

'We urgently need another flying method,' Mr Wonka said. 'Are those Angel Canes up to scratch yet?'

Charlie shook his head and pointed at Felicity Custard, who was now barely floating at all.

'Why do you need to fly?' Winston Little asked. 'Is it something to do with the Oompa-Loompas?'

'You should tell us. Maybe we can help. We *are* children, after all,' said Felicity Custard, and Jim Roarman nodded in agreement.

'We *should* tell them, Charlie,' Mr Wonka said. 'We're almost out of time and most certainly out of ideas.'

Charlie considered it. 'All right then,' he said.

'Now, before we begin,' Mr Wonka said, itching to get started, 'you must understand that this is entirely Violet's fault.'

Violet opened her mouth to protest – but then decided that technically he was correct.

Charlie explained everything: the gum, the missing reindeer and the children without **PRESENTS.**

Mr Wonka added that Santa had been fished out of the chocolate river and was drying off in a secret room.

'A fantastic chocolate shell is hardening round him as we speak – you could make *real* Santa chocolate moulds with that, Charlie. Just a thought,' said Mr Wonka.

'So, you *know* Santa?' Felicity Custard said in awe. 'I bet I'm lucky enough to meet him too.'

'This is the twist!' Winston Little cheered. 'We have to save Christmas for Santa. If we do, do we get to meet the Oompa-Loompas?'

'Give the children chocolate instead of presents!' Jim Roarman roared. 'Every child would love special Wonka chocolate bars.'

Charlie got to his feet. 'That's a great idea, Jim. Though we'll need a way to deliver them . . . and without the glass elevator . . .'

'There must be *one* room in this factory that has something in it we could use,' Felicity Custard said. 'You said yourself the place is huge; maybe there are things that you've forgotten about.'

'You're right,' Charlie said. He thought and he thought and then an idea burst into his mind – bizarre and bubbly, bottled and brilliant. His eyes grew wide. 'Oh my, I think I know just the thing,' he shouted. 'Come with me!'

❄

Charlie led them out of the **SCRUMPTIOUS SNOW ROOM** into a corridor lined with all sorts of BUTTONS and PIPES and LEVERS. They passed door after door and the place looked dustier and dustier.

'This is the oldest part of the factory,' he said. 'A lot of these inventions didn't make it to the shops – they were too wild. But they'll live here forever.'

He came to a halt outside a door coated in a thick layer of dust. Slowly, he wiped his hand over it to reveal an old plaque:

FIZZY LIFTING DRINKS.

'I don't remember this one,' Violet said.

'That's because by this point in the tour you had

already turned into a giant blueberry and were off being juiced,' Charlie explained.

'Charlie, my boy,' Mr Wonka cried, patting him on the back. 'This could work!'

'The bubbles in the drinks lift you up like a balloon and you burp to come back down,' Charlie said with a smile, remembering what Mr Wonka had told him all those years ago during his visit to the factory. He turned to the excited children. 'I have an important question, esteemed guests . . . How good are you at burping?'

❄

So that is why, if you looked up on that particular Christmas Day, you might have seen a strange sight – three children, Violet and Charlie, a flock of elves and one chocolate-coated Santa, drinking and burping their way through the clear winter sky, armed with sacks full of Wonka chocolate.

They dropped chocolate down chimneys – every flavour you could get – until it was snowing chocolate.

They got almost halfway round the world before handing the present-delivering over to Santa and his elves.

It was time for the children to return to the factory for their feast and they arrived back, burping and chattering excitedly about their adventure. Inside, they found the table laid and waiting for them in the Chocolate Room.

All Charlie's family were seated already, along with the Oompa-Loompas and the rest of the elves.

'OOMPA-LOOMPAS!' Winston Little bellowed. He was too distracted to even notice the elves.

'It's fine,' one muttered, looking offended. 'We just make *all* your toys.'

Mr Wonka was hopping about, taking Christmas crackers out of a basket and placing them gently on the table. 'No one touch them!' he cried. 'They're a surprise – and incredibly unstable.'

Everyone inched back from the table.

Charlie stood marvelling at the glorious Christmas scene in front of him. The table itself was made from shiny set caramel. His mother and father were busy placing big bowls of potatoes on the table, next to a huge steaming turkey that his grandparents were all *ooh*ing and *aah*ing at. Flying Angel Canes floated overhead and edible tinsel was wrapped round every chair. Marshmallow foliage adorned the table, along with scattered festive gobstoppers and gingerbread men. Beautiful chocolate candles twinkled and dripped delicious melted chocolate into cups placed carefully beneath them.

'Come on, Charlie! Come on, everyone, sit down!' Mr Wonka cheered.

The competition winners rushed to their places.

When Jim, Felicity Custard and Winston took their seats, they found a small present on their plates – wrapped in purple paper with a matching purple bow. They opened their gifts, and each of them held up a wad of gum. There was one for Violet too.

'The Oompa-Loompas have created a new gum, for undoing side effects,' Mr Wonka explained.

Winston, Felicity Custard and Jim pocketed theirs, but much to Charlie's surprise, Violet didn't look happy. Quite the opposite, in fact. Her smile had slipped into a sad frown.

'Violet,' Charlie said. 'What's wrong? The gum will reverse the purpling. And it's gum – your favourite.'

She squished it between her fingers, then slowly placed it back in its wrapper and pushed it aside.

'You're not going to chew it?' Charlie asked.

Violet shook her head. 'Thank you, but I like being purple.'

'*Why?*' everyone asked at once.

'Because it reminds me of this **MAGICAL** place and all of you,' she said. 'If I'm not purple any more, one day I might just forget. If I'm purple, I know I never will.'

Charlie beamed at her and the Oompa-Loompas launched into a Christmas jingle.

Mr Wonka raised a cracker.

'Merry Christmas to all!' he boomed, pulling both ends of the cracker himself.

BANG!

Sparks flew out from it, along with a burst of shredded chocolate and glitter. And just when they thought it was all over, a tiny sleigh, crafted perfectly out of boiled sweets, and pulled by chocolate reindeer, shot out and soared around their heads.

'And to all –' Charlie cheered – 'a good chocolate!'

Adam Kay

To healthcare staff everywhere

Please do not attempt to make this marvellous medicine at home.
Or any medicine, for that matter.

'But I don't want to go to Grandpa George's house,' moaned Gigi, from the back of the car. 'He's boring.'

'It'll be fun!' replied her mum. 'Well, maybe not *fun*, but . . .'

Her dad was fed up with all this – he'd been listening to the same discussion since Junction 8 of the M5. 'Enough! We're going to Grandpa George's house for Christmas, and that's that.'

Actually, sorry for interrupting, but I should probably fill you in on a few important details. First of all, this is a Christmas story. You might have guessed that because it's called 'George's Marvellous Christmas', it's in a book called *Charlie and the Christmas Factory* and the previous paragraph includes the word 'Christmas'. But I need to warn you that it's not a normal Christmas story, with a lovely happy ending. Sorry about that. If that's a problem, then you should probably skip to the next chapter.

If you're still here, then I'll tell you who these people in the car are – it might help you understand what's going on. The last time we met George Kranky, he was an eight-year-old boy who had just experienced the strangest couple of days of his life. Involving a gruesome grandmother and some rather marvellous medicine? Of course you remember; I knew you would. Well, it's quite a long time after all of that. In fact, it's so long afterwards that the people in this car, wearing the brightest and ugliest Christmas jumpers you've ever seen, are:

George's daughter, Katy.

Katy's husband, Pip.

And last, and grumpiest: Gigi, their eight-year-old daughter, which makes George her grandpa, because that's generally how this stuff works. Right, back to the car.

Gigi pressed her head against the window and stared out, as the big office blocks and squished-together houses of the city began to blur into acres upon acres of green. And with acres upon acres of green came Gigi's two most dreaded things in the world. No, not mushrooms and homework. Peace and quiet.

'BOOOOOORING!' she yelled, so loudly that a cow looked up.

'There'll be lots to do at Grandpa's house,' said Pip.

'Like what?' replied Gigi. 'Get bored to death by his hour-long stories, then listen to him snore like a warthog in his armchair?'

'Stop that right now!' said Katy. 'Your grandpa worked hard all his life, and he deserves a nice quiet retirement! Did you know that he worked in medicine and came up with jabs and vaccines which saved lives all over the world?'

'Well, yes. You've told me about thirty-five times.'

'Careful, young lady!' said her dad. 'Or there won't be any presents for you tomorrow.' And then he gave her the Raspberry-Sauce Look, which was a look he reserved for when he was extremely cross, like the time Gigi accidentally spilled a full bottle of raspberry sauce on to his laptop. Which might have been how the Raspberry-Sauce Look got its name.

Gigi was sitting in a sulk with her arms folded and her bottom lip poking out when the car turned left on to Grandpa George's road. On Gigi's street in London there were 68,000 separate houses all in a row (OK, that might be a tiny exaggeration), but where Grandpa George lived, out in the countryside, there were only two. His neighbour, Malcolm Gripe, lived in the house next door, as neighbours generally do, and was a nasty little weasel of a man who complained about everything that George did, from the noise to the smell to the explosions. (I'll come to the explosions a bit later.) And it wasn't just George he complained about – he held the record of writing the most ever letters of complaint to the local newspaper (13,428. And 3,989 of them were about bin collections alone). As Gigi's car pootled past his house, Malcolm Gripe screamed, 'Slow down!' and 'Careful of my precious camellias!' even though the car was travelling at ten miles per hour and was nowhere near his flower bed. Gigi stuck her tongue out at him, which probably didn't help matters, to be honest.

They turned left into the gates of George's farm and crawled up the steep driveway to his ramshackle old house.

'Right! Out we get!' said Pip. 'And remember not to touch the doorbell!'

Oh yes, the doorbell. George liked to invent things. Last Christmas, he installed an ingenious doorbell designed to electrocute burglars – slight problem: it also electrocuted the postman, delivery drivers and any visitors. Besides, burglars tend not to use the doorbell.

All a bit weird, if you asked Gigi. And, as far as she was concerned, if there was one thing worse than being boring, it was being boring and weird. 'He better not have made me one of his ridiculous inventions as a Christmas present,' Gigi said, as her dad heaved their bags out of the boot.

She still shuddered when she remembered Repeatcorn, the massive fluffy toy sweetcorn that George made her last Christmas, which repeated anything you said to it. It had been quite fun for the first ten minutes, but then it malfunctioned just as Katy said, 'Gigi, you didn't flush the toilet.' And then it said, 'Gigi, you didn't flush the toilet' constantly on repeat, day and night, until eventually they buried it in George's garden.

The door swung open and there was Grandpa George, spectacles a bit **WONKY,** looking a little flushed, moustache slightly singed and . . . was that smoke coming off his hair? He'd obviously been doing one of his ridiculous experiments, but Gigi had learned it was best not to ask . . . otherwise he'd tell you all about it and that was – you guessed it – weird and boring.

'Hello, poppet!' said George, producing a slightly warm toffee from up his sleeve. 'Are you happy to be back on the farm for Christmas?'

Gigi felt like saying, 'Of course I don't want to be stuck on a farm at Christmas with a load of boring old people, miles and miles away from my friends and any bookshops or cinemas or places to get pizza. Oh, and I hate being called Poppet too.' But her dad shot her the Raspberry-Sauce Look, and she remembered his threat about not getting presents the next morning, so she said, 'Oh yes, Grandpa! I'm **VERY EXCITED!**'

It was almost convincing.

Once they had all hung their stockings from the mantelpiece (Gigi went for the big blue one, which would fit the most presents in) and chosen their bedrooms (Gigi went for the big yellow one, so it would fit all her presents in), George called everyone to the big oak dining table for dinner. It was gleaming with tinsel and glistening with fairy lights, the bright red tablecloth was dusted with squirts of fake snow and in the middle was a huge dish that contained . . . actually, Gigi wasn't sure. Pasta, maybe? But it could just as easily have been trifle.

'Umm. What are we eating, Grandpa?'

George looked very proud of himself. 'It's a new taste sensation I'm trying out: banana and mushroom lasagne.'

Gigi glanced at her parents, who, instead of vomiting all over the tablecloth, said things like, 'Ooh, sounds interesting!' and 'What a delightful idea!' If being an adult meant pretending to like disgusting meals, Gigi wasn't sure she ever wanted to be one. She decided to say nothing.

If your family is anything like mine, when they get together, they share memories of years gone by. Maybe your aunt brings up that time you ate a nappy when you were two. Or your brother reminds everyone of the birthday you got your head stuck in the toilet seat. Well, the Kranky family were no different. As they ate, George started to tell his LOOOOOOOONG stories. Well, one particular looooooooooong story, about what happened back when Grandpa George was Gigi's age and lived with his miserable, mean old grandma.

Gigi rolled her eyes at her mum and mouthed, 'Not this one AGAIN!' She didn't have a calculator with her, but she reckoned this was at least the 638th separate time she'd heard it. Maybe even the 639th.

'My Grandma was the ghastliest, grumpiest, grizzliest grouch,' said George. 'We lived together in this very house, and every day she would point her horrid, thorny, twiggy fingers at me and order me about, and her brown triangle-teeth would gnash away in fury. She'd tell me I was lazy and selfish and useless, and her breath was so bad it would make the flowers die.'

Gigi started fiddling with the pepper grinder, until it made a strange whirring sound and hundreds of peppercorns fired out of it like a volcano full of fireworks, so Katy had to throw a napkin over it.

'That might need a tiny bit of adjusting,' said George. 'Right – where was I? Ah, yes! So, I grabbed a saucepan and tipped in all sorts of horrendous-sounding lotions and ointments and powders, with terrifying names like DISHWORTH'S FAMOUS DANDRUFF CURE, and FLOWERS OF TURNIPS, and TOOTHPASTE.'

'Toothpaste isn't terrifying,' muttered Gigi under her breath.

'Well, before I knew it, she'd drunk the potion and she grew and grew until she was as tall as the house. So I had to cook up a new potion to make her smaller again, but . . . I got it a bit wrong. Or maybe not wrong at all, depending on how you look at it. She got smaller, and smaller, and smaller . . .'

Gigi knew the story so well that she joined in. 'Until – ***PING!*** – she disappeared altogether,' Gigi mouthed along. But then her parents gave her a huge Raspberry-Sauce Look, and she urgently stopped.

Grandpa lowered his voice to a whisper. 'But sometimes, in the middle of the night, I dream that she didn't actually disappear at all. I dream that she's climbing into my ear and screaming, "Make me big again! As tall as the sky! So I can crush you under my foot!" and then I wake up, covered with sweat, like I've just climbed out of the bath in my pyjamas.'

Gigi didn't believe a word of it – not even the little words like 'of' or 'but' or 'and' – no more than she believed in ghosts or goblins. A little old lady towering up into the air like a redwood tree, before shrinking to the size of a speck of dust, then disappearing altogether? No way. Nope. Not a chance.

Just as everyone was forcing down the last of their cornflake and cabbage crumble (which tasted even worse than the lasagne), Gigi's mum and dad announced they were going to go for a drink with some old school friends at the pub in the village.

Gigi thought this sounded pretty dull – a bunch of grown-ups talking about the traffic on the A473 and kitchen worktops and how much houses cost these days – but she was still desperate to go with them. It was either that or be left alone with her grandad and pretend to be interested in the new voice-activated dishwasher he was constructing, then taste his vomit-sounding leek and lentil ice cream. Or, worst of all, listen to that nonsense story about his made-up medicine for the 639th (or was it 640th?) time.

Gigi did everything she could to persuade her parents to take her along with them. She promised she'd be the best-behaved child in the history of children, that she'd sit quietly in a corner and she wouldn't ask for anything (except for some peanuts), but her mother said she was far too young and would have to stay at home. Besides, there were peanuts in the kitchen cupboard. Katy and Pip each gave George and Gigi a kiss on the cheek as they stepped out into the freezing December air.

'Make sure you behave for your grandad, now, Gigi!' said Katy. 'And don't forget to leave out a carrot and a glass of brandy for Santa and his reindeer. They'll be glad of it when they drop by.'

And then they were gone.

Gigi sighed. 'What shall we do, then?' She hadn't brought any of her usual books and games with her, even though her mum told her she should. Gigi had wanted to make sure there was enough room in the car for the mountains of presents she was certain she'd get in the morning. She picked up the remote control from the TV, then immediately dropped it on to the carpet when it started buzzing like an electric toothbrush full of wasps. She remembered it was generally safer not to touch anything electrical in George's house. 'How about . . . umm . . . a game of Snap?'

But by the time she'd finished her sentence, George was already fast asleep in his big comfy armchair, snoring so loudly it sounded like a tree being attacked by a chainsaw.

What was she supposed to do now? Count his nose hairs? Bedtime was ages off! While George snored away like a dustcart, Gigi looked round the room, searching for something to do on her own.

❄

On a shelf, she found some test tubes from her grandpa's experiments and practised her juggling with them. But it wasn't long before she dropped the lot.

CLATTER!

CRASH!

CLANG!

Malcolm Gripe certainly heard it – Gigi froze as a muffled, 'Stop making so much noise!' drifted through the wall. It didn't wake George, though.

What now? She stacked every single log in the fireplace into a huge pyramid and stood back to admire her work . . . until they tumbled down on to the floor.

SMASH!

BASH!

CRUNCH!

'I'll call the police if you don't pipe down!' yelled Malcolm Gripe. But still George slept like a baby. A baby rhino, by the sounds he was making.

Hang on, wasn't there something she was supposed to do? Of course! She had to sort out brandy and a carrot for Santa and the reindeer.

A carrot would be easy, surely. On a farm? There must be millions of them! She bounded out of the back door and was marching purposefully ahead when she heard her name being whispered by an extremely spooky voice that definitely wasn't Malcolm Gripe's.

'Giiii-giiiiii!'

She JUMPED the height of a scarecrow and was about to run inside when it said, 'You didn't flush the toilet,' and she realized she was stood in the exact spot where the Repeatcorn was buried. She kept walking towards the vegetable patch and yanked a carrot out of the ground. Easy!

Next: brandy. Hmm. Where might that be? There was none in the kitchen, none in the rickety little cabinet where Grandpa kept those sticky old bottles of gin and wine, and none in the utility room either. The cupboard under the stairs, perhaps? Nope, just a vacuum cleaner, lots of overcoats and some spectacularly smelly shoes.

She thought about waking her grandpa up and asking for help, but he was still snoring like a helicopter coming in to land, so she went back outside to carry on her search. It was dark and a bit scary, and she didn't really know where she should look, but the moon was peeping through the clouds and she could see the old greenhouse at the bottom of a path. She wandered in – there were a lot of plants, and most of them looked like old dead twigs, because it was winter. She picked up a plant pot, just in case it somehow had a tiny bottle of brandy underneath – but instead, a large family of spiders scuttled out. No, thank you very much – she wouldn't be investigating the greenhouse any further.

Hmm. How about Grandpa's tumbledown old shed? She could see its tiny window glinting in the moonlight, as if it were winking at her. Gigi trudged down to it and prised the door open. It creaked loudly, like Grandpa's back when he got out of his chair. She peeped inside, just as the moon snuck behind a cloud and everything went pitch-black. *Oh dear*, she thought to herself. *Well, you're here now. You might as well go in.*

She shivered as she crept into the shed. The air was as cold as Bigfoot's big toe and she could hear strange scurrying sounds – it suddenly felt a lot more like Halloween than Christmas. Gigi fumbled around on the wall for a light switch, and soon a cobweb-covered bulb blinked to life. **MUCH BETTER!**

Actually, it wasn't necessarily better, because it meant she could now see what was making those sounds. Ugh! There were tens of thousands of earwigs and slugs and beetles, all slithering and scratching about on the floor around her. But this was no time to be squeamish – she was on a mission. She couldn't let Santa down – not on Christmas Eve! She spotted a shelf covered with jars, bottles, tins and pots – one of those must have some brandy in! She looked at the labels. She couldn't see any brandy, but she could see . . .

CANARY SEED

FLOWERS OF TURNIPS

DISHWORTH'S FAMOUS DANDRUFF CURE

Hang on. She knew those names! She'd heard them at boring dinners a minimum of 639 times – they were ingredients from her grandpa's silly story! A thought occurred to her, like a non-cobweb-covered lightbulb turning on in her head. She didn't know much about brandy, but she was pretty sure that Santa must be bored out of his Christmassy skull with it – drinking the same thing in millions and millions and millions of houses. She got bored if she had spaghetti two nights in a row. And she was sure she could do a lot better than brandy. She could make something an awful lot more **MARVELLOUS.**

Before she even knew what she was doing, Gigi grabbed an old tin bucket that was hanging from a rusty nail on the wall, and began emptying pills, liquids, pastes and goodness knows what else into it. Like her grandpa always said, the best recipes are a kind of experiment. (Even though most of his recipes were a total disaster.)

SPLAT!

SPLASH!

GURGLE!

RATTLE!

She waved every single lotion and potion under her nose as she took them from the shelf.

This one smells like old socks! she thought, as a huge blob of HELGA'S HAIRSET splatted into the bucket.

Next came some FOWL PEST POWDER. *And this one smells like fox poo! Gross!* She reached for another bottle. *And this one smells like milk that's been left in the sun all day*. She looked more carefully – it *was* a bottle of milk, best before 1 November 1973. Still, in it went, lumps and all. She poured and sprinkled and doused until she'd emptied everything on the shelf.

She peered inside the bucket – it was more like a gooey, lumpy slop than a delicious December beverage. There was no way Santa was going to drink so much as a sip of that. How could she make it more festive? ***OH!*** She spotted another shelf with exactly what she needed. A squidge of the squirty fake snow – hopefully her grandpa wouldn't mind. And then a quick shake of **GLITTER,** a short string of tinsel, a broken bauble and an old party hat from last year's Christmas dinner.

Well, that looked slightly better, but it was still a bit . . . grey. Then she spied one final ingredient sitting by itself in a corner: a big tin of dark brown gloss paint. She slopped some into the bucket until the mixture was a warm, golden, reddish-brown. Perfect!

As she stirred her slimy, soupy mixture, Gigi found herself chanting a strange rhyme that suddenly popped into her head and refused to leave until she said it out loud, over and over.

'I command this rancid goo
To be the finest festive brew!
Some like chocolate

Some like candy
Make Santa like this
More than brandy!'

Gigi ran back into the house with a small glass jar of her potion – her grandpa was snoring like a washing machine doing an extra-fast spin, which was the noise he always made when he was about to wake up. Quick as a *FLASH,* Gigi put the miraculous Christmas mixture next to the carrot in front of the fireplace, seconds before Grandpa's snoring stopped, and his eyes blinked open.

'Did I miss anything?' he said, yawning.

Gigi stood and beamed at him, trying not to look suspicious. 'Oh no, Grandpa, I've just been sitting quietly and reading my book.'

Doctors are very good at telling if people are hiding something. Like when a patient hasn't quite been honest about how fifteen Smarties ended up inside their left nostril. Or when a patient is too embarrassed to show them a boil on their bum. And, even though he was retired, George felt like his granddaughter might have had a little secret bubbling inside her. 'Is there anything you'd like to tell me, poppet?' George asked.

'Nothing at all, Grandpa!'

'Well, Santa won't come if we aren't fast asleep, and there's no point waiting up for your mum and dad – they'll only be . . . high-spirited. Time to hit the hay.' (Which Gigi always thought was a very weird expression for people who sleep on mattresses.)

They shuffled up the rickety stairs, and Gigi went into the nice big bedroom she'd chosen and jumped into bed. She pulled the duvet up to her nose and before long she started to feel that weird and floaty sensation that tells you you'll be nodding off to sleep any . . . second . . . now . . . but instead she was jolted awake by an enormous BOOM. Not just a small **BOOM,** like a Christmas cracker bursting open, or a medium-sized **BOOOOOM** like thunder outside your window, but a huge, WHOPPING SHOCKER of an explosion that went **BOOOOMMM!!!!!!** Then there was silence. Followed by the distant sound of Malcolm Gripe yelling, 'I'm trying to sleep over here, you loathsome louse!'

Gigi wasn't any kind of expert, but this didn't seem great. She leaped out of bed so she could run downstairs and see what on earth was going on. But, when she opened her bedroom door, there were no stairs at all, rickety or otherwise. They had vanished. Gone. No longer there.

Other little things that she noticed were missing included:

- The upstairs landing
- The living room
- The garage
- Two other bedrooms
- The utility room

All she could see was her grandpa, standing outside his bedroom, his mouth wide open. Everything else in the house had disappeared into thin air. Except . . .

It wasn't just thin air. Because in place of the upstairs landing, the living room, the garage, two other bedrooms and the utility room was the biggest person you've ever seen, dressed in a very recognizable shade of red. Where the fireplace had been, there was now a **GIGANTIC** boot, with a colossal silver buckle that glimmered and twinkled in the lights of the Christmas tree which, by some miracle, was still standing.

When Gigi and her grandpa looked up to where the roof used to be, they saw a waterfall of shiny white hair that looked very much like an enormous beard. Unless she was massively mistaken, and she wasn't the sort of eight-year-old who was mistaken very often, this was Santa Claus. Only he was the size of a spaceship. His bright blue eyes were as huge as cinema screens and his grinning mouth was as wide as a zebra crossing.

Gigi expected her grandpa to go through the roof (not that there was a roof any more) and give her the biggest telling-off in the history of tellings-off. She was clearly going to be grounded with no sweets or fun for at least five years. Maybe until she was at university. She'd never see her friends again! But George didn't seem cross in the slightest. He seemed intrigued, interested and almost . . . **EXCITED.** He had a glint in his eye that shone like a supernova.

'I knew it!' shouted Grandpa gleefully. 'That brandy

you left out for Santa by the fireplace. It wasn't brandy at all, was it, Poppet? It was . . . something slightly more marvellous than that!'

Gigi nodded very slowly.

'Yippee! I *knew* we had another scientist in the making,' said George, hugging his sides with delight. He would have hugged Gigi, but he couldn't get near her on account of the landing having vanished.

George was interrupted by a sound like an aeroplane's engine. They both looked up to see Supersized Santa clearing his throat. He lowered his **HUMONGOUS** palm down to their level, and they both stepped onto it, as if they were hopping into a lift.

Santa dropped them off in the biggest field in the farm. (The other two fields weren't big enough for him to fit in.) Then he let out a massive sigh. It wasn't like any sigh you've ever heard before – it was more like a huge gust of wind. In fact, it made a tree bend so far backwards that it nearly snapped in two.

'Well,' he said. 'This probably isn't the Christmas Eve any of us expected, is it?'

From where Gigi was sitting, that was the understatement of the century. Santa was about a million times too big to fit into his sleigh, let alone squeeze down a chimney! This was a disaster. And not just for Gigi. Millions of children all over the world were about to have an extremely miserable Christmas Day, with empty stockings on their mantelpieces, and it would be all *her* fault. Gigi thought back to every single time she'd heard her grandpa's story and every single time she'd said that it was nonsense. She suddenly felt extremely bad for not believing him. But the truth was that the marvellous medicine was quite clearly real. This was **HUGE.** But, unfortunately, so was Santa.

George could see how worried she looked, so he said, 'We're scientists, aren't we? We solve problems. And the first step is to find out exactly what went into that potion. Now, did you put PIG PILLS in there?'

'I think so . . .' said Gigi, but she didn't sound particularly sure. 'It's all a bit of a muddle right now.'

Santa tried to help. 'I distinctly detected the tang of BRILLIDENT FALSE TEETH CLEANER, if that's any use?'

'Come on, concentrate!' said George. 'If I don't know exactly what Santa swallowed, I won't be able to make the medicine to shrink him back down. So tell me . . . just how many squirts of **NEVERMORE PONKING DEODORANT** did you spurt in there?'

Santa tapped his ten-tonne toe on the ground, and the whole field shook like there had been a reasonably sized earthquake. But George still carried on talking. 'You remembered to squeeze in some **TOOTHPASTE**, right?'

Santa then cleared his throat so loudly that one or two robins fell from the trees.

Gigi and her grandpa looked up at Santa again. 'Everything OK up there?' asked Grandpa. 'Apart from, umm, the obvious.'

'Well, I might have a suggestion . . .' boomed Santa.

'Great,' said Grandpa. 'What do you think we should put in the shrinking potion?'

'I was actually wondering,' boomed Santa again. (He could only really do booming these days.) 'How about if I just stay . . . on the big side?'

'Oh, of course!' said George. 'And we make the rest

of the world massive too? If I hired a plane, then I could rig up some kind of pump-action sprayer device and have the medicine rain down on everyone and everything. It'll probably take a few weeks, but I don't see any reason why it –'

Santa rolled his eyes. 'No, I meant –'

George interrupted. 'Oh! So, you're retiring! I guess you've been at this game for a long old time. No harm in putting your feet up now and –'

'I think what Santa actually meant,' said Gigi, 'is that he *likes* being that big.'

'Exactly! I'm going to be able to get around the world so much faster than with this lot pulling me.' Santa gestured towards his slightly miserable-looking reindeer. 'No offence, lads. The only issue is how I get down the chimneys . . .'

'Well,' said Gigi. 'I don't suppose you're any good at basketball?'

'Good?!' replied Santa. 'You're looking at the gold medallist in the North Pole championships nine years running.'

Santa stood up slowly, almost bopping his head on a cloud. 'Let's see if this works!' he said, then scooped up a huge pile of presents from his sleigh and began flicking them off his palm like peas.

WHOOSH!

ZOOM!

ZZZZZIIIIIIP!

Over the fields they flew, off to the villages, plopping right into each chimney with perfect precision. George and Gigi watched, their mouths hanging open like the back of a bin lorry.

'This is brilliant!' bellowed Santa. 'Can you imagine how dirty my suit normally gets? I have to bring a couple of spares with me. And it's so embarrassing changing in a conservatory – anyone could see!'

'And you're absolutely sure about this?' asked George. 'I'm pretty certain I can whip up a batch of shrinking potion for you.'

Santa was really, really, really, really sure.

'I reckon I can be in bed with my feet up by midnight at this rate,' he roared. 'Although, come to think of it, I might need to buy a bigger bed. Right, best be off. Thanks again!'

And with that, Santa carefully stuffed a dejected Dasher, Dancer, Prancer and Vixen into one pocket; a downcast Comet, Cupid, Donner and Blitzen into another; then bounded off with a smile as wide as a football pitch.

His first step made a huge crater right in the middle of George's prized potato patch. Oops.

His second step knocked over the fence that George had only just put back up after the high winds in October. Double oops.

'What's that blasted racket?' screamed Malcolm Gripe.

Unfortunately, Santa's third step smashed down on Malcolm's house, squashing the building and its moany inhabitant as flat as a piece of printer paper. Oh well. The camellias were fine, though.

Car alarms shrieked, dogs howled, cats screeched, the ground bounced like a trampoline, and Santa's **HO HO HOs** faded into the distance.

George and Gigi were still staring at each other in stunned silence when Katy and Pip arrived back from the pub. Katy had her key in her hand, ready to open a door that was now just a stack of splinters.

'Dad! Gigi!' she shouted. 'Oh my goodness! Are you OK? What happened? Why is the house just a pile of bricks and a Christmas tree?'

Katy and Pip stood with their arms folded, waiting for an explanation.

Gigi stepped forward, shaking like a jelly on a roller-coaster. 'I've . . . got something to say . . .'

At which point George stepped in front of her. 'Don't worry, poppet. I'll tell them.' He took a very deep breath and told them everything. By which I mean, he told them a load of balderdash. 'I wanted to see if using dynamite to cook the Christmas turkey would be any quicker than using the oven when . . . **BOOM!** The house exploded. It could have happened to anyone.'

'Dad!' yelled Katy, giving George the biggest Raspberry-Sauce Look that Gigi had ever seen.

Gigi wasn't sure that George's story was very

convincing, but then again, the truth about a colossal Santa Claus would probably have sounded even less convincing.

Katy started to tell him off, so George let out a huge exaggerated yawn and said he was exhausted and should probably head to bed. Well, not bed exactly . . . how about if everyone slept on the bales of hay in the barn?

'Oh, so **THAT'S** what you mean by "hit the hay"!' said Gigi, and her grandpa winked at her.

Pip had a much better idea, which didn't involve sleeping anywhere near mice or earwigs: the pub in the village had a couple of rooms to rent. They began to walk down the driveway, past the big pile of bricks that used to be George's farmhouse, when Katy suddenly shrieked, 'What's that?!' and pointed over to a huge footprint in the ground, where Malcolm Gripe's house used to be. George and Gigi smiled at each other, and George said, 'I think some . . . tectonic plates must have moved . . . yep, that's it.'

Gigi grabbed her grandpa's hand, and they walked behind Katy and Pip, only stopping to roll away a white beard-whisker the length of a lorry. 'You must be tired,' said George to Gigi, and even though she was ABSOLUTELY EXHAUSTED, she said, 'Not in the slightest, Grandpa!' because she didn't want this day to end.

She couldn't believe she had ever thought her grandpa was boring, or his tales were nonsense, or his inventions were weird – not for a millionth of a millisecond. All she wanted to do now was hear more of his spectacular stories.

'Oh!' squeaked Gigi. 'We'll need to design you a new house!'

'Of course!' said George. 'Think of all the **AMAZING** gizmos and gadgets and widgets I can fill it with! A spinning kitchen, so the window always faces the sun!'

'And a special lab for your amazing experiments!' added Gigi. 'On the roof, maybe? With a special glass lift to take you up there.'

Grandpa giggled and almost toppled into another enormous footprint. 'Well, if I build a shiny new lab, I'm definitely going to need a shiny new assistant. You don't know anyone who might fancy the gig, do you?'

Gigi hugged George so hard, it was a miracle she didn't break a few of his ribs.

'Oh, this is the best Christmas present ever!' squealed Gigi, which was lucky because the rest of her presents had been destroyed when the house fell down.

'I'll start drawing up your contract, poppet,' said George.

Gigi stopped in her tracks, folded her arms and spoke to her grandpa in her very sternest voice. 'If I'm to accept this position,' she said, 'you're going to have to stop calling me "poppet".'

George looked surprised. 'Oh, I'm so sorry – I had no idea whatsoever you didn't like it, Gigi.'

'Not "Gigi" either. That's just a nickname. I was named after a very brilliant person, and from now on, I want to be known by what's on my birth certificate . . . Georgia.'

George smiled so wide that the corners of his mouth almost touched his eyes. Gigi, sorry – **GEORGIA** – rushed on ahead, turned on her very sweetest smile and grabbed her parents' hands. 'Do you think I could stay with Grandpa until the new term starts? It's only a couple more weeks! I promise I'll do all my homework on time for a year!'

'I think Grandpa might actually have to come and live with us until his house is fixed,' Katy replied, and Gi– Georgia squealed so loudly that you could hear her fifteen villages away. Malcolm Gripe would definitely have complained – if he hadn't been squished, of course.

Now, if you stopped reading there, you might have thought this story had a happy ending. But I told you at the start that it wouldn't, and I don't break my promises. And, as the more observant of you might have noticed, there's one paragraph left to go . . .

As George walked past the tumbledown old shed, he heard a quiet voice drifting up from the ground. *Good old Repeatcorn*, he thought to himself. If he'd have looked down at that very moment, he would have seen a rusty tin bucket, still full to the brim with his granddaughter's magical brew. But what he definitely wouldn't have spotted was a very, very, very ancient, titchy-tiny, microscopic speck of a woman lowering herself in using a walking stick no bigger than an ant's tongue, shrieking 'Time for my revenge . . .' and about to take a very, very big gulp of it . . .

Adam Hills

It was Christmas Eve in Australia, and the sun was hot.

In the **BIGGEST, WIDEST,** deepest river in Australia, two crocodiles lay with their heads just above the water. One of the crocodiles was GIGANTIC. The other was not as big.

'Do you know what I want for Christmas this year?' the Gigantic Australian Crocodile asked.

'No,' replied the second crocodile, who, as mentioned, was not as big. In fact, his friends called him 'Notasbig', so we'll do the same.

'What do you want for Christmas?' asked Notasbig.

The Gigantic Crocodile grinned, showing hundreds of sharp white teeth. 'For Christmas this year,' he said, 'I would like lots and lots and lots of presents.'

'You'll never get lots and lots and lots of presents,' the Notasbig one said. 'You're rude and you're greedy and you're nasty to all the other animals. You'll be lucky if you even get one present.'

'HO, HO, HO,' laughed the Gigantic Crocodile, in a way that made him sound like a slightly naughty Santa Claus. 'I bet, that by the end of Christmas Day,

I'll have more presents than you've ever seen in your whole life!'

'Not a chance!' the Notasbig one said. 'No one will give even a single present to a crocodile who is as rude and greedy and nasty to all the other animals as you are.'

'HO, **HO,** *HO!*' laughed the Gigantic Crocodile again. (This time he sounded like a really naughty Santa Claus.) 'Well, in that case, I'll just have to take some presents for myself.'

'Take some presents for yourself!?' repeated the Notasbig one. 'From where?'

'From the town,' said the Gigantic Crocodile with a wicked grin. 'I'll leave the water and go through the bush to where the houses are. Then I'll steal all the presents from all the little children.'

(In Australia, anywhere that is full of trees is called 'the bush'. Unlike forests, which can sometimes seem neat and orderly, the bush is wild, messy and cluttered. A bit like a teenager's bedroom, but with snakes.)

'Steal presents from children?' echoed Notasbig. 'I suppose that's better than eating them.'

'Oh, but this is much more fun,' said the Gigantic Crocodile. 'This way I get loads of presents and make children miserable at the same time. I go home happy and I get to watch them cry!'

'Well, you really are the rudest, greediest and nastiest crocodile in the whole river,' Notasbig replied.

'Yes, I am,' said the Gigantic Crocodile. And just in case there was any doubt, he flashed his hundreds of teeth, which gleamed like sharp knives.

'You're also the biggest crocodile in the river,' said the Notasbig one. 'The children will see you coming from miles away.'

The Gigantic Crocodile was indeed the biggest crocodile in the river. Sometimes, in Australia, people are given nicknames that are the opposite of how they look. For example, a tall man might be called 'Tiny', or someone with red hair might be called 'Blue'. In this case, though, the Gigantic Crocodile was actually gigantic.

'Tommy rot!' cried the Gigantic Crocodile. 'No one will see me coming because I have secret plans and clever tricks. In fact, as well as being the **BIGGEST** crocodile in the river, I am also the **CLEVEREST.'**

Between you and me, Notasbig knew that any crocodile (or person) that calls themselves the cleverest or the most brilliant or the strongest at anything, usually isn't as clever or brilliant or strong as they think they are.

'Maybe you should try being nicer to people,' said Notasbig. 'Maybe then someone would give you presents.'

'I've never been nice to anyone in my entire life,' replied the Gigantic Crocodile. 'And I'm not about to start now. It sounds like too much hard work. Stealing presents will be easier.'

Notasbig shook his head and turned to swim away. He knew that some crocodiles (and people) just refuse to listen to good advice.

The Gigantic Crocodile swam to the side of the river and crawled out of the water. A **TALL,** furry animal was standing on the bank, drinking from the river. It had a long tail, huge hind legs and a TINY pouch for its baby. This was Hoppy-Dops the Kangaroo.

'G'day, g'day,' said Hoppy-Dops, eyeing the Crocodile suspiciously. (Hoppy-Dops knew the crocodile well enough not to trust him.) 'Where are you off to on Christmas Eve?'

'I have secret plans and clever tricks,' said the Crocodile.

'Tut, tut, tut,' replied Hoppy-Dops. 'I'll bet you're going to do something rude and greedy and nasty.'

The Gigantic Crocodile grinned at Hoppy-Dops and said:

'I'll wiggle my tail and shuffle my feet,
And steal myself a treaty, treat, treat.'

'What kind of treat?' asked Hoppy-Dops.

'Try to guess,' said the Crocodile. 'It's something you find under a tree.'

Hoppy-Dops looked shocked. 'You don't mean you're going to steal a Christmas present?'

'Of course I am,' said the Crocodile.

'Oh, you horrid, greedy, bumptious brute!' cried Hoppy-Dops. 'I hope someone catches you and locks you away in a cage.'

The Gigantic Crocodile laughed a deep, rumbling laugh at Hoppy-Dops, then waddled off into the bush.

Before too long, the Crocodile met a small nuggety animal with coarse grey fur. It was Wimble the Wombat. Wimble was busy digging himself a hole, and didn't notice the Crocodile at first.

The Gigantic Crocodile snuck up behind the Wombat and bit him on the bottom. You see, not only was the Crocodile rude and greedy and mean and selfish, he was also desperate for attention.

'Ow!' cried Wimble in a gruff voice. 'Who did that?' He turned to find the Crocodile grinning at him with his gleaming teeth. 'Oh, it's you, is it, you grubby crocodile. Why don't you go back to the big wide river where you can get up to no good on your own?'

Wimble had only met the crocodile a couple of times, but that was enough to know how much trouble he could cause.

'I have secret plans and clever tricks,' said the Crocodile.

'You mean greedy plans and nasty tricks,' said Wimble.

The Crocodile grinned and said:

'I'm off to steal from someone's tree,

To find a lovely present for me.'

'Oh, you selfish beastly beast!' cried Wimble. 'Oh, you rude and rugged reptile. I hope someone sends you far, far away where there's no one for you to annoy!'

The Gigantic Crocodile laughed again, even deeper and rumblier (because he knew that no one could ever stop his plans), then disappeared into the thick, thick bush.

A bit further on he saw a fluffy ball of fur sitting high in a tree eating gum leaves. It was Fuzzyface the Koala. Fuzzyface was new to this part of the bush and unfamiliar with the Crocodile's wily ways.

'Hello,' said Fuzzyface. 'My name's Fuzzyface, what's yours?'

'What's mine?' boomed the Croc. 'WHAT'S MINE??' He was clearly annoyed that the Koala didn't know who he was. 'I'm the biggest, cleverest and strongest crocodile in all of Australia!'

'And apparently the rudest,' said Fuzzyface to herself quietly.

'What was that?' snapped the Croc.

'Nothing,' said Fuzzyface meekly.

The Crocodile frowned at her, so Fuzzyface changed the subject. 'And what are you up to today?' she asked.

'I have secret plans and clever tricks,' said the Crocodile.

'I see,' said Fuzzyface, who really couldn't have cared less about secret plans and clever tricks. 'Would you like to take a leaf?'

'I have better things to take than leaves,' said the Crocodile.

'There's nothing better than leaves,' said Fuzzyface.

'Ah ha,' said the Crocodile.

'Your gift is OK if you just want a meal,

But the present I want, I am going to steal.'

Fuzzyface's face started to **SHAKE.** Even her fur seemed to become less fuzzy. 'Did you say you're going to steal a present?'

'Yes!' said the Crocodile. 'I'm going to take loads of presents. Right from under the children's Christmas trees.'

'Oh, you awful, annoying Croc,' cried Fuzzyface. 'You mean and muggish creature. I hope the trees all fall on you and crush you underneath them like a raisin under a piano.'

The Crocodile grinned up at Fuzzyface and said, 'Maybe your tree will fall down, and take you with it.' And quick as a flash, with one huge bite of his huge jaws, he bit through the tree that Fuzzyface was sitting in, and **DOWN** it came. Just in time, Fuzzyface grabbed hold of another tree, swung herself **UP** on to a branch and scurried away. She vowed to tell everyone about the mean, rude, selfish crocodile she had just met.

A bit further on, the Crocodile met a small brown and white bird with a long beak, sitting in a tree and laughing to herself. It was Cackledackle the Kookaburra, and her laugh was famous for being **LOUD** and raucous – so much so that people even sang songs about it.

'G'day there,' chuckled Cackledackle, who always tried to see the best in people. 'What brings you up here so far from the river?'

'Ah,' said the Crocodile. 'I have secret plans and clever tricks.'

'I hope it's not something rude and selfish,' chortled Cackledackle.

'Rude and selfish?' cried the Crocodile. 'It's fun and helpful.'

'It's lovely and super
It's fun and it's duper
It's sure to give you a lift
It's great to receive it
You better believe it
Everyone loves a gift.'

'Are you giving out gifts?' said Cackledackle Kookaburra with a giggle. 'I must admit, that is a fun and helpful thing to do.'

The Gigantic Crocodile laughed so hard that his teeth rattled like keys in a backpack. 'Crocodiles don't give gifts,' he said. 'We take them. And sometimes we take feathers too, for decoration.'

Very quickly, the Crocodile jumped up and snapped his jaws at Cackledackle Kookaburra. He just managed to grab hold of a couple of the bird's tailfeathers before Cackledackle shot straight up into the air.

For the first time in Cackledackle's life, she didn't feel like laughing.

At last the Gigantic Crocodile came out on the other side of the bush. The hot, hot sun was setting now, and he knew that all the little children would soon be going to bed.

When the children wake up, he thought to himself, *they'll have* LOTS *and LOTS and* ***LOTS*** *of presents under their trees. And that's when I'll put my secret plans and clever tricks into action.*

The Gigantic Australian Crocodile lay down in the long grass and fell asleep, dreaming of stealing Christmas presents.

Back in the bush, the other animals had gathered together in a clearing.

'I just met the Gigantic Crocodile,' said Fuzzyface the Koala. 'He told me he's going to steal Christmas presents from children. Then he bit my tree and made it fall down!'

'I saw him too,' said Cackledackle Kookaburra. 'He told me the same thing. And he took some feathers from my tail!'

'He bit me on the bottom!' cried Wimble the Wombat.

Fuzzyface looked concerned 'What should we do?' she asked. 'He's mean and rude and selfish and greedy.'

Everyone was silent. No one seemed to know what to do about the mean and rude and selfish and greedy crocodile.

'I'll tell you what you should do,' said a voice from up high. All heads turned skywards to see a small furry animal hanging from the branch of a tree. It was Old Grandma Possum. She had dark grey fur, long white whiskers, and her strong tail was dotted with sliver flecks. She moved very slowly.

Grandma Possum cleared her throat as if she was about to speak, then said nothing. No one could tell if she was doing it to create tension or if she had forgotten what she was going to say.

Eventually Fuzzyface spoke up.

'What?' she cried. 'What should we do about the Gigantic Crocodile?'

'You stop him!' said Grandma Possum.

'But how?' cried Hoppy-Dops. 'He's bigger than us.'

'And meaner,' said Wimble.

'And ruder,' said Fuzzyface.

'And . . . well . . . just all of those things,' said Cackledackle.

'That might very well be,' said Old Grandma Possum. 'But you're all smarter than him. His plans won't be anywhere near as clever as he thinks they are.'

The animals thought for a moment, then they all huddled together in the middle of the clearing and began to *WHISPER*.

Back at the edge of town, the Gigantic Crocodile was waking up after a good night's sleep. The sun was rising now on Christmas Day, and he knew that soon the children would be opening their presents. He crept through the **LONG** grass at the edge of the bush and spied a holiday park.

'Ah ha,' he whispered. 'All those families are spending their holiday away from their homes, which means they probably won't have big trees. It's time for Clever Trick Number One!'

The Gigantic Crocodile snuck over to a patch of grass in front of a caravan. He knew that Christmas trees were tall and green, and that they were usually very narrow at the top and very **WIDE** at the bottom. Gently, carefully and ever so quietly, the Gigantic Crocodile did a crocodile headstand. He spread his little crocodile arms out on the ground to make them look like the bottom branches of the tree and pointed his tail straight up into the air like a church spire.

'Oooh, look outside!' shouted a little boy called Emilio. 'There's a gigantic nobbly Christmas tree.'

The Crocodile heard the door of the caravan open, and the sound of small footsteps approaching.

'Maybe we should open our presents under this tree,' said Emilio's brother, Leon. 'It's way bigger than the tiny one in our caravan.'

'That's the best idea you've ever had,' said Emilio. 'Let's put all our presents under the gigantic tree now!'

The Gigantic Crocodile heard the footsteps go back to the caravan, then he heard the door **SLAM.** There was rummaging and rumbling, the opening of a door, and then the return of footsteps. He almost laughed out loud at how well his plan was going. He licked his lips and began to dribble with excitement.

Suddenly there was the sound of something jumping through the bush. The noise seemed to get closer and closer until . . . Hoppy-Dops the Kangaroo came bounding towards the caravan!

'Look out, Emilio; look out, Leon!' cried Hoppy-Dops. 'That's not a Christmas tree. That's the **GIGANTIC CROCODILE,** and he wants to steal all your presents!'

Emilio and Leon shrieked and ran back into their caravan as fast as they could, carrying all their presents with them.

Hoppy-Dops hopped over to the tree-that-was-actually-a-crocodile, leaned back on her own tail, then used her hind legs to kick the Crocodile as hard as she had ever kicked anything in her life. The tree-that-was-actually-a-crocodile **CRUMPLED** into a ball and went skidding and tumbling back into the bush, crashing head first into the base of a tree.

But crocodiles are tough and stubborn. It is difficult for even a kangaroo to hurt them. The Gigantic Crocodile bent himself back into shape and checked that nothing was broken. There was a large dent in the trunk of the tree where the Croc's head had collided with it, but apart from that, everything was in the right place.

The Gigantic Crocodile picked himself up, huffed a bit, then began creeping through the long grass again.

Soon he spied a picnic area with a barbecue.

'Now for Clever Trick Number Two,' he said to himself. 'This one is certain to work.'

No one was using the barbecue at that moment, but the Crocodile knew someone would be along soon. Australian families love having barbecues at Christmas because the weather is so lovely and warm.

The Gigantic Crocodile waddled over and stood a little distance away from the barbecue – but not too far. He laid down on the ground and curled his hands and feet underneath him. He then unfurled his tail and curled it back over the top of his body towards his head. Finally, he tilted his head back as far as it would go.

'HEH, HEH, HEH,' chuckled the Crocodile to himself. 'And **ho, ho, ho.** I look just like Santa's sleigh.'

To be fair to the Crocodile, he did kinda look like Santa's sleigh – if Santa's sleigh was green and rough and had nobbly bumps all over. Before long, he heard the voices of a family approaching. The children of this family were called Polly and Max.

'Ooh, look,' said Polly. 'Santa left his sleigh behind.'

'It's a nobbly old sleigh,' said Max, who was very observant.

'We should open our presents on it!' said Polly. 'It'll

feel like Santa's giving them to us personally.'

'I don't know . . .' began Max, but Polly cut him off.

'Oh, go on, Max, please!' she cried.

'Fine then,' said Max eventually. 'But you have to go get them.'

The Gigantic Crocodile opened one eye and saw Polly's feet scamper back to the barbecue, where her parents were trying to get it to light. She picked up a **HUGE** bag and came running back to the sleigh-that-was-actually-a-crocodile. The Crocodile heard the bag opening and could almost see the wrapping paper on the presents. *Only a few more seconds*, he thought, *and those presents will be within my reach.*

At that moment, there was a flash of grey as Wimble the Wombat came careering out of the long grass and barrelled into the Crocodile's bottom, sending him somersaulting tail-over-head.

'Run!' cried the Wombat, 'All of you, run! That's not a sleigh, it's the Gigantic Crocodile and he wants to steal all of your presents!'

The children ran back to their parents, making sure to take their presents with them, and Wimble ran back into the bush. The Gigantic Crocodile was left sprawled upside down with his head on the ground and his tail in the air.

He righted himself, cursed the Wombat, and waddled back into the bush to hide for a while.

'Gumnuts! Now I'm going to have to collect lots and lots of presents all in one go,' he said to himself. 'It's a good thing I prepared Clever Trick Number Three.'

The Gigantic Crocodile crept round the edge of the town, taking great care not to be seen. Soon he spied a huge house with loads of Christmas decorations. There was a big red mechanical Father Christmas in the front yard, a fake reindeer on the roof, and **LOTS** and **LOTS** and **LOTS** of Christmas lights.

'If they have lots and lots and lots of Christmassy things outside,' said the Crocodile to himself, 'I'll bet they have lots and lots and lots of presents inside.'

The Crocodile crept up to the front of the house and stole some tinsel from one of the windows, then snuck behind a tree. There was puffing and panting and the sounds of reptilian straining, and a minute later the crocodile emerged – looking like a surfboard that had been wrapped up as a present.

(Actually, he emerged looking like a Gigantic Crocodile who had tried to make himself look like a surfboard that had been wrapped up as a present.)

The crocodile had tucked in his arms and legs and flattened out his tail. The tinsel was wrapped round him, but the end of it was dragging on the ground as he attempted to hop towards the front door.

'Ho, ho, ho,' he laughed to himself. (This time he sounded like a slightly tired Santa.) 'When they see me, they'll take me inside to where all the other presents are. Then I'll steal them for myself.'

When the Crocodile made it to the front door, he poked out one finger and pushed the doorbell, then quickly tucked his arm back in again. He heard footsteps inside the house and the unlocking of a door, then a child's voice.

'Mum, Dad!' cried the child. 'Someone's left a present at the door. It looks like a surfboard!'

'Really?' came an adult voice from inside the house.

This particular child was called Becky, and she peered closely at the surfboard-that-was-actually-a-crocodile.

'Yep,' answered Becky. 'A big, bumpy, green, slightly scaly surfboard.'

'Well, bring it inside and we'll open it with all the other presents,' said the adult voice.

Just then there was a **SWOOSH** and a ***SWISH,*** and something came swooshing and swishing out of the sky. It was Cackledackle Kookaburra, and she did not look happy.

'Look out, Becky! Look out! Look out!' cried Cackledackle. 'That's not a surfboard, that's the Gigantic Crocodile, and he plans to steal all your presents!'

Becky screamed out loud and slammed the door shut, right in the Crocodile's face.

Cackledackle flew back to her tree, and the Gigantic Crocodile toppled backwards, towards the mechanical Father Christmas. He tripped and tumbled, bounced and stumbled, then teetered over the robotic Santa for a second, before crashing down on it with an **ENORMOUS** thud and a tiny jingle.

The crocodile lay grumbling in the wreckage of the mechanical Father Christmas. To the casual observer, it would have been hard to make out where the crocodile ended and the Santa began.

'Grrrr,' said the Gigantic Crocodile to himself. He was angry, annoyed and slightly embarrassed.

But not yet beaten.

'I think I just came up with Clever Trick Number Four. This one will definitely work!'

Before anyone came back out of the house, the Crocodile removed all the clothes from the mechanical Father Christmas, tucked them under his arm and waddled into the long grass.

The Gigantic Crocodile walked a bit further round the edge of town until he spied a beach. In Australia, some families celebrate Christmas on the beach so they can cool down from the hot, hot sun. The sand was golden, the sea was bright blue and the children's beach towels were green, yellow, red and orange.

The Crocodile chuckled and began to put on the clothes he had stolen (he even found a place for the beard).

The mechanical Father Christmas had been much smaller than the Crocodile, and the clothes were way too tight.

The Gigantic Crocodile took a deep breath in and fastened the final button of the trousers. He then tried to stand on his two hind feet and walk like Father Christmas. Very clumsily, the Crocodile waddled towards the beach with a big grin on his face. He looked like a toddler who had just learned to walk (or a crocodile who was trying to look like a human).

'Ho, ho, ho,' said the Crocodile loudly. **'HO, HO, HO!'** He now sounded like a frazzled, desperate and trying-too-hard Father Christmas.

All the faces turned towards him, and the children beamed with joy.

'It's Santa!' cried one of them, with a wide grin. His name was Ethan.

'Santa's a lot bigger and greener and teethier than I remember,' said an older child, whose name was Anne-Marie. She took off her glasses and gave them a wipe, as if not trusting what she was seeing.

'Let's invite him home,' said Ethan, who was now brimming with excitement. 'He must be tired after delivering all those presents.'

'I want to take him to my house!' cried a third child. This boy was called Alfie. He had heard the commotion and desperately wanted to be a part of it.

'No, I want him to come to MY house!' said another child, called Helen. (She was Alfie's older sister and seemed to have forgotten that Alfie's house was also her house.)

More children gathered around now, and they all wanted a visit from the Santa-that-was-actually-a-crocodile.

'Hmmm,' said Helen, trying to keep everyone happy. 'Maybe Father Christmas can visit everyone's houses.'

'I'd love to see all your presents,' said the Crocodile out loud. *And steal them all for myself*, he thought silently.

'Don't take him home! Don't take him home!' cried a voice from a nearby tree. It was Fuzzyface the Koala. 'That's not Father Christmas, it's the Gigantic Crocodile. And he hasn't been delivering presents, he's here to steal them.'

Ethan, Anne-Marie, Alfie, Helen and all the other children screamed as they ran back to their families. A few angry adults reluctantly peeled themselves from their deckchairs and began to walk towards the Crocodile, who panicked and speed-waddled past the children, towards the sea. As he did so, the button on his trousers popped off and they fell down on to the sand.

'You can try to stop me all you want!' cried the Crocodile as he dived into the waves. 'But I'll just keep coming up with more secret plans and clever tricks. You'll see!'

The Crocodile swam out to sea, and Fuzzyface jumped from tree to tree as she returned to the bush. When Fuzzyface the Koala reached the clearing, the other animals were waiting for her.

'How did it go?' asked Cackledackle.

'Did we stop the greedy, nasty selfish brute from stealing presents?' asked Wimble the Wombat.

'We stopped him for a bit,' replied Fuzzyface. 'But he said he'd just come up with more secret plans and clever tricks. I'm sorry,' she said softly. 'I tried. I really tried.'

The animals were silent once again. No one seemed to know what to do.

Then Cackledackle had an idea.

'I know,' she said. 'Why don't we ask Old Grandma Possum? She knew what to do last time.'

'That's a great idea,' said Wimble.

'Old Grandma Possssummmm?' cried Cackledackle.

'Old Grrandmaaaa Possssummm?' shouted Fuzzyface.

'Olllldddddd Grrrandddmaaaa Posssummmmm!!!' yelled Hoppy-Dops.

'There's no need to shout,' said Old Grandma Possum, who was hanging upside down from a branch above their heads. 'I'm right here.'

'Sorry,' said Cackledackle, 'but we've tried everything to stop the Gigantic Crocodile from stealing the children's Christmas presents, but he keeps coming up with more secret plans and clever tricks.'

'What should we do?' asked Wimble.

'Well,' said Old Grandma Possum. 'The only solution is for all of you to get together and grab him by the tail. Then you need to swing him **ROUND** and **ROUND** until you're able to throw him into the hot, hot sun, where he'll be sizzled up like a sausage.'

'We're not strong enough to do that!' cried Fuzzyface.

'You will be if you all work together,' said Old Grandma Possum gently.

The animals looked at each other. All at once, they knew what they had to do.

Back in the long grass on the edge of town, the Gigantic Crocodile was busy thinking. 'I've got it!' he cried to himself. 'It's time to try out Clever Trick Number Five.'

But just then, he heard a rustling and a **RUMBLING** and a rushing in the bush. Suddenly he saw Wimble the Wombat, Cackledackle the Kookaburra, Hoppy-Dops the Kangaroo and Fuzzyface the Koala all coming towards him.

'We've all had quite enough of your clever tricks!' said Hoppy-Dops.

'Oh yeah?' said the Gigantic Crocodile. 'And what are you going to do about it? You're little and I'm gigantic!'

One by one, the animals approached the crocodile. As they gathered at his feet, he looked down on them all with a flashy grin. They couldn't hurt him!

The Crocodile watched, bemused, as the four animals grabbed him by the tail and dug their feet into the ground.

'Now what are you going to do?' asked the Crocodile, smiling with glee (and slightly misplaced confidence).

Wimble, Cackledackle, Fuzzyface and Hoppy-Dops began to swing the crocodile round and round. At first they swung him slowly, then they swung him faster . . .

And FASTER.

And **FASTER.**

And **FASTER STILL.**

Soon the Gigantic Crocodile was just a blurry circle going round and round above their heads.

Suddenly they let go of the Crocodile's tail, and he went shooting up into the sky like a great green rocket.

Up and up he went.

Higher and higher.

Faster and faster.

He was going so fast and so high that soon the Earth was just a tiny dot, miles below.

He *whizzed* on and on.

He *whizzed* far into space.

He *whizzed* past the Moon.

He *whizzed* past stars and planets.

Until, at last . . .

With the most tremendous **BANG**, the Gigantic Crocodile crashed head first into the hot, hot sun.

And he was sizzled up like a sausage on a barbecue.

'Hoorrayy!' cried Wimble, Cackledackle, Fuzzyface and Hoppy-Dops.

'Old Grandma Possum was right!' said Wimble.

'Let's run back and tell her it worked!' cried Cackledackle.

Back at the clearing, Old Grandma Possum was woken by the sound of cheers and whoops.

'It worked!' shouted Hoppy-Dops. 'Your plan worked.'

'Good,' said Old Grandma Possum, wiping the sleep from her eyes. 'I thought it might.'

'But how did you know what to do?' asked Wimble.

'Well,' said Old Grandma Possum, 'when I was a young possum, my elders told me a story about an Enormous Crocodile in Africa. His name was slightly different, and he came from a different place – but he was just as greedy and rude and nasty and selfish as the Gigantic Australian Crocodile.'

Old Grandma Possum looked around and saw that more animals had gathered to hear her speak. There was a cockatoo and a galah, a snake and a spider, a wallaby and an echidna.

'There will always be rude and greedy beasts,' said Old Grandma Possum to the crowd around her. 'And when we tell stories about the old beasts, we teach each other how to deal with the new ones.'

'Tell us the old story!' cried Cackledackle.

'Yes, please!' said Wimble.

'Yes, tell us the story of the Enormous Crocodile,' said Fuzzyface.

'We're all listening,' said Hoppy-Dops.

Old Grandma Possum looked around the clearing and saw that every set of eyes was on her. She took a deep breath, cleared her throat, and began to speak.

'In the biggest, brownest, muddiest river in Africa, two crocodiles lay with their heads just above the water.

One of the crocodiles was enormous. The other was not so big . . .'

Nadia Shireen

'What's you thinking is the best thing about living in England?' the Big Friendly Giant asked as he strode into his cave and set Sophie down on a shelf.

'The rain?' Sophie replied. 'Tea and scones? Hedgehogs?'

'No,' the BFG said. He pointed to the black-and-white striped snozzcumbers piled up in the corner. 'It is that I is not having to eat them disgusting things any more.'

'Well, I can understand *that*,' said Sophie, with a little shiver. Snozzcumbers were the most revolting things she had ever tasted.

The BFG began hunting around for a sack to fill up with **DREAM** jars. He wore tatty leather sandals, had large soft ears and a crinkly, craggley face. Sophie remembered the night when he'd plucked her from her bedroom in the orphanage, and grinned. They had shared some wild ADVENTURES together. Of course, the biggest had been getting rid of the child-guzzling, bone-crunching, horrible giants who also used to live in Giant Country. That had been a *very* satisfying mission.

Although the BFG was a **GIANT,** he was most definitely *not* a child-guzzler. He was, in fact, a dream collector. Of course, you or I cannot collect dreams. We cannot recognize the way they dance through the air like wispy clouds. Nor can we hear them buzzing about our heads. But the BFG can. He catches them with a LONG butterfly net and plops them in large glass jars. Then, every evening, he gallops miles and miles, over land and sea, to blow happy dreams through the windows of sleeping children.

Sophie craned her neck to look at all the jars of dreams the BFG had collected over the years, but she still couldn't see the very top of the shelves.

'How many dreams do you think you have?' she asked.

The BFG stroked one of his ears thoughtfully. 'I is thinking it is somewhere between nine thousand and twenty-three zillion,' he said, with a little nod. 'Yes, that sounds about right.'

'It's amazing,' said Sophie.

'Just you be careful high up on that shelf,' said the

BFG. 'I don't want you splattering all over my floor like a potato.'

Sophie giggled. 'Do you mean tomato?' she said. 'They're much squishier.'

'What I is saying and what I is meaning is two entirely different things,' sighed the BFG. 'You should be knowing this by now.'

'I know,' said Sophie, not wishing to hurt the BFG's feelings. 'I'm sorry.'

The BFG gave her a little nod.

She turned her attention back to the jars. There were rows and rows of them. The dreams themselves were different colours, and floated behind the glass like soft, glowing eggs. Each jar had a label, upon which the BFG had scribbled a description of the dream trapped inside. Sophie read some of them:

My cat can speak but only I understand her. She tells me she likes it when I stroke under her chin but doesn't like the vacuum cleaner. She also says she deliberately left a dead mouse in Dad's slippers because he said a rude word about her.

The next one was much longer:

I discover that I can make people do a silly dance just by saying 'jellybaby'. I make my little sister dance during breakfast. I shout 'jellybaby!' through the bathroom door and my mum starts dancing in the shower. Then I walk to the bus stop and shout 'jellybaby!' and everyone in the queue starts jiggling and waving their arms about. I get to school and Mr Mackintosh is doing a very boring assembly, so I stand up and hoot 'jellybaby!' The whole school starts leaping about and it is total chaos. Then my mum shakes me awake and says, 'No more sweets for you before bed, young man.'

'Silly,' said Sophie, rolling her eyes. She looked at another one:

> ***One day I decide to eat an entire jar of honey. It is so delicious that I start eating honey for breakfast, lunch and dinner until one day I wake up to find I have wings and yellow fuzz all over my face. I am a bee! I buzz around the house and fly through an open window. Mr West from next door is hanging out the washing and faints when he sees me buzzing happily through the air.***

Sophie snorted and shook her head. 'That one is even sillier!' she said.

Then she spotted a cluster of jars that looked quite different. She weaved her way towards them, and gasped as she got closer.

'Aha,' said the BFG. 'You is finding the cracklers! They is extra special dreams for extra special times.'

These particular jars shone as if they were filled with glitter. The sparkles gently swirled and danced behind the glass.

'Oh! They're so lovely,' said Sophie. She read two of the labels:

My birthday cake is so massive, a crane has to lift it through the window of our flat. I cut it open and loads of sweets tumble out. I gather them up in handfuls and chuck them over the side of the balcony, and all the kids outside catch them and cheer.

It is Eid and my mum is stressing over having to make dinner for everyone, so I click my fingers and the dining table is magically full of food. Then I click them again and the house is all tidy and decorated. Mum goes and has a relaxing bath and asks why I can't do the clicky thing every day.

Sophie giggled. 'How do you know when it's the right time to give someone a **CRACKLER?** Do you have a special calendar or something?'

The BFG tapped the side of his head.

'You is forgetting that I is a very old giant. I keep lots of dates and facts up in here. For instance, I know that every December, a lot of you humans is going utterly bananas about CRINKLEMAS.'

'Crinklemas? I think you mean Christmas,' laughed Sophie.

The BFG frowned a little, and Sophie clamped her hands over her mouth.

'I'm so sorry,' she said. 'I don't mean to keep correcting you. Yes, you're right, lots of people *love* Crinklemas.' Sophie thought about her previous Christmases. She had spent each and every one of them in the orphanage, where she had lived since she was a baby. The woman who ran the place – the dreadful Mrs Clonkers – was strict, mean and miserable.

'Your face has gone all glumpy,' said the BFG softly. 'I thought all chiddlers loved Crinklemas?'

Sophie shook her head. 'I think many do,' she said. 'But it wasn't much fun where I lived.'

A big fat tear rolled down the BFG's cheek. 'I is dumbsilly because I keeps forgetting you are a norphan,' he sniffed. 'Did you not get any presents? Not even one?'

Sophie shook her head. 'Nope. Mrs Clonkers didn't allow it. I'm sure other orphanages weren't as horrible as ours. Just my bad luck. But the *one* good thing about Christmas Day was that Clonkers would go to her horrible brother's house for lunch. So we'd have a couple of lovely hours without her.'

'But . . . but did you not get to have a scrumdiddly-umptious glorious Crinklemas feast?' asked the BFG.

'Oh no,' said Sophie. 'Clonkers would leave a tray of boiled-egg sandwiches out for us on the kitchen table and that would be that.'

The BFG sniffled some more, eventually blowing his nose into a **MASSIVE** hankie. Sophie reckoned it was about the size of a duvet. For a moment she wondered if it was *her* duvet, but then she saw the initials *BFG* had been neatly embroidered on to one of the corners.

'What about you?' asked Sophie, who felt it was sensible to change the subject. 'What do you do over Chris – I mean, Crinklemas?'

The BFG settled back in his chair and folded his arms across his chest. 'Well,' he said. 'I is glad you asked. I usually has quite a busy time in Crinklemas. I has to help a VERY IMPORTANT FRIEND.' He paused and smiled.

Sophie raised her eyebrows. 'Who?'

'FATHER CRINKLEMAS himself!' said the BFG, his eyes shining.

'No!' said Sophie. 'Really?'

The BFG nodded.

'I would never fib about such a thing. I has been helping Father Crinklemas for many years now. It's the least I can do, ever since . . . well.' He suddenly looked a little sheepish.

'Since what?' asked Sophie.

The BFG gave a big sigh. 'You must remember I has been living a long old life,' he said. 'And lots of strange things have happened over the years. Some of them has been good things and some of them has been . . . *bad* things. Anyway, a long time ago, I is scribbling a letter to Father Crinklemas telling him I has been a very good giant that year and could I please, if it's not too much trouble, have a dream-blower?'

'Oh yes!' said Sophie. 'It's over there in the corner.'

'Yes, indeed it is. You is a clever girl, though you like interruptings a lot. Anyway, writing that letter was a very bad idea. Because LOVELY jumbly old Father Crinklemas came to Giant Country for the very first time – *especially* to deliver my present. He landed his big old sleigh outside my cave, which had been pulled along by his 120 reindiddlers –'

Sophie blinked. Had she heard the BFG properly? She didn't want to interrupt him again, but she *had* to ask.

'Sorry, but do you *really* mean 120 reindeer? I thought he had twelve?'

The BFG gulped. 'Well, that's the thing,' he said, his voice dropping to a whisper. 'After those horrible bone-crunchin' giants finished with them, there were only twelve left.'

'Oh no!' cried Sophie.

'Oh yes!' said the BFG, nodding. 'It was terrible!

Those brutes gobbled the poor reindiddlers up, antlers and all. "Merry Christmas to us!" they hooted. We gathered the rest of them and hid inside the cave. Father Crinklemas put *all* of those giants on his Naughty List that day,' said the BFG with a heavy sigh.

Sophie couldn't quite believe what she was hearing. 'Then what happened?' she asked.

'Well, of course I is feeling terrible about the whole thing,' continued the BFG. 'If I hadn't written my letter, those poor reindiddlers would still be scampering about happy as fleas! I knows I has to fix it somehow.'

'You mustn't blame yourself,' said Sophie gently. 'It was those nasty brutes who hurt the reindeer, not you.'

'Father Crinklemas said the same thing,' muttered the BFG. 'But I is feeling terrible all the same. "These poor hoofers won't be able to drag this sleigh all around the world," Father Christmas had said. "There are only twelve left! It's just not fair on them."

'The two of us sat together for a long, long time, scritching our noggins and trying to think of a plan. Poor old Father Crinklemas was pacing about muttering this and that, stroking his beard with worry. Well, I was feeling so bad for him I thought maybe he needed a little drink and a snack to cheer him up. And *that* is when I is suddenly having the most whoppsy idea!' The BFG jumped up and ran to a cupboard in the corner of the cave. He dashed back, holding a huge green bottle, which was half full of bubbly liquid.

'Frobscottle!' said Sophie, with a grin.

'Exunckly!' said the BFG.

Frobscottle was the most **DELICIOUS** drink in the world. But it was so bubbly, it made whoever drank it whizzpop. Sophie had often watched the BFG flying noisily and rudely through the air, like a parping rocket.

'I loaded up the remaining reindiddlers with gallons and gallons of the stuff. Father Crinklemas tied them to his sleigh and WHOOSH! You've never seen anything fly so fast! Those reindiddlers happily **WHIZZPOPPED** their way around the globe, powered by delicious galumptious frobscottle.'

'You're a smart cookie,' grinned Sophie.

The BFG stopped and looked down at Sophie. 'A clever biscuit?' he marvelled. 'I has never eaten one of

them but I will be sure to try it. Anyway, the frobscottle worked a treat. So now I is loading them up with it every Christmas Eve,' said the BFG.

'But what about the horrible giants?' asked Sophie. 'How did you keep Father Christmas and the reindeer safe, especially after last time?'

The BFG got up and walked over to the shelves where his dream jars were kept. This time he reached up to what must have been the very highest shelf, but it was so high Sophie couldn't even see it. He lifted down a huge tatty old cardboard box and plonked it on the table with a thud.

'Every single year I has to untangle these finicky Crinklemas lights,' said the BFG, frowning. He started to empty the gigantic box, piling metres upon metres of wire and lightbulbs into a heap. Sophie had never seen so many fairy lights in one place before.

'They are the most fiddlesome lights ever, but back when those stinky giants lived here, they had a very important job to do,' said the BFG. 'Because every Crinklemas Eve afternoon, I crept out to where those horrible brutes was sleeping. And I expertly tangled them up in these colourful lights! Has you ever seen people trying to untangle these fiddly Crinklemas twinklers? It's impossible. They're just too twisty.'

Sophie nodded. 'We could see the village church from the orphanage,' she said. 'And every year the vicar and his wife would get into a horrible tangle trying to decorate it. They would get so frustrated their faces would go bright red, and the vicar's wife would always have to pop outside to buy a pint of milk and calm down.'

'The giants hated it,' said the BFG. 'I'd tangle them up good and proper. I'd also leave the lights flashing on and off, which made them all so angry they'd start biffing each other in the face.'

'Why didn't you leave them tangled up forever?' asked Sophie.

The BFG shook his head. 'If I'd left them tied up too long, they'd have chewed through the glass and wires and destroyed the whole lot. No, what I did was, once Crinklemas Day was over I'd walk past and say, "Oh, you poor giants, what a terrible tangle you've got yourselves in! Here, I can unravel you in a jiffy!" And, because they is so very lunkheaded they let me.'

'You were ever so **BRAVE** to get that close to them,' said Sophie.

'Oh, they still liked to bash me about a bit and no mistake,' said the BFG. 'But it is worth it if it is keeping them out of the way. It meant Father Crinklemas and his happy **WHIZZPOPPING** reindiddlers could still get all those presents delivered by Crinklemas morning.'

'You're a good egg,' said Sophie.

The BFG beamed. 'And you is a delightful chicken,' he said graciously.

'What else do you do for Christmas?' said Sophie.

'Well,' said the BFG, 'it's a time for doing extra good turns, is it not? So while I is skiddling all about the place blowing dreams into windows, I is doing some good turns along the way.'

'Like what?' asked Sophie.

'Has you ever seen some very big Crinklemas trees around the place? You know, those absolute **WHOPPERS** you is seeing near ice rinks and parks and fancy buildings?'

Sophie nodded excitedly.

'Yes, yes! One of the girls went into London for a doctor's appointment last year and she saw the huge one in Trafalgar Square!'

The BFG chuckled. 'Yes, I knows that one well,' he said. 'It's a present from the people of Norway, is it not?'

'Yes,' said Sophie. 'It's quite a nice story, really.' Sophie pushed her glasses up her nose a little, which she sometimes did when she had something important to say. 'The Norwegians have given us a tree every year since 1947, to say thank you for helping them during the Second World War.'

'Is that so?' said the BFG, raising an eyebrow. 'Lovely human beans, the Norwegians. Anyway, every year, I is reaching up and putting the star on top of that tree. I is putting angels and stars on the tops of big Crinklemas trees all over the place, so that you human beans don't go up ladders and fall off and break your necks.'

'But don't people *see* you?' asked Sophie.

'You is forgetting that I is a sneaky and clever giant,' said the BFG. 'Nobody is seeing me.'

The BFG drummed his enormous fingers on the table, and then wandered over to where his dream trumpet leaned against the cave wall. He picked it up. 'What a lot of trouble you caused us, little dream-blower,' said the BFG, giving the long brassy pipe a polish.

Sophie watched as her huge friend wandered about inside his old cave. She thought about the fantastic adventures they had been on together. And now, here she was, little orphan Sophie, living right by Buckingham Palace! It was hard to believe. What would the girls at the orphanage have made of it all? She shook her head and gave a little chuckle.

'What's that you is thinking now, little Sophie?' said the BFG.

'Oh, just about the orphanage,' she replied.

'So you isn't missing it too badly?' asked the BFG.

'No way,' laughed Sophie. 'There's nothing to miss! Well, apart from the other girls. I hope they're OK.'

If there had been any happiness at all in Sophie's life – before meeting the BFG – it was because of them. She remembered how, a few months ago, little Olivia had somehow managed to sneak a pack of bubble gum into the dorm room. After lights-out, she had carefully divided it up into pink, squidgy chunks and shared them out. The girls giggled silent giggles, blowing secret bubbles in the middle of the night.

Sophie gave a big sigh. She looked up again at the dream jars clustered together on the shelf, the specks of glitter floating around like dancing sparks. Slowly, a smile spread across her face.

'I've got an idea,' she said to the BFG. 'You can deliver just about any dream you like to anyone in the world, can't you?'

The BFG nodded. 'Oh yes,' he said. 'I is popping them in my suitcase, and then I is blowing them through bedroom windows with my special dream-blower. Easy as crumpets!'

Sophie pointed at the cracklers. 'And those special, sparkly dreams. The cracklers. Are there any Christmas dreams in there?'

'Oh yes!' nodded the BFG. 'Oodles of them.'

Sophie clasped her hands together. 'Could you mix

some of them together and make the most perfect Christmas dream ever?' she asked.

'Of course!' scoffed the BFG. 'I is doing that easier than you is tickling a flea.'

'I was just thinking,' continued Sophie, 'why don't we mix up the perfect Christmas dream? Then you could blow it into my old dormitory at the orphanage! It would give the girls the best Christmas they've *ever* had.'

The BFG was perfectly still for a moment. Then he leapt from his chair, and started whooping, hollering and hopping all over the place. 'It's a **RAZZTWIZZLER** of an idea! It's a total and utter **WINKSQUIFFLER!** You is brilliant, young Sophie. How do you think up such brilliant things with that titchy little head of yours? It's a miracle.'

Sophie grinned.

'We is going to make a PHIZZWIZARD,' nodded the BFG. 'Which is the VERY best kind of dream it is possible to be having.'

Sophie gasped. 'Yes!' she cried. 'Oh, yes, please!'

The BFG found an enormous empty glass jar and

plonked it on the table next to Sophie. It was almost as big as her. 'Right!' he said, rubbing his huge hands together. 'This is where we is going to mix up the ingredients for our Phizzwizard. What is we putting in this dream of yours, little Sophie?'

Sophie closed her eyes for a few seconds, trying to imagine the loveliest things about Christmas. They pinged open.

'Well, let's start with a Christmas tree. A real one, I think, because they have the most fantastic smell. And we should cover it in decorations, tinsel, fairy lights . . .'

The BFG nodded and darted over to the dream jars, clinking them about, reading labels and wittering to himself.

Sophie glanced at the pile of snozzcumbers and decided to have a little fun. She dragged a couple of the smaller ones into the middle of the cave and stood one up on its end, as if it were a tree trunk. She snapped the other snozzcumber into little pieces, and squished the chunks into the trunk, so they stuck out like branches.

'What the jiggins is you doing?' said the BFG.

'Ta-daaa!' said Sophie, waggling her hands at her creation. 'It's a Snozzcumber Christmas tree!'

The BFG laughed. 'It's not bad, little Sophie,' he said. 'But I think it is needing *lights*.'

He draped some of the fairy lights round the snozzcumber tree, and then proceeded to hang them across the barren walls of his massive cave, zigzagging them high across the ceiling.

Sophie hopped up and down with excitement and, without entirely realizing she was doing it, she started to hum and sing.

'Ugh! What on earth is that terrible racket?' said the BFG, clutching his enormous flappy ears.

'It's a Christmas carol,' said Sophie. 'A very famous one, actually.'

'Well, you is sounding like an elefunt trapped in a washing machine,' moaned the BFG.

'It's called "The Twelve Days of Christmas",' said Sophie, ignoring him. 'I can teach it to you if you like.'

'Oh well, of course I is knowing *that* song!' said the BFG, rolling his eyes. 'I'm not totally cloth-headed. But you is getting the words all wonky. Here, I can sing the whole thing *properly*.'

He stood up straight, cleared his throat and began to bellow:

'On the twelfth day of Crinklemas my true love
sent to me . . .
Twelve hummers humming
Eleven vipers sniping
Ten frogs a-leaping
Nine donkeys dancing
Eight spades a-digging
Seven swans a-grinning
Six bees a-buzzing
Five gooooold bins
Four falling birds
Three clenched hens
Two purple gloves
and a party in a spare tree.'

There was silence for a few seconds before Sophie remembered to clap.

'I suppose you is wanting Crinklemas songs in your dream and all?' asked the BFG.

Sophie nodded.

'Definitely. Mix in a few Christmas carols, and maybe

some of the **FUN** new ones you hear on the radio.'

The BFG set down more and more **SPARKLY** jars.

'Right, I'd better start mixing these dreams up before they get as jumpsy as a joghopper,' said the BFG, rubbing his hands together.

He unscrewed the lid of the large, empty glass jar. Then he lifted a smaller dream jar and unscrewed the lid. **SLOWLY,** he poured the dream – which looked like a deep green blob of smoke – into the bigger jar.

'There we go,' he said. 'I always like to start my Phizzwizard recipes off with a nice, calm dream. It is making the whole process a lot easier.'

Slowly and carefully, the BFG measured out different-sized blobs of dream into the big jar. He was frowning with concentration, looking more like a top chef in a posh restaurant than a **BIG FRIENDLY GIANT.** The various blobs didn't seem to mind sharing a jar at all.

'They look like tropical fish,' said Sophie, 'the way they glide gently around each other.'

The BFG shuddered. 'I will take your word for it,' he said. 'To me fishies is frightsome.'

'Now, we need to think about food,' continued Sophie. 'We need to make the best Christmas dinner ever! Roast turkey, stuffing, roast potatoes, parsnips, gravy, cranberry sauce – this is making me hungry.'

The BFG was plonking down jars as quickly as Sophie was talking. Inside each jar danced shimmering dreams, all of which were about food.

'Ew! What's that one?' asked Sophie, pointing at a particularly greenish-looking jar.

'You is wanting Crinklemas eats, isn't you?' said the BFG, peering at the jar label. 'It's a dream all about something you is calling "brunkle sprouts".'

'Oh NO!' cried Sophie. 'Anything but sprouts!'

The BFG frowned. 'But you is saying this is a proper Crinklemas feast. Aren't these brunkle sprouts part of it?'

Sophie sighed. 'I suppose so. I've just always hated them. But you're right. Hating them is part of Christmas too, I suppose.'

'Down the hatch!' cried the BFG, adding the great green blob into the dream jar.

'OK, we need crackers, hats, party games and a cosy

fireplace,' said Sophie, thinking about what Christmas looked like on television. She had always dreamt of snuggling in front of a cosy fireplace, drinking hot chocolate.

'And of course, all chiddlers is wanting buckets and buckets of presents, is they not?' asked the BFG.

'Oh yes,' said Sophie with a nod. She gave a heavy sigh. She wondered what it would actually feel like, to pick up a present and see her name written on the gift tag.

'Actually,' she said quietly. 'There doesn't need to be buckets of presents. And they don't have to be big or expensive. Just a little something under the tree would be nice, maybe.'

The BFG nodded, tipping more dream blobs into the jar while Sophie stared into space.

'Maybe there could be stockings hanging down from the fireplace,' she murmured. 'With everyone's names embroidered on to them. The whole family.'

The BFG stopped what he was doing and looked at Sophie. 'What you is describing,' he said softly, 'sounds very warm and **WHOPPSY-WHIFFLING.** You is helping to make a most wonderful gift, Sophie. Even though you has never been given nothing at all. You is quite the kindest little girl I has ever met.'

Sophie blinked a few times and then laughed. 'Hang on,' she said. 'Aren't I the only little girl you've ever met?'

The BFG hooted. 'You is quite right! Now here, let's stir this dream up together.'

He placed what looked like a **HUGE** egg-beater into the jar, which had a circular wooden handle at one end and two metal whisks at the other. By now, the jar was full of **TWINKLING,** colourful floating blobs of dream. Sophie cranked the handle round and round, and the blobs started to swirl and froth as they blended. The sparkles seemed to multiply, gently floating out from the jar and dancing their way to the top of the cave.

'Wahoo!' said the BFG. 'This is going to be a humdinger of a Phizzwizard, Sophie! Keep going!'

Sophie grinned as the Phizzwizard started to take shape. It was now a huge, sparkling silver thing. Tiny rainbows seemed to dart through it, like SHOOTING stars.

'That's it! You've done it,' said the BFG. And he

rested the egg-beater on the table while Sophie wiggled her arms around.

'Phew!' she said. 'Tiring work.'

'That's why you is deserving some of this,' said the BFG, and he presented Sophie with a bottle of frobscottle. 'Cheers!'

Sophie gulped down the frobscottle and let the glorious sensation of fizzy raspberries and cream dance on her tongue.

The BFG took the bottle from her and took a mighty swig.

And then . . . they waited.

'It's coming!' said the BFG. 'I can feel it. **1, 2, 3 – BLAST OFF!'**

And the BFG did the most tremendous whizzpop.

Sophie collapsed into giggles, and then they both started whizzpopping uncontrollably.

'Whoopee! Now this is what I call a Crinklemas crackler!' cried the BFG, dancing around and making rude noises. Sophie could barely speak, she was laughing so much.

'Please! No – no more,' she panted, clutching her stomach.

She sat down to catch her breath, grinning in the glow of the fantastic Christmas Phizzwizard.

Eventually, Sophie's breathing returned to normal.

'It's beautiful,' she said, with a happy sigh.

'Yes, it is,' said the BFG.

And they looked at the jar for a long time.

'The thing is –' Sophie began. And she looked at the BFG.

'Hmmm,' said the BFG. 'It is not *quite* as spliffling as it could be, is it?'

Sophie shook her head. 'It just needs – a certain *something*, doesn't it?'

'Goats!' hooted the BFG. 'Of course! It needs goats!'

'Not goats, though it's a lovely idea,' said Sophie. 'No, we need something else.'

They sat thoughtfully for a while.

Sophie looked around her. It all felt so festive, what with the snozzcumber tree, the twinkling fairy lights and the bottle of bubbly frobscottle still warming their bellies. Then she looked at the BFG, who was happily humming his special version of "The Twelve Days of

Christmas". She smiled, and a warm glow spread through her body from somewhere deep inside her.

'Ooh!' said the BFG, his ears flapping and his eyes growing wide as he looked at Sophie. 'Well, well, well. Just look at that, you clever thing!'

'What?' said Sophie.

The BFG gently stood up and crept over to the other side of the cave. He picked up his dream-catching net.

'You is glowing, Sophie! Look, it's all around you,' he said.

Sophie looked around.

'What is? I can't see anything,' she said.

The BFG chuckled.

'I forget you humans is maybe not seeing or hearing all the magical and mystical things in the universe like us giants do,' he said. 'But by goggles, I think you've done it! You've found our missing ingredient.'

Sophie looked confused and started waving her arms over her head.

'What is it?' she said. 'I can't feel anything either.'

The BFG chuckled.

'It's nothing bad, little Sophie,' he said. 'Just you stay perfectly still.'

Slowly, the BFG swooped and scooped at the air around Sophie's body.

'Lovely,' he said. And with another smooth movement, he tipped whatever he had caught into a jar, and screwed the lid on tight.

Sophie peered at the jar. Inside was a mysterious soft, red smoke. When Sophie looked closely, she saw tiny white and turquoise **SPARKLES** floating around like snowflakes on the wind.

'Oh!' she gasped. 'It's so lovely! What is it?'

'That, dear Sophie, is Crinklemas Spirit! It is very special indeed. You is making it when you is feeling all warm and happy inside. I think it's just the thing our Phizzwizard needs.'

He unscrewed the Phizzwizard jar and tipped in the magic ingredient. The effect was astonishing. The cave filled with a golden light so BRIGHT Sophie had to shield her eyes for a few moments.

'It's perfect,' she whispered.

The BFG beamed.

'Well, there's enough dream in this jar for each and every chiddler in your norphanage, Sophie. More than enough! I can blow this Phizzwizard into hundreds of windows on Christmas Eve.'

'Brilliant!' said Sophie. 'Oh, I can't wait! I wish I could see their faces after they wake up.'

The BFG picked up the jar. 'I just has one last thing to do,' he announced. 'You just wait there, little Sophie.'

He marched over to the other side of the cave and busied himself with something for a couple of minutes. There was some clinking and clanking, as well as a little bit of murmuring. Then the BFG returned to Sophie with his hands held behind his back.

'Close those peepers for me,' said the BFG.

Sophie did as she was asked.

'There . . . now you can be opening them,' he said with a smile.

Sophie opened them and saw, under the snozzcumber tree, a small package. It was the shape of a much smaller dream jar, which had been wrapped in some scraps of torn newspaper. Sophie could see the contents **GLITTERING** through the glass where the paper hadn't quite reached. An old bootlace had been tied into a messy bow, and there was a gift tag attached. Sophie held it up and read it.

'I know it is a bit early,' said the BFG. 'But I is thinking it would be nice for you to be getting a present as well for once.'

Sophie stared at the label for some time. Then she looked up from the jar and ran to the Big Friendly Giant. Standing on her tiptoes, she gave him the biggest hug she could manage.

'Merry Crinklemas, Sophie,' said the BFG, gently hugging her back.

'Merry Crinklemas, BFG,' she whispered. 'It's already been the best one ever.'

MATILDA AND THE NAUGHTY LIST

Elle McNicoll

18th of December

Dear Father Christmas,

I hope this letter finds you well, and, more importantly, that it finds you on time. I apologize for writing to you when it is so close to Christmas. I appreciate that a correspondence in October, or even November, might have been more agreeable. You must forgive me, but it has been an eventful term at Crunchem Hall. Our previous headteacher has vanished without a trace. There was an incident with a board and some chalk. It's a long story . . .

I'm writing to you – as you must already know – about what I would like for Christmas. However, I am also sharing a change of address. I no longer live with my parents, Mr and Mrs Wormwood. I now live with Miss Jennifer Honey and have enclosed our new address along with this letter, for your convenience.

I was also wondering if you could clear something up for me, if that is not too impertinent. For nearly every Christmas I can remember, the presents I had asked for in my letter to you appeared under the Christmas tree – evidence that made me believe, at first, that I was on the Nice List (which is exactly where I have always wished to be). However, those same presents were always passed along to my brother by my parents, who told me that it was because I was, in fact, on the Naughty List. My father further explained that you had left those presents for me to see, but you had instructed my parents to give them away to make sure I fully understood the consequences of my misbehaviour.

This year, I would very much love to be on your Nice List. So although I understand that some of the things I have done in the past year might seem like naughtiness, I feel I can plead my case for them. Should you have any concerns, I would be happy to discuss this matter further. Would it be too forward of me to ask exactly which list I am on? Perhaps you could be kind enough to let me know.

If I am on the Nice List, I would only like books this year. Simply because I have a lot more homework these days, now that I've been moved up to join the eleven-year-olds, so I do not get to visit the library and my friend Mrs Phelps as often as I would like. We also do not have a library at school. Miss

Honey has suggested I create a little book corner in the common room instead, which I have done.

I would like some Virginia Woolf, Toni Morrison and anything that you yourself have been enjoying in your reading. And maybe some chocolate. That is all I need, I think. If it is not too much trouble.

This is my first Christmas with Miss Honey, and I so would like it to be good. I know Miss Honey has not thought of herself at all this year – but I have. Would it be too much to ask if she could have some new gloves? Her current pair are very worn.

Yours sincerely and happy Christmas,

Matilda

Matilda sealed the letter inside its envelope and then sat on it for safekeeping. She was out in the garden, perched on the wooden swing, which was tightly strung up to a sturdy tree branch. It was mid-December, and the frost was **SPRINKLED** across Matilda and Miss Honey's garden like icing sugar on a cake.

'Shall I give you a push?' Miss Honey asked, as she made her way from the house to the tree.

'Yes, please.'

'Is that a letter for Santa?'

'Yes. I'm trying to talk myself on to the **NICE LIST.'**

'Matilda,' Miss Honey said, with a surprised little laugh. 'I'm sure you've always been on the Nice List.'

'No. My parents were very clear that I was on the Naughty List.'

Miss Honey pursed her lips. She always tried to avoid speaking ill of Mr and Mrs Wormwood, even though they were two people who were very easy to speak ill of, she felt. However, this time, she made an exception. 'I'm sure that had far more to do with your mother and father than it did Santa Claus.'

Matilda hugged the envelope close but did not say anything. She often never needed to, with Miss Honey. She leaned against one of the ropes of the **SWING** and let Miss Honey push her gently, as the snow started to fall.

❄

It was the final week of term before Christmas and Matilda was sitting on the little patch of grass beside the old school building. She was huddled with Bruce, Lavender, Hortensia and Nigel. There was an excited **SPARK** in the air, in spite of the frost. This was Matilda's first Christmas at Crunchem Hall, and the first for many of its students without the formidable former headteacher, Miss Trunchbull.

'Last year,' Hortensia spoke breathlessly, 'she threatened to use Maisy Andersen as stuffing. And if anyone brought their teacher a present, she confiscated it. Kept it in her office and never gave it back.'

'I heard she once caught some older children making

snow angels,' Nigel added. 'So she made them stand with their arms out like wings for **HOURS**. She said if they dropped them, she would throw them out of the window to see if they could really fly.'

Matilda let her friends reminisce about their old shared enemy. She had nothing more to say about the awful woman who had tormented and tortured the students. Matilda was content – quietly happy in the knowledge that she had been the one to lead the revolution against Miss Trunchbull.

Although she did still have the occasional bad dream about The Chokey – the small, dark and dank cupboard full of rusty nails and broken glass was never very far from Matilda's mind.

But a **BRILLIANT** mind is always on the move and something caught Matilda's eye and diverted her thoughts.

'Is the headteacher's office bigger than we think?' Matilda suddenly asked, leaning forward and squinting at the side of the old school building.

Her friends were surprised by the question, but they quickly broke into smiles. They had grown quite used to

Matilda. Her cleverness was a never-ending well of amusement for them and they liked hearing about her adventures in Year Six, with the eleven-year-olds.

'It always feels like a snug little office,' Lavender offered up. 'Why?'

'Because –' Matilda said, moving **SWIFTLY** from their spot on the grass to the school building. She ran her finger along the side of the outer wall, while her friends scurried after her – 'the first few classrooms should end here. Then the office. Then the lunchroom. But this wall seems far longer. It's as if one of those rooms is bigger than it seems.'

Before she could continue, the lunch bell rang. Keen to be in the warm, Matilda and her friends rushed towards the school doors, **PUSHING** and PULLING alongside the other pupils who were just as eager to get inside. While the Trunchbull had described central heating as 'an insult to "survival of the fittest"', Mr Trilby (the new headteacher of Crunchem Hall) was a huge supporter of students not freezing to death during their lessons, and hypothermia at the school was now at an all-time low.

'Know what this school really needs?' Matilda said to Lavender, as they made their way to the student common room. There were five minutes until the final bell and they usually made good use of the beanbags by the radiator.

'A tuck shop,' Lavender said instantly.

'A library,' Matilda said. Her tone was firm, and it had that familiar little edge of defiance, the kind that alerted Lavender to Matilda's mood. Although she was a tad disappointed at giving up a full-time sweet shop, Lavender understood that her best friend was a *changer*. Someone who got notions and ideas in her head and then set about making them happen. If Matilda wanted a library at Crunchem Hall, Lavender knew it was only a matter of time until they had one.

'There's the reading corner,' she said optimistically.

'There is,' acknowledged Matilda, as the two girls entered the common room. 'But it's a bit small. Miss Honey and I thought we could expand it by getting donations from people. Then we could set up a proper library . . .'

Matilda's words died as her eyes landed on the exact reading corner they had been speaking about. It was normally a nice and tidy part of the room, with some small, splintery shelves, which were always full of donated books. Although there was usually the odd novel left on the carpeted floor, it was generally a well-preserved little space that the students respected.

However, at that moment, one of the older girls was sitting on a throne made out of the books. Dickens, Austen and Hardy were all being used to prop up this newcomer. She had gone for the hardbacks on the bottom, with the older paperbacks on top. It was an **UNSTEADY**-looking seat, but the girl didn't seem to be worried. She appeared to be holding court, her icy blonde hair slicked back in a ponytail and her cold eyes surveying the room.

'She's sitting on the books,' murmured Matilda, shocked by the audacity of it.

Matilda enjoyed being in a class with the older children, even if there was a significant age difference between her and everyone else. Most of the pupils had been really welcoming and interested in the fact that Matilda was so smart for her age. All of them except –

'Hernia,' Matilda said softly, her gaze pinned to the older child like a dart to its board.

Lavender snorted. 'That's her name? Hernia?'

'Unfortunately, yes.'

'Everything all right, girls?'

Matilda and Lavender turned to face the voice: Mr Trilby, the new headteacher. He had been the deputy head when Miss Trunchbull was in charge and, after the disappearance of said headteacher, he had taken her place. Mr Trilby ruled with a great deal more benevolence, although Matilda thought he seemed a tad absent-minded.

'Sir,' Matilda said, her voice calm and **STEADY**. 'Hernia Pinch is sitting on the books.'

Mr Trilby frowned and then glanced over at the reading corner. 'Ah. I see.'

'Those are for everyone,' Matilda maintained. 'And she's –'

'Sitting on them, yes, I know. Now, Matilda –' Mr Trilby was speaking in a way that Matilda instantly recognized as an attempt to placate her – 'Hernia is very new to this school. I'm sure she's not doing it to be mean or disrespectful.'

Matilda was not an angry child. She was not a callous individual. She was the sort of individual who would turn the other way if a hungry-looking person ate a few extra grapes in the supermarket – grapes they could not afford to pay for. Matilda was **FAIR.** She was someone with a very steely moral barometer. One that told her that sitting on other people's shared property was not acceptable. She did not need to be placated. She needed justice.

'Miss Honey tells me that the two of you are planning a little library in here,' Mr Trilby added, his smile a little desperate as he attempted to steer Matilda and Lavender away from the older children. 'What a Christmas treat that would be for everyone!'

'It will be decidedly difficult to make a little library if the only books we have are **SQUASHED** and **BROKEN,'** Matilda said, looking pointedly at where Hernia was sitting.

'I understand that, Matilda, but again, I don't think she is doing it **MALICIOUSLY.** This is a new environment for Hernia. You remember what it's like to be new?'

'Fine,' Matilda said, choosing to be the more mature party. 'I will allow her the benefit of the doubt.'

'Thank you. It's noted and appreciated.'

'Besides, a small corner of the student common room really isn't BIG enough for a proper library, Mr Trilby,' Matilda said, trying to take advantage of the brownie points she had just earned. 'We should really be given a **BIGGER** space.'

'I do agree, Matilda,' the headteacher said despondently. 'But it's the only room Crunchem Hall has to spare, at present. Unless another room magically appears, we'll just have to make do.'

He gave her a weak little pat on the shoulder and then left.

'So, what's the plan?' Lavender asked, for when it came to her best friend Matilda, there was always a plan.

'Negotiation first,' Matilda said.

The small girl made her way over to her older classmates with a cool and composed air. Hernia Pinch, who normally towered over Matilda like a palm tree over a coconut, still seemed to loom a little, even while sitting on a pile of books.

'Hello, Hernia,' said Matilda, giving a polite smile.

The older girl met the younger with a sneer – the kind of sneer that filled Matilda with disappointment and dread. The headteacher had been wrong. This was not a simple case of misunderstanding. In fact, this particular sneer alerted Matilda to the fact that Hernia was probably sitting on the makeshift library books for one very specific reason.

To ruin them for everybody else.

Nevertheless, Matilda persisted. 'I just wanted to let you know that those are library books. For everyone.'

Hernia stood to her full height before pointedly looking down at the throne she had made out of copies of Brontë and Dickens. 'These books?'

'Yes,' Matilda said courteously. 'Although they can be **STURDY,** I just wanted to make sure you weren't trying to damage them. Because they're for everybody.'

Hernia frowned. She stood up from her pile of books and, for a fleeting moment, Matilda wondered if she had been mistaken and misread the situation after all. It did happen, occasionally. While a mathematical equation was easy for her brain to work out, other people were the ultimate puzzles. She had lain in bed night after night at the Wormwood house, trying to rationalize the things her parents did. While the thirteen-times table was always going to be unchanging, and therefore possible to understand and predict, human beings were completely different.

Matilda waited to see if the complex cluster of cells before her was going to behave like a nine when it was crossed with a thirteen. She had been civil but frank. Therefore, it would be proper for Hernia to return the favour.

Instead, the older girl used her foot to kick over the little fortress of books. They fell to the floor in a slow, undignified heap – a **LANDSLIDE** of dry paper and cracked spines. Matilda watched impassively, urging her face to remain expressionless despite the cold flicker of rage that was tickling her ribcage.

'Oops,' murmured Hernia, with a steely, spiteful smirk. Some of the older children snickered, though they were naturally cagier when it came to Matilda.

'The books are for all of us,' Matilda said, fixing Hernia with a hard stare. 'It's the Crunchem Hall Library.'

'Library?!' cried Hernia, kicking the heap of books across the floor and bellowing in amusement. 'Hardly! A pile of dopey, second-hand copies of books no one wants to read, what kind of *library* is that? My old school had a *whole floor* of books.'

This hit Matilda like a lance. She felt the sickly green infection of envy inside her. 'Well, we do not have a floor. Just this small corner with books people have kindly donated. All the more reason for you to help care for them.'

'I'm not caring for some dusty old pile of rubbish,' Hernia replied. 'I like new things. You don't even have Shakespeare. I was named after a Shakespearean character, and naturally every library should have brand-new copies of him. Without him, it's not a library.' She looked Matilda up and down with deliberate disdain. She gave the books one final kick. 'How old are you anyway? You're in my year – I see you sometimes – but you're way too small. Do you even know how to read?'

'Oh,' Matilda said softly, with the smallest of smiles. 'You really are new.'

The final bell rang shrilly, and most children in the common room rushed for the exit. Many followed the school rules to the letter, as if they were still afraid that Miss Trunchbull would come **LEAPING** out of a broom cupboard should they fall behind.

As Matilda rejoined Lavender, she turned to address Hernia one final time.

'There is no Shakespearean character named Hernia. *A Midsummer Night's Dream* has a woman called *Hermia*. Perhaps that is who you mean. She was a **BEAUTIFUL**, if slightly selfish, daughter of Athens. A hernia is when an organ or tissue pushes through weakened muscles in the body, causing a swelling to protrude outwards. At best, irritating. At worst, life-threatening.'

❄

At lunch the very next day, Matilda's friends watched her move towards their table, and they knew, simply by looking at her, that she had just had one of her ideas.

'What's the plan?' asked Nigel, without any preamble, as Matilda sat down with the group.

Matilda gave Nigel a warm smile of appreciation. Then her expression grew more serious, as she readied herself to make a plan. She never had a malevolent air about her when it was time to execute one of her plans, for Matilda took no great pleasure in punishing people who needed punishing.

(**MISCHIEF** is an occasional chore that children are required to undertake. Much like adults and jury duty.)

However, there was the slightest **GLIMMER** of cunning in her eye.

'More like *who* is the plan,' said Bruce.

'Hernia Pinch,' answered Matilda. 'And we don't have a lot of time.'

'She's a real bully,' Bruce said quietly, glancing around the lunchroom. 'Called me a liar when one of the bigger kids told her about what happened with Miss Trunchbull.'

'Well then, I have the perfect job for you,' Matilda told him grimly.

So, Matilda, Bruce, Lavender and Nigel all put their little heads together and plotted. As soon as orders were dispatched, they set to work.

❄

Days later, during Crunchem Hall's first-ever Christmas lunch, they were ready.

By the time Hernia Pinch sauntered into the lunchroom, Matilda and her friends were at their posts, ready to execute the plan seamlessly. Lavender had made her way to the **MOUNTAIN** of Christmas crackers at the front of the lunchroom. She placed a particularly large and glittery cracker on top of the pile, knowing its weight and glamour would prove irresistible to Hernia. Nigel and Matilda busied themselves at the pudding section of the canteen, before nodding to Bruce. He was waiting in the cutlery section, ready to put on the performance of a lifetime, while the other members of the group hurried back to their table. They would get a proper view of the proceedings from there.

Hernia, oblivious to their scuttling, swiped up a tray and headed for the canteen. She paused upon reaching the batch of Christmas crackers. Her fingers snatched up the largest on the pile, the one that had been so meticulously placed there by Lavender. Hernia put it on her own tray with a smug look of TRIUMPH, and then demanded some turkey and trimmings from the dinner staff. While they obeyed, Bruce geared himself up for his part in the plan.

Just as Hernia reached the puddings, Bruce stepped forward. He channelled all of his skills into appearing desperate for a very specific, very delicious-looking serving of lime jelly. Hernia noticed his hand reaching out for the plate, and a different sort of **HUNGER** entered her blue eyes. She stepped in between the younger boy and the jelly, grinning down at him.

'Not in the mood for something with chocolate, Bogtrotter?'

Bruce scowled up at the tall, waif-like girl and her

cruel eyes. The only positive thing about school during the Trunchbull's reign had been the sense of solidarity between all of the students, regardless of age or gender – everyone had come together because of their common enemy. But now, it seemed Hernia had stepped in to fill the school-bully space that Miss Trunchbull had left behind.

'You don't know what you're talking about,' was all Bruce said to Hernia, his voice quiet and assured. He made a great show of reaching for the lime jelly once more, prompting Hernia to grab it for herself.

'Bad luck, Bog,' she said, smirking triumphantly as she left him in her wake.

But rather than being upset, Bruce was silently delighted. Everything had gone according to Matilda's plan.

He waited a few seconds and then dashed back to their table, **SLIDING** into the empty seat next to Lavender. The four friends watched surreptitiously as Hernia sat down with her tray of Christmas lunch.

'I'm now worrying that I calculated the cracker incorrectly,' Matilda murmured to Lavender.

'Not a chance,' her friend said.

They all watched as Hernia decided to pull the cracker with herself. A singular choice, at Christmas, but she was obviously eager to snatch whatever present lay inside. As it broke in two, a cloud of powder burst free from the cardboard, coating Hernia in purple dust.

Purple dust that immediately got to work.

The sound of Hernia sneezing and snorting brought silence to the rest of the lunchroom. Students of all ages laid down their cutlery to see what the commotion was. The sneezes continued and Hernia was quick to slap away any helping hands from others at her table.

She furiously swiped at the remains of the cracker, only to hold up her hand and find the thin paper crown stuck to it with super-superglue. No matter how she batted her hand, it remained in place. Matilda was mildly disappointed that the crown had become glued to Hernia's hand rather than her hair, but no plan was ever perfect.

The *pièce de résistance* lay inside the lime jelly.

They all watched as Hernia tried to carry on with her lunch, attempting to retake the high ground by ignoring the paper crown now stuck to her hand. She took a bite of the jelly and the entire room held their breath.

Lavender and Nigel had found the poor dead beetle. It had been lifeless by the side of a drain at the entrance to the school. Matilda liked to believe that this beetle would appreciate knowing that its death was now contributing to a noble cause.

Noble, because the scream Hernia Pinch let out was so piercing, so **SHRILL,** so unbelievably satisfying, that Matilda knew it would serve as a balm to every one of her victims in that lunchroom.

Hernia was still bellowing as she snatched up the final piece of the cracker – the slip of paper that usually featured a joke. This one merely read: ***libri sunt sacri.***

'What on earth is that?' shrieked Hernia, perhaps afraid that it was some deadly spell.

'My Latin is not perfect,' Matilda said curtly, 'but loosely translated, it reads: BOOKS ARE SACRED.'

❄

'I know it was her!'

Matilda remained calm as she stood in front of Mr Trilby's desk, Hernia's loud **BELLOWS** only a few centimetres to her left. After the beetle discovery, everything had turned into chaos. The lunchroom was now a crime scene, with turkey, potatoes and leftover sneezing powder scattered all across the floor.

Hernia had instantly accused Matilda, and Mr Trilby summoned them both to his office to investigate.

Matilda had no intention of denying it.

'She did this to me,' Hernia said, her eyes sparkling with pure, incandescent rage. 'She did it out of revenge for her stupid books.'

'Books?' Mr Trilby said, turning to Matilda. 'What about the books? The library books? Matilda, we have already discussed this.'

Matilda took in the small, pokey office where the three of them now found themselves. Mr Trilby behind the headteacher's desk, Matilda and Hernia before it. While most of Miss Trunchbull's personal items had been removed, there was one shot still sitting on the desk. The ball used in the shot put – the shot – was a still and chilling reminder of an old memory. Matilda's eyes moved, almost automatically, from the small item to the wall. To the only other reminder of their old headteacher.

THE CHOKEY.

Matilda stared at it. Marvelled at it. She sometimes wondered if it had been an aspect of the entire experience she had simply made up. There was something too awful about it. The trophies, the medals, the photographs and the large javelin – they were all gone. But The Chokey remained, haunting all of them like a ghost who refused to move on.

'Matilda, did you have anything to do with – with this?' asked Mr Trilby.

Matilda was pulled back from her thoughts to the conversation in the room, but her eyes remained upon The Chokey. 'I did.'

'See!' shrieked Hernia. 'I told you! She admits it.'

'I do,' Matilda said quietly. 'She damaged the library books. And she did it on purpose.'

Matilda was not going to go into any sort of detail about why she found that to be such a repulsive act. To any civilized person, it was already extremely obvious. The books were shared items, there for everyone to use. To destroy any kind of book was an act of violence, but to do so to a story meant for hundreds of readers – it was unthinkable.

Perhaps it was The Chokey. Perhaps it was Hernia. Or perhaps it was the vivid memory of a copy of Melville's *Moby Dick* being ripped to shreds. Whatever the cause, Matilda was prepared to fight. She was not going to allow this kind of behaviour to occur unchecked.

'Matilda, I'm surprised at you,' Mr Trilby said softly, disappointment leaking out of his voice like water from a loose tap. 'You're better than this.'

Matilda threw him a sharp glance. 'Why is The Chokey still here, Headteacher?'

Hernia snorted derisively. 'Chokey. So stupid.'

'Why is it still here?' Matilda asked again, ignoring the bully to her left.

'We haven't got around to getting rid of it, Matilda. But now, don't change the subject!' Mr Trilby said, with an exasperated sigh. 'You can't play pranks on your classmates without retribution.'

'I was doing it in response to her treatment of the books,' Matilda pointed out. 'If I get punished for punishing, then is someone going to punish you for punishing me?'

Mr Trilby blinked, clearly lost.

'Why do grown-ups get to hand out punishments for bad behaviour, but not children?' Matilda asked. 'Hernia mistreated some valuable items. Items that other students, Miss Honey and I spent hours accumulating so that this school could finally have a little library in time for Christmas. And she trampled all over it.'

'It's a stupid library. Barely a library at all,' retorted Hernia.

'Well, there isn't room for a real one,' Mr Trilby said, his tone both frustrated and apologetic. 'I'm sorry, girls, but this is all just –'

His words were cut off by a **KNOCK** on the office door. Miss Honey peered inside and, after giving Matilda a surprised look, she addressed Mr Trilby.

'Can I borrow you for a moment, Headteacher?'

'Uh.' Mr Trilby glanced at the two girls in front of him. He was a reluctant disciplinarian, Matilda could tell, so Miss Honey's arrival was certainly welcome. He got to his feet, dusted off his tweed waistcoat and made his way to the office door.

'Try and work this out between yourselves while I'm gone,' he said pleadingly.

Matilda turned to look at Hernia, assembling her thoughts.

'This whole school is weird,' snapped the other girl, her lip curling in disgust.

'What's wrong with weird?' Matilda challenged. 'Besides, it's not weird. It's just . . . recovering.'

'Recovering?' sneered Hernia. 'Ah, yes. From this fake bogeyman you've all cooked up.'

'Not fake,' Matilda said, almost inaudibly. 'Real. And Miss Trunchbull would have made even you afraid.'

'Unlikely.'

'What makes you think you can damage our books?' Matilda pressed. 'Or bully Bruce Bogtrotter? Or anyone, for that matter.'

'You're all pathetic. Your silly little book corner! Your weird stories and . . . that thing!'

The older girl jerked her thumb towards The Chokey.

'Why would an entire school make up an evil headteacher?' Matilda said bluntly.

'Maybe she wasn't made up, but she was exaggerated. And where did she go? **VANISHED** into thin air?'

'Maybe she went to Spain,' muttered Matilda.

'What?'

'Nothing.'

'You are the creepiest kid in this entire school. To be fair, your friends are a close second. But you? You're weird. Why is a six-year-old in a class with the eleven-year-olds? I don't care how good at your two-times table you are, you're not smart enough to be sitting with the rest of us.'

The words were like stones thrown against a greenhouse window – loud and aggressive. But Matilda was protected. An impenetrable glass wall stood between her feelings and the impact of Hernia's insults. She had spent most of her life being shouted at and told she wasn't good enough, and she knew how to shield herself. However, in recent weeks, Matilda had grown used to the gentle tone of Miss Honey, and the **CHEERFUL** voices of the other teachers at Crunchem Hall.

She was a little out of practice when it came to blocking out the sound of hateful bullies.

Hernia continued to pelt angry words at Matilda, a little bit of spittle flying free from her **SHARP,** angry tongue. Matilda chose to step away from the taller girl, her eyes resting once more on The Chokey wall.

She thought about bullies.

Hernia was nothing she had not seen before. In fact, she almost felt sorry for the girl – sorry enough to even start regretting the prank. Hernia was obviously intimidated by books and the people who enjoyed them. She may never have had a Mrs Phelps or a Miss Honey. Perhaps adult bullies were so much worse than child bullies, Matilda wondered, as she continued to stare at The Chokey.

Hernia was powerless.

Matilda was not. Her **MAGICAL** powers had been dormant since moving into the older class, but as she stared stonily at The Chokey wall, the hot flickers of anger started to heat up the parts inside her that had once wielded her magic.

'Stupid little worm,' Hernia's voice said, though it sounded far away to Matilda, as if she were shouting from the other side of a train platform. 'Pathetic.'

Bullies yelled at their victims to shrink them. They did it to try and make them feel small. But all bullying ever seemed to do to Matilda was make her stronger. **BIGGER.** More powerful.

So, when Hernia Pinch yelled one final 'stupid', Matilda let go. The anger, the frustration, all of it went firing into The Chokey wall with the power of an explosion. Both girls jumped in shock as the wall suddenly **CRUMBLED,** breaking apart before their eyes.

The Chokey, once the most feared thing in all of Crunchem Hall, was now broken.

The two girls approached the mess of stone and rubble with the caution of two explorers who had discovered an ancient crypt.

'Wait,' Hernia said breathlessly, staring at the broken nails of The Chokey, now spread across the debris. 'It was real!?'

'All of it was,' Matilda said, kneeling down.

'I'm . . .' Hernia looked taken aback. The word **'SORRY'** seemed to be waiting in the back of her throat but it never came. She looked sorry, though. Matilda decided that it would have to be enough.

'Miss Trunchbull,' Matilda told her conspiratorially, 'she was . . . a creative punisher. Not like Mr Trilby. In fact, if she had seen the pranks I pulled on you today – if she had still been headteacher – I would probably have been thrown out of the classroom window.'

While Hernia was too stunned to speak, Matilda's focus was elsewhere. Now that the wall was crumbling, she noticed that the room behind The Chokey wasn't one of the classrooms. There was, it seemed, a whole hidden antechamber – another little room with no windows, one that nobody seemed to know about. She recalled the mystery of the outer wall, where she had traced it, wondering how the rooms joined up with each other.

'A hidden room,' Matilda said in wonder. 'That's . . . perfect.'

❄

Matilda's punishment from Mr Trilby was not much of a punishment at all. She, with the help of Hernia, was instructed to furnish the newly discovered room behind The Chokey with all of the donated books. It was to be the new Crunchem Hall Library. Matilda accepted the punishment with grace, remembering to be grateful that it was not a hammer throw or an **ENORMOUS** cake. She even decided to make a peace treaty with Hernia.

As the two girls were unloading a wheelbarrow of books, Hernia spoke softly.

'This is my first Christmas without my dad.'

The words hovered between them like an OUTSTRETCHED hand of reconciliation. Matilda took a moment, staggered by Hernia's honesty. When she finally did speak, it was with gentle understanding.

'Mine too,' Matilda said. 'But I'm looking forward to it. I live with Miss Honey. I hope you can have a good Christmas with your mum. Families can look . . . all kinds of ways.'

Hernia slowly shelved the books Matilda had already alphabetized and categorized. 'Miss Honey seems nice.'

'She is. Though I expect she'll be cross with me after what I did to you.'

It was clear that the two girls would never be best friends. They would probably never be good friends. But they could be civil. They could nod to one another in the corridor. They could pull a Christmas cracker, so long as it was not full of purple powder.

They worked together in a comfortable silence and although Matilda was **ECSTATIC** to finally have a library at Crunchem Hall, she regretted that she had probably put herself on the Naughty List in order to get it.

Matilda walked home, the air cold enough for her breath to be visible, but too dark to see it. As she reached the entrance of the vast building that they now called home, her mouth dropped open and she almost dropped her schoolbag. The **WHOLE** house was lit up like a Christmas tree, with the warm glow of a fire visible in the sitting room at the front. It was like a doll's house had been stuffed with fairy lights.

She made her way inside and gasped in appreciation of the house's warmth and the smells of chocolate and orange. Miss Honey emerged from the kitchen with a tray of something that smelled even better. Her face made Matilda feel another flicker of shame about what had happened earlier.

'I'm sorry.'

Miss Honey gave her a sympathetic smile and offered her a biscuit. 'Matilda. Some day you may have to come to terms with the fact that you are not responsible for righting every wrong in the world.'

'Not the world,' Matilda said. 'Just the school.'

'Leave that to Mr Trilby, myself and the rest of the staff.'

'But none of you did before; I had to do it.'

The words shot out before Matilda could stifle them.

'I know,' Miss Honey said, her voice as gentle and as warm as the soft centre of the biscuits she was holding. 'But things are different now.'

They moved to sit by the fire, where two stockings hung in anticipation of Christmas Eve.

'I think I've bumped myself off the Nice List,' Matilda said candidly.

'Oh, I don't think so,' Miss Honey said reassuringly, a spark glittering in her kind eyes. 'I think Father Christmas knows you very well, Matilda.'

❄

When Christmas morning arrived in the Honey house, it brought a **MIRACLE.**

Matilda had been awake since four o'clock in the morning, but she had forced herself to remain in bed. When it was finally time to creep across the landing to Miss Honey's room, the two of them walked quietly down the LARGE staircase, hand in hand, while the little girl held her breath.

The sight that greeted her at the foot of the stairs, in the middle of the sitting room, was enough to wipe away a year of bad memories. There were more books than Matilda had ever seen in one room before (outside a library). Everything she had asked for was wrapped in a ribbon and boasting a tag with **'MATILDA'** written upon it. Virginia Woolf, Toni Morrison, *Anne of Green*

Gables, a book of speeches, some comic books, a brand-new hardback edition of *The Odyssey*. Matilda was completely delighted – so delighted that it was impossible for her to express it, the feeling was too big for words. There was jam. A box of pencils. Beautifully embroidered blankets and a pair of tiny slippers. Chocolates. Hair ribbons. A bear with wellington boots.

Then, best of all, a shiny, laminated card that proclaimed Matilda the very first member of the Crunchem Hall Library.

Miss Honey watched and marvelled at the gratitude and wonder the little girl was showing at a modest pile of presents. She could not help but find it moving, to see Matilda so in awe of the gifts.

'He gave me everything I asked for,' Matilda finally said.

'Me too,' Miss Honey said quietly. 'This is the **BEST** Christmas I've had in so many years.'

As they sat by the fire, eating scones for breakfast and sipping hot chocolate, it must have looked from the outside like two people who had only ever known the warmest, cosiest and **HAPPIEST** of Christmases.

In actual fact, it was two lost little girls who had found home in one another. And they would never be out in the cold again.

The Giraffe and the Pelly and the Runaway Baubles

Nathan Bryon

'Ten, nine, eight, seven . . .!' we yell from the tops of our lungs. The whole class races to the window as the snowflakes fall on to the school playground. This is an **OFFICIAL** countdown to Christmas. It proper feels festive now and I get the warmest feeling in my belly.

Beyond the frost-covered panes of glass we spot Fumbi's dad, his Afro twinkling with snow. Alice's mum slips and slides on the ice outside the school gate. Her limbs fly out in what looks like a terrible new dance move.

We can't help laughing. Behind them, Walleed's stepmum and dad are taking home a giant Christmas tree. She's carrying the stump, sagging beneath the weight, cheeks red. He's messing about up front, phone angled above his head as he tries to take a selfie of him and the tree and his Christmas jumper. It has reindeer on it, and elves – all green and red and festive.

'. . . THREE, TWO, ONE!' we all cry in a last cheer, and when the school bell rings, we realize that we have finally – officially – at last – broken up for the Christmas holidaaaaaaays!

Even on a normal day, most kids race out at 3.30 p.m.

Mums and dads, grandparents and childminders wait in the playground, ready to take their kids home for warm mince pies, cartoons and chilling. Not me, though. I never go home straight after school. I go to an after-school club called Power Squad, for kids whose parents have to work late at their super boring jobs.

But if I'm totally honest, I don't mind going to Power Squad. Especially not today, because today we are getting the club ready for **CHRISTMAS.**

Our parents are coming after work and we're all having an early Christmas dinner! Which means – if my calculations are right – this year I will be eating a whopping four Christmas dinners. Count them!

One at the club

One at home

One with Uncle Fred (who's just got divorced from his wife, Melissa)

. . . and one with Aunty Melissa.

As I think about the gravy, the pigs in blankets, the crispy roast potatoes, even the Brussels sprouts (which will definitely make me fart), my tummy rumbles.

BIG WIN. Quadruple dinners.

We go outside and line up in the snow at the playground fence, waiting to be walked over to Power Squad in Henwood Lane. There's a sharp nudge from my classmate Theo.

'Where are they, Billy?' he asks, brow furrowed. He's talking about my friends, the Giraffe, the Pelly and the Monkey. They run the Ladderless Window-Cleaning Company, not far from where I live, and we met when they first moved here. We even had an adventure together, catching a famous BURGLAR called the Cobra. They somctimes help me run my sweet shop, The Grubber, and I help them with the Ladderless Window-Cleaning Company. I've told Theo all about them, and they're supposed to be here for our Christmas party. But there's no sign of them yet. Maybe I made a mistake . . .

'I don't know,' I say, 'but I'm freezing my baubles off!' I'm trying to sound casual, but I'm starting to feel sad not to see my best friends in the whole world. I look around our icy school playground. I reminded them at least a million times. Maybe I should have reminded them a million and one times.

A few of my Power Squad classmates start to grumble.

'We've been left behind again, just like the parsnips at the end of Christmas dinner!' Jackson says.

But before I can respond, I hear a sweet singing voice echoing off the rooftops. The Giraffe! My heart bursts with excitement.

Jingle jangle jingle bells,
Ol' Pelly made us late,
Please accept our apologies,
With a slice of Christmas cake.

The grown-ups at the school gates suddenly move apart and we see the Giraffe's **LONG** legs appear.

She's wearing a Santa hat and ice skates. She moves gracefully across the icy school playground and turns a pirouette, hooves spinning through the air. Our jaws drop. What a dance! If we had score cards, she would have tens across the board, no doubt at all. Seriously, she needs to join a giraffe ballet troupe one day!

But it soon becomes clear that the Giraffe hasn't quite worked out yet how to put the brakes on. 'Sorry. Sorry! SORRY!' she calls as she speeds forward, eyes wide and long legs circling, and we all run over to stop her from planting her snout into a wall. The Monkey follows behind on another set of skates, showing off as usual. But suddenly he looks like Bambi on ice, limbs slipping and sliding as he ploughs into Walleed's stepmum and dad, who are still carrying the tree. The Christmas tree goes flying out of their hands and rolls across the playground in an explosion of pine needles.

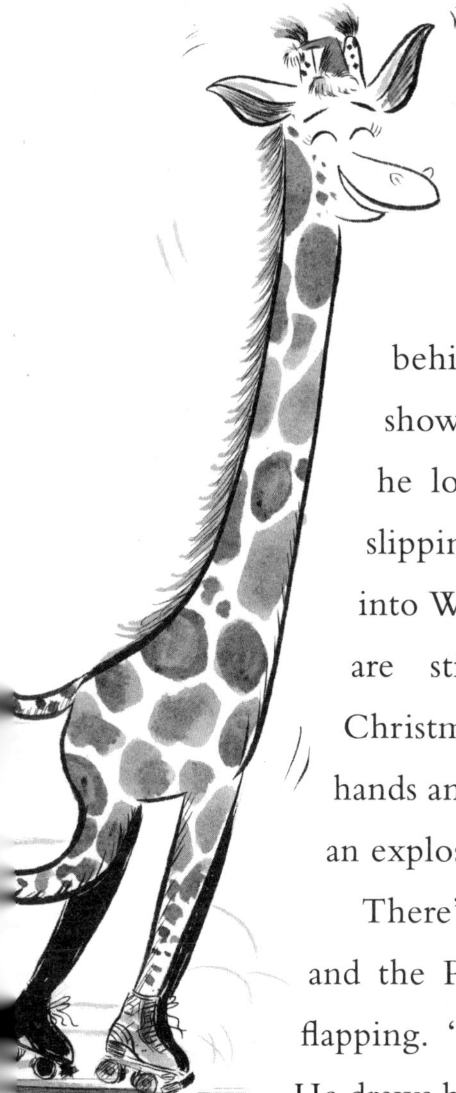

There's a sound from above. I look up and the Pelly is flying overhead, wings flapping. 'Sorry to be so late!' he cries. He draws back the top half of his Patented

Pelican Beak. Pelly has this amazing ability to slide the whole of his top beak all the way back into his head, and with this neat trick, he shows us the presents and cakes stuffed inside. I can tell that they're presents because the shapes are all squares and oblongs and there's a gift label hanging out. 'We were Christmas shopping!' he mumbles.

I can't help but hope that one or two or even three of those gifts are for me. But mainly, I'm just glad to see them, and I feel my face split into a big grin. 'I told you they'd be here!' I cry to Theo, whose mouth has been **WIDE** open since they appeared.

The Monkey is still careering about on his skates and it looks as though he is about to tumble into another set of parents carrying a huge cake.

'Woah, **woah**, WOAH!'

Just then, the Pelly flies down and saves the day. He scoops the Monkey up, nestling his friend among all the presents in his beak. Together, they head high into the sky. That was a near miss!

Now, finally, we are ready to go to Power Squad. We sing our friends' song as we go:

Jingle jangle jingle bells,
Ol' Pelly made us late,
Please accept our apologies,
With a slice of Christmas cake.

We run like a stampede of wild animals, excited to crack on with today's big project. There always needs to be a big project at Power Squad. Especially at Christmas!

From the outside, Power Squad's headquarters looks like the sort of building a queen lives in. It's proper grand, with **MASSIVE** stone pillars that reach high into the sky, and tons of windows that are always **SPARKLINGLY** clean (thanks to the Ladderless Window-Cleaning Company!). The building used to be the town hall, so loads of important people must have been here – but no one as important as me and the Power Squad kids.

The inside is messier than my bedroom, though. Mice are nesting in an old lampshade and spider webs hang from the ceiling. There are cracks in the wall that poor Maria, who runs the Squad, is always trying to fix. Sometimes the lights go on and off without warning.

The main problem right now, though, is that this place doesn't look CHRISTMASSY. It's all cold and grey. But with the help of the Giraffe, the Pelly, the Monkey and me, that is about to change . . .

'Hello, my friends!' A hand waves above a smiling face. Maria is the real queen of Power Squad. Her smile is **SO** bright that if you stared at her pearly whites for too long you'd need sunglasses. Every day, Maria dresses in the most colourful clothes. Once she came to the club wearing a disco-ball jacket. She brought out a big speaker and spun around and we all danced in the **SPARKLES** shining from her jacket. Today, she's wearing a whole Christmas outfit – boppers in her hair, a jumper with a reindeer flying across it and big, dangly earrings in the shape of jingle bells. She's a walking, talking Christmas!

'My favourite kids!' she cries, welcoming us with her arms open wide and bundling us into a hug. She's the literal best!

'Let's make Christmas royally brilliant!' From behind her back, she reveals a bag that spills over with bunting, baubles and strings of fairy lights. Power Squad will soon look better than any Santa's grotto.

Maria goes straight in, calling out commands.

'Giraffe! Take the bunting!'

'Theo! Baubles!'

'Pelly, why don't you fly this up to the roof?'

Each time Maria yells an instruction, we give her a big salute and reply, **'YES, SERGEANT!'** I can tell she's trying not to laugh. She plugs her phone into the speaker, and suddenly, blazing hot Trinidadian Christmas songs echo around the space, making us all dance and wiggle and groove as we work.

Then Maria, smiling, hands me her list. I feel a swell of pride that she trusts me with it, and I read it out to the others:

- ★ Decorations
- ★ Grubber sweets
- ★ More decorations
- ★ Bunting
- ★ Christmas hats
- ★ Tinsel
- ★ Christmas tree

Did I mention decorations?

We have **A LOT** to do, and not a lot of time before our parents arrive. But with Maria in charge and the Ladderless Window-Cleaning Company on our side, we've got this.

❄

A few hours later, and we're all still working really hard. The Pelly has flown super high to help decorate the roof. The Pelican's **ENORMOUS** beak can easily fit two, three, maybe even four children comfortably, so me and Theo climb in and fly up to put Christmas hats on the ugly gargoyle heads that hang from the building. The

Giraffe has wrapped the pillars in colourful tinsel, and the Monkey has made a bundle of Christmas lights into a lasso. He tosses them up high then uses them to scale the side of the building so he can secure them to the roof. And then, all together – the Giraffe, the Pelly, the Monkey and me – we clean and scrub and polish and buff those windows until they shine like mirrors. Everything looks brilliant.

The Christmas tree is now covered with baubles and tinsel and glittery stars, chocs and toffs and candy canes, as well as **TUMMYTICKLERS** and **SPITSIZZLERS, FIZZWINKLES** and **GOBWANGLES,** even some fiery **SCARLET SCORCHDROPPERS,** and all sorts of treats I brought from The Grubber. Its branches are so full that it looks like it could fall over at any moment. When Maria isn't watching, we munch on some of the candy. **DELICIOUS!** Jackson accidentally eats a Scorchdropper and smoke billows out of his mouth and nose.

'I don't know why we're still doing this,' Theo grumbles as we all laugh. 'We'll never get the rest of the decorations up before the adults get here!'

Now is not the time for him to turn grumpy. We only have one hour left before our parents arrive for the grand light switch-on event. We want to surprise them.

'Don't worry, Theo!' I tell him. 'It's just about having fun. It's Christmas, after all.'

Theo grins reluctantly and gives me a nod. 'What do you want for Christmas?' he says.

'Want?' I ask.

'You know, presents and stuff.'

I shrug. But before I can answer, the Monkey looks at me from up high on a pillar where he's tying more lights and I know what he's about to say.

'A bright turquoise apron, chockful of pockets for stuffing with sweets. That's all Billy ever talks about!'

'Mac has one of those, but in red,' Theo says. 'For all her paint supplies. She looks SO COOL!'

'Be quiet, will you?' I mutter. But it's true. I already know Mac has one of those. Actually, Mac inspired me to add one to my wish list. Mac also inspired me to get my trainers, my watch . . . even my haircut. She's my style inspiration. But I don't want her to know that.

Yet.

Mac is Maria's daughter. She's so cool, I'm surprised she hasn't turned into a walking, talking ice cube. Right at this moment, Mac is painting a huge Christmassy mural on a wall. It's a picture of Santa Claus skateboarding down a ramp. I always try to impress Mac, hoping she'll invite me to go hang out with her graffiti crew, but I usually end up doing something to embarrass myself. Like the time I leaned on one of her murals thinking it was dry and got covered in spray paint. I'd made such a mess by the time I noticed, the Pelly, the Monkey, the Giraffe and I had to get our cleaning stuff out to clean it all up. Luckily, she found it funny.

Maria checks the time on her phone and claps her hands together. 'Time to finish up!' she calls out. 'Parents will be here soon.'

We all race around, adding the final touches. The Giraffe drapes felt snow on the roof while the Monkey hangs a giant snow globe over the entrance. The Pelly hops to my side. 'Shall we have a final gander?' he says, and I clamber into his beak so we can do a last circuit of the building, inspecting all the details. I tick everything off on Maria's list.

Tick.

Tick!

TICK!

Inside, we all take a minute to look around. The place looks **AMAZZZZZING,** considering how run-down and in need of repair it is. Even Theo's eyebrows raise in surprise. I feel a pulse of pride in my chest.

Suddenly, Maria cuts the music. 'Come on, everyone! Time for the Mighty Christmas Light-y Switcher-On-er Extravaganza!'

Our parents had crowded around the entrance, all dressed up, heads arched up to the sky. Theo's dad has a pair of deer antlers on his head, Jackson's mum is wearing a dress covered in sequins, and Walleed's parents are back from their Christmas tree retrieval mission wearing matching musical sweaters that sing 'Fa, la, la!' when you press a button.

Is this for real? Have they made all this effort, just for us?

Then I glimpse two other parents. The ones that I care about most. My mum and dad are here, mixing with the crowd. Dad wears tinsel around his neck. Mum has red holly berries dangling from her ears. The Giraffe slowly lowers her head to let Mum put a tiny Christmas hat on each of her horns. I run over to stand with them.

Maria's face splits into a wide smile as she claps her hands together. 'Thank you for being here! Your children have put so much work into Power Squad tonight. They wanted to make it just right for all of you. And now, it's lights time.'

She reaches for a power switch on the side of the building and yanks it down, and suddenly the car park is lit up and **GLITTERING** in the snow, the lights shimmering in the window panes. Maria's proud face beams almost as bright as the lights.

But then *FLASH!* **BANG!** SIZZLE and **FIZZLE!** The lights all go out! Leroy – our chef – races out of the kitchen. Sweat beads his forehead, despite the cold.

'Thedinnerisoff,everythinginthekitchenisn'tworking, doesanyonehavethenumberforatakeaway?'

From across the car park, Mac and I share a panicked glance.

'Could you say that again?' Maria asks. I mean, I love fast rap lyrics as much as the next person, but that was too quick even for me.

Leroy takes a deep breath. 'The ovens have blown their fuses. Ain't no cooking today.' He looks around and asks again, 'Does anyone have a takeaway app?' I know he must hate this, because he's all about everything being cooked from scratch and with love. To be fair, nothing is better than Leroy's food.

'Hey!' Maria calls out. 'Anyone know how to fix an oven?'

The parents shake their heads and begin murmuring between themselves.

Then, something **BUZZES** in my mum's pocket. She pulls her phone out and looks at the screen. 'It's Uncle Otis,' she says. She puts her phone on speaker so Dad and I can hear. 'Hi, Otis.'

'Sandy! Sandy! This is Otis!'

'Yes, I know,' my mum says, rolling her eyes.

Uncle Otis goes on, barely pausing for breath. 'I have an emergency. It seems like a job for the Ladderless Window-Cleaning Company. Are they with you?'

My mum hands the phone over to me.

'Go on then, Uncle Otis,' I say. 'What is this big problem?'

He starts talking at super-speed like Leroy did. 'Billy, weneedyourhelp,lotsofChristmasbaublesanddecorations haveblownoffandaretumblingdownOxfordStreet.'

'So, what you're saying is – the giant Christmas baubles are on the run? And you need us to catch them and put them back where they were?' I ask.

You might not expect it, but the Ladderless Window-Cleaning Company doesn't just clean windows. Anyone who knows us knows we do all sorts of things, from picking fruit from the tallest trees to catching thieves.

The Pelly nods enthusiastically. The Giraffe's eyes light up and the Monkey leaps from foot to foot. 'A mission, **A MISSION!'** he says excitedly.

'There was a big storm last night. It must have loosened all the decorations because there are baubles all over the place and more keep flying free! But it's not just the baubles, the lights, the tinsel, the chocolate coins. Without Oxford Street decorations looking their best, Christmas might as well be cancelled.'

Oxford Street is where everyone in London does their Christmas shopping. Every year giant Christmas baubles are hung out in rows, dangling from the Christmas lights that hang above the shops and shoppers.

The Pelican shakes his head. 'We can't have that,' he mutters.

'Can you help us?' says the voice down the phone.

I look round at Giraffe, Pelly and Monkey – and I know we're all thinking the same thing. 'Don't panic!' I tell Uncle Otis. 'We're on our way!'

The Pelly opens his beak to let me in, while the Monkey clambers up on to the Giraffe's neck.

'TO OXFORD STREEEEET!' the Giraffe cries.

'Indeed,' the Pelly proclaims in a muffled voice. We take off, ducking beneath the doorway and flying out into the freezing air. The Giraffe gallops after us as streetlights flicker on.

'Good luck!' Mac calls, giving me a two-thumbs-up. 'You're the best.'

I send her a little salute as we swoop out of Power Squad and the Monkey begins to sing:

We're off to save Christmas,
You won't want to miss this,
The baubles are out of control!
We're galloping and gliding
And swooping and striding,
The Oxford Street trinkets are rogue!

But there's no need to fret,
Not all is lost yet,
Oxford Street will soon be aglow.

For we're the fantabulous, miraculous
Wonderfully splendiferous,
Ladderless Window-Cleaning Co!

❄

Oxford Street is always busy. Every day. Like, anytime of the week. At Christmas, it's on a whole other level, and there's no sign of Uncle Otis.

Luckily, the Giraffe makes space wherever she walks, so we stick close and she wades through shoppers, each carrying ten shopping bags (which should be an Olympic sport, because it's basically weightlifting). We weave through tourists, who immediately stop taking pictures of everything Christmassy and turn to gape at our little troupe. We dodge around entertainers dressed up as reindeers, who stop mid-song as the Pelly flaps overhead with keen eyes. We step over a small band of carolers, who all quieten down, mid-*Silent-Night*. 'There!' the Giraffe shouts.

And there are the rogue baubles that Uncle Otis warned us about.

As the Pelly settles on the pavement, baubles big enough to knock down Father Christmas himself fly past us.

'Woah!' I cry, leaping out of the way as a bright red bauble whips past me. Red, gold, green . . . all of them like giant billiard balls, pinballing around the pavements.

'Watch out!' a newspaper seller cries.

'Rogue decorations heading left!' a stall-holder warns, calling at the top of his voice.

This is CHAOS.

The Giraffe raises her eyebrows at me, which is hard to do when you're five metres tall and a giraffe. 'This looks like our hardest job yet,' she says.

I nod. Maybe too hard.

We take shelter in the doorway of a giant toy shop – except the Giraffe, who is much too big – just as another bauble knocks down a police officer.

'Arrest that bauble!' he cries.

The rest of us turn to each other. The sparkling Christmas decorations from a shop's window light up our faces with their warm glow and something else lights up in my chest. I'm not giving up – especially when Mac believes in me. Didn't she say we were the best?

'Watch out!' The Monkey, clinging to a pillar, spots another giant bauble, as red as Rudolph's nose, rolling towards us at full speed.

If the Giraffe was Indiana Jones she'd run the other

way right now, just like he does in that old movie *The Temple of Doom*, and get out of the way of the boulderous bauble just in time. But the Giraffe is way braver than Indiana Jones and instead she bows down, using her neck like a ramp, and the bauble rolls up and off her head, flying through the sky.

'Yes, Giraffe!' I cheer.

Tourists watch the ball **FLY** through the sky and land in the arms of a giant inflatable Santa a little way down the street.

A few metres down the road another giant bauble is shaking in the wind, about to fall off the Christmas lights. If it lands on the pavement, a whole load of Christmas shoppers are going to be hit by a giant bauble!

That's when I see the coolest thing I have ever seen in my life. Just as a massive gust of wind finally breaks the bauble free, the Monkey scrambles to the top of the Giraffe's neck and leaps into the Pelly's beak as he flies by. The Pelly glides higher and higher, and then the Monkey jumps into mid-air, catches the giant bauble in one hand, and sails to land on the wires for the lights, dragging the bauble with him. He reconnects the bauble to the string of lights hanging over the street, his furry fingers working in a flurry as he ties knots. It's a Christmas decoration slam dunk! Proper teamwork.

I clap hard, **CHEERING,** and the other shoppers join in. The Monkey lets go of the wire and lands perfectly, giving a deep bow to his new fans, who gape and gasp. But then we hear some more shouts. It's the police officer who was knocked over before.

He points. 'Baubles on the run!'

We follow the noise, turning the corner into Carnaby Street. 'Billy,' the Giraffe calls down, and I climb to the top of her neck – feeling her muscles flex beneath my feet – and spot a bauble about to crash into a shopfront. But we are at least 200 metres behind it. We're not going to get there in time . . .

'I'll get it!' the Monkey shouts, and he clambers up the side of the building at a speed that would make even Spider-Man jealous. The Pelly flies ahead as the Giraffe gallops through the crowd, her long legs weaving between people as though she's on a football pitch.

The people down below take pictures on their mobile phones – snap, SNAP, **SNAP!** I suppose this doesn't happen every day.

But this bauble isn't slowing down – it's going to smash into the shop and ruin a perfect gingerbread Christmas display. The Monkey isn't going to make it in time!

I cover my eyes. But instead of the sound of broken glass, we hear the strain of flapping wings.

Hoping the Pelly hasn't been hurt, my eyes fly open. The Pelly is swooping right into the path of the bauble! Everyone knows that the Pelly's beak is like Mary Poppins's bag – it can fit in a **GIANT** amount of stuff. But I don't think even the Pelly knew if he could hold a bauble this huge – which is what he's about to do now.

Hopefully. Maybe.

'Go, Pelly!' the Giraffe calls as I cling on to her knobbly horns. We all watch the Pelly dive after the bauble as it bounces off a kerb and up into the air, and then with a huge breath in – POP! – just like that, the bauble is sucked into his beak like an Everlasting Gobstopper. Immediately, the Pelly swoops round and drops it down on to one of the Giraffe's horns. Then the Giraffe stretches her **MAGICAL** neck and keeps stretching and stretching and stretching until it's extended out to twice its normal length, with me still perched at the top. She angles her head, trying to get the bauble neatly on top of one of the Christmas lights. But she needs some help!

I reach out and direct the bauble with my hands as I call directions. 'Just a little bit over to the left. Right! Left again!' And then we've done it. The bauble hooks over the string of Christmas lights and we're safe.

Phew. That was A LOT!

The people below cheer us on as though we're festive superheroes. And I feel like one!

The Pelly wafts his wings to redirect a bauble about to crash into a bus, the Giraffe is kicking random baubles out of the way, and the Monkey is riding a great golden bauble, spinning his feet to drive it safely into a bush. This could be chaos, and yet . . . it isn't. It feels as though we are rocking this together.

Finally, we hang up the last bauble, the biggest one of all. We settle it on the roof of a shop that's covered in

Christmas decorations. And now everything looks right. The baubles and lights fill the streets with a glow that wasn't there before. Not like this.

My only regret is that Mac wasn't here to see all of our hard work.

The police officer from earlier strolls past and gives us a thumbs-up. He doesn't even seem surprised to see a giraffe, a monkey and a pelican.

'Good work!' he calls, as I slide back down the Giraffe's elongated neck. ***WHEEEE!***

Uncle Otis suddenly appears and rushes over. 'At last!' His voice carries ahead of him, echoing off the shop fronts. 'But there's still one bauble missing! And I think . . .' He gasps for breath. 'I think it's heading towards Buckingham Palace!'

No! Is this FOR REAL?

I thought we'd done our job, that we could rest and enjoy some Scrumdiddlyumptious Hot Chocolate. Clearly, hot chocolate will have to wait.

'Get on, Billy! We had better get to it!' the Giraffe calls. I climb back on to my long-legged, long-necked friend and we race down Regent Street, towards Buckingham Palace. Strangers double-take left and right as we pass by.

'Giraffe by the zebra crossing!' a young girl calls out.

'Monkey incoming!' That's the police officer again, directing people out of the way.

'Pelican overhead!' a boy shouts, pointing.

And you know what? I feel proud of my friends. We're on a proper mission.

We race down the Mall, the wide road leading to the palace. We'd be able to spot a sparkly glimmery bauble immediately, but there's nothing here other than the parks, the swans and a lot of very awestruck tourists watching us gallop past.

'Is this meant to happen?' I hear someone ask, as he takes hold of his child's hand.

'I don't know, Dad,' she says. 'Maybe it's interactive art or something.'

We arrive outside the palace gates.

Immediately there's a shout from the direction of one of the Buckingham Palace balconies. Did the King stub his toe, I wonder? Did a corgi nip someone's finger? Did the royal household run out of crumpets? I climb further up the Giraffe, trying to get a closer look.

Unbelievable!

There's the King. The actual King of England! He's in his dressing gown, wearing fluffy slippers with little bunny ears. He also has a right alarmed look on his face. He calls out at the top of his royal lungs, pointing at something down below. I follow his line of sight . . . and see the last bauble rolling down the Mall on a crash course with the palace. We thought we'd seen the biggest bauble that could ever exist already, but this was even **BIGGER!**

'Excuse us! Giraffe coming through!' the Monkey calls out from the Pelly's beak, and the Giraffe and I navigate our way through the crowd as quickly as possible.

'We need something to stop it,' I say, glancing around. 'Something long like a . . .' My mind goes back to my favourite old movie hero, with his trilby hat and his bullwhip, braided together with long strips of leather. '. . . something like a lasso!'

The Monkey's eyes light up. He races back to the gates. 'Begging your pardon, miss; excuse me, sir,' he says, as he deftly unravels scarves from person after person. Pink, yellow, red . . . all the colours in the world. He carries an armful of wool back through to us and drops it at our feet. 'Will this do?'

I understand straight away. 'We MAKE a lasso!' I cry.

'Right you are!' the Monkey says.

We all grab scarves and work together to tie them in knots. The Pelly uses his beak to clamp the scarves while the Monkey and I tie the knots. The Giraffe's teeth are perfect for pulling the scarves tight, and before we know it . . . we have a lasso!

The Monkey raises the scarf-rope in a hairy fist and starts to spin the makeshift lasso above his head. 'One, two, three . . .!' we all chant, and the Monkey sends the loop of the lasso over the top of the bauble, just as it crashes through the palace gates.

We watch, waiting to see if the lasso will catch hold. Then, yes! It wraps around the bauble and the Monkey pulls the rope tight. We all heave on the scarf-rope as hard as we can. I feel my muscles tremble. The bauble careers off to one side for a moment, but then – no! – the scarves break free and fall to the ground. The bauble crashes down, spins round, and is headed again straight for the palace. This is a disaster!

Immediately, the Giraffe sprints after the bauble, her long legs moving faster than any giant Christmas decoration. She gets right in the bauble's path, lowers her head to the ground, and extends it out as far as it will go, and just like a pinball machine, the bauble runs up between her horns, along her LOOOOOOONG neck and . . .

No! It falls to the ground again, picking up even more speed.

'Pelly!' I cry. 'Can you help?'

My pelican friend takes to the sky and flies after it. I've never seen the Pelly flap his wings *so* hard. Then he swoops down low and snaps the bauble's hook in his beak. He tries to fly up, but the bauble's been travelling so fast, the momentum is too strong, and it spins right out again. He swoops back to the three of us.

I call out to the rest of the gang. 'We'll need to work together to stop that bauble!'

The Monkey gathers a couple more scarves. But he needs LOTS more if our plan is going to have a chance of working. Luckily, that's when the crowd of people at the broken-down gates start chucking all their scarves at the Monkey. 'Monkey, take mine! Monkey, use this!' they all cry.

'Thanking you kindly,' he says, and he quickly gathers them up and makes an even longer, stronger lasso. The Monkey then takes a deep breath and aims. Once again, he chucks his lasso over the flying bauble, just like a cowboy, and it lands perfectly around the middle! He loops the end of the lasso around a tree stump, then me, the Monkey, the Giraffe and the Pelly all pull – hard. I can feel my face turn red with the effort. The Pelly is flapping, the Giraffe's long legs are trembling . . . and the bauble starts to slow down! But the force of the momentum against the pull of the lasso spins it high up into an arc, up, up, up towards the palace . . . where it gently lands on the palace roof. It hasn't destroyed anything at all. In fact, the palace looks more festive than ever.

We're all sweating and totally out of breath – but triumphant. 'We did it!' I cry.

'Amazing! Astonishing! Remarkable!' A booming voice sounds out from the royal balcony. The King gives us a massive double-thumbs-up. 'Thank you, all of you, you **MAGNIFICENT** creatures,' he says. He leans over the balcony. 'Now, does anyone have time for tea and crumpets?'

'But what about the bauble?' I cry. Yes, it looks pretty up there, but that's not where it belongs.

The King raises a finger, and a butler arrives at his side holding a mobile phone in a white-gloved hand. The King takes it daintily. 'I know just the right people to call,' he tells us with a wink.

We join His Majesty for our tea and crumpets, and just as we finish, there's the beep of a horn from outside the palace. We go to the window to see an army of black cabs lining the Mall. 'Taxi's here,' the Pelly announces, and he flies back up to the bauble and gives it a gentle nudge with his beak. It rocks and sways and then – ever so softly – rolls down a palace column to land in a cloud of snow. We rush down and help to nudge it out of the gates, where a black cab trundles right up to us. Then the taxi drivers use their bumpers to gently roll the bauble back up the Mall towards Oxford Street. As we follow, we toss the scarves back to their owners, who cry out with happiness.

'You saved Christmas!'

'You saved the palace!'

There's a last call from the King, back on the balcony. 'Well done! You're all heroes!'

HEROES. That's a good word. I feel my chest fill with pride. I can't wait to tell Mac about all of this. We've done a lot of saving today.

More cheers from onlookers follow us as we make our way back to Oxford Street, where we find Uncle Otis again. He beams.

'I wondered where you'd got to,' he says, eyes widening with surprise when he sees the taxis – and the bauble.

'Oh, we had a very important appointment at Buckingham Palace.'

His eyes grow even wider, and he shakes his head. 'I'm not sure I understand, but I'm glad you're back. And with the final bauble!' Then he looks at the Christmas decorations high above us, and his brow creases in a frown. 'But how are we going to get it back up there?'

'Oh, don't worry about that,' I tell him.

I huddle with the Giraffe, the Monkey and the Pelly,

sharing my plans. They all nod.

'Good show,' says the Giraffe.

'Masterful!' exclaims the Pelly.

'In a jiffy,' agrees the Monkey.

Then I climb up the Giraffe's neck while the Monkey clings to the Pelican's back. The Giraffe extends her neck out long, long, longer than I've ever seen it, and the Pelly opens his beak wide, wide, wider than it's ever been, and the Monkey and I balance and roll and steady the bauble as we lift it up into the air. We can hear gasps from the crowd below. Then, the four of us manage to hook the last runaway bauble on to a previously bare section of Christmas lights.

When we land back down at street level, Uncle Otis rushes over and gives me the biggest hug. **'WOW!** I'm so impressed. You, Giraffe, Monkey and Pelly really saved Christmas on Oxford Street, Billy.'

He hugs the others too, though I'm not sure the Pelly really likes it, and he can only reach as high as the Giraffe's elbow. 'Now, get whatever you want,' he says, casting out an arm to take in all the shops. 'This is on me, as a thank you.' He pauses and looks me in the face. 'What do you want, Billy? What would really make Christmas for you?'

I take a gulp of air. That's a big question to answer. A very big question.

The Monkey, the Pelly and the Giraffe start miming something to me, pulling imaginary clothes over their heads. What are they saying we should get? A superhero's cape? A big furry hat? Platform snow boots? Then I finally understand! A multi-pocketed apron, just like Mac has. Maybe we could all have matching ones, with our names on the front? We would look like a real team. Mac would be so impressed. I tell Uncle Otis what I'm after, and he leads us into his favourite department store. The security guards all applaud as we walk in. The shop assistants zip around our group like bees, sizing us up for our aprons.

We all pose in the mirror.

The Giraffe's is a bit short.

The Monkey's is a bit long.

The Pelly's catches on his wings and squashes his feathers.

Something's not right . . . it doesn't feel that cool wearing them.

I think back to what really makes me feel happy. The Grubber Sweet Shop. The Ladderless Window-Cleaning Company. My mum and dad. All the fun we have at Power Squad. And then I think about how we left Henwood Lane today with everyone feeling sad about the broken oven, the cobwebs and mouse nests, and the cracks in the walls that Maria is always trying to fix.

Quietly, I slip off my apron and let it fall to the floor. One by one, my friends do the same. I can tell that we've had the same idea. A Very Good Idea.

'What's wrong?' Uncle Otis asks.

'I have another thought,' I say, my friends nodding in agreement. 'Instead of getting something for ourselves, could we help our after-school club?' I swallow hard. 'Maybe with a new kitchen? Something to fix the walls? Even just some paint?' I know it's cheeky to ask. This won't be cheap, but if I can't help my friends, what else can I do that would make me happy?

Uncle Otis's smile spreads again. That great big smile

that he has. He nods.

'Of course. But it's getting late. For now, why don't we have a fabulous dinner made up that you can take with you to eat right away?'

'NO WAYYYYY!' I cry.

'WAY!' Uncle Otis cries.

The Monkey claps his hands together in delight and hops on to the Giraffe's back, hand on his chest:

How delightful, what wonderous glee!
To receive such a fabulous treat!
A festive bonanza
(I hope there's banana)
For our friends, our families, and me!

'Better make some phone calls, Billy,' Uncle Otis says as we clap the Monkey's singing.

I call Maria. 'Everyoneneedstogetthetableslaid,Ihave managedtosortusoutabigChristmasdinner.'

Maria pauses a moment, trying to decode my super-speed speech. 'Billy, are you saying you've sorted us out a Crimbo dinner?'

'YESSS!' I say as I hear everyone else cheering.

'That sounds amazing,' Maria says, 'but how will we get it here? It's a long way, after all.'

Uncle Otis takes the phone from me and speaks down the line, his voice rich with excitement. 'Leave it to me, Maria! Just get everyone ready.'

❄

A short time later, we watch as top chefs from all the fancy Oxford Street restaurants cook on giant barbecues lining the pavements. We take in the aromas wafting up and down the street. All of the Christmas shoppers have gone home and now Oxford Street is just for us. And only us! The snow has stopped. The lights are lit. I glance up at the last bauble we managed to fix and realize how lucky we are.

Thirty minutes later, the world's **LONGEST** limousine arrives. It has black-tinted windows and looks SUPER glamorous. We all ooooh and ahhh at the fancy car, trying to guess who it's for, when we realize, it's for us! The chefs start loading the food on to the rows and rows of seats all the way down to the end, along with Christmas crackers and candles, napkins folded like swans and wobbling desserts on silver platters. Right at the back, I climb in with Uncle Otis, the Monkey, the Pelican, and finally the Giraffe, who sticks her head up through the open sun-roof.

When we arrive, everyone is gathered outside the front. Maria is grinning. Theo is laughing. Mac is waving from the back. Even Leroy looks **EXCITED.** He may not be cooking, but he is getting a delicious dinner from some of London's best chefs! The chefs and helpers get to work inside the club, lighting candles so we can see, then putting down platters with every meat, vegetable and Christmassy side you could think of, with ten different types of gravy and vats of cranberry sauce. They've made special dishes for my friends: roasted honey walnuts for the Monkey, a huge salmon wellington for the Pelican, and the most magnificent dish made from the pink and purple flowers of the Tinkle-Tinkle tree that you've ever seen for the Giraffe. There is even a band on the upstairs landing with a choir playing Christmas songs. Maria goes over to them and asks if they know any Trinidadian ones, and they do!

Before everyone settles into their seats, Uncle Otis comes over. 'Will you turn on the lights?' he asks.

I turn to look at him. 'But I thought the electricity went out?' I ask.

'I sent someone ahead,' Uncle Otis says.

This is . . . awesome. Then, I stop to think. We're here, in the club. Every day, this place is made to feel like home. And there is one person in the whole world who makes that happen. I look over at Mum and Dad, who give me a nod. They already know what I'm thinking.

I take a deep breath. 'Could Maria help?'

Uncle Otis lays a hand on my shoulder and squeezes. 'Of course,' he says with pride.

I take Maria's hand and, together, with everyone behind us, we walk outside. It feels as though thousands of people are watching us, but I recognize everyone's faces immediately. Theo, Fumbi, Alice, Walleed, Jackson . . .

Maria and I head towards the lever. Voices settle around us, then Uncle Otis starts calling out: 'Five, four, three . . .' The whole crowd join in. '. . . two, one!' It reminds me of the countdown we all shared at our classroom window.

Maria puts her hand out and I follow. Then I signal to the Pelly, the Giraffe and the Monkey. They all clamber to join us. Our hands, our paws and our hooves all gather over the lever. Then we pull it down as Maria and I yell together: **'WE SAVED CHRISTMAS!'**

The Power Squad lights flicker on, sparkling, shining, shimmering – even better in my eyes than the baubles and tinsel and lights of Oxford Street – as the reflections dance off the sparkling windows.

This really is the start of Christmas.

I look around at everyone from the Power Squad staring up in awe. Forget my turquoise apron. Watching all my friends and family enjoy Christmas really makes me feel COOL. And then hunger wins out, and we all file back in and settle down in our seats in front of the food.

I look up to see Mac on the other side of the table. She waves me over.

'Come and sit down,' she says, patting the spare chair next to her.

OK!

She gives me a long look, smiling. 'You've done something great today. You know that, right?' Snowflakes have started to fall again and gather on the windows. 'Otis told us what you did. You know . . . saving Christmas.'

'Well, it's not all about me,' I say.

She looks so impressed that I capture that moment in my heart. I did a good thing today.

'I hope you don't mind, but I brought something for you.' She reaches beneath the table and pulls something out of her backpack. It's a roll of black material. I unravel it and inside is a load of paint supplies sticking out of little pouches: paintbrushes, chalk, stencils and pencils, and spray cans in burnt umber and aquamarine, toffee brown and Christmas-tree green, lemon-sherbet yellow and giraffe orange – all the colours you could think of.

'For me?' I ask, pulling out the cans of impossible gold and dazzling silver.

'Want to join me and my crew and help paint?' she asks.

'YES!' The word flies out of my mouth before I can stop it and Mac's face flushes with pleasure.

Mac believes in me. She really does! I look over to my friends – the Giraffe, the Monkey and the Pelican. I can see from their smiles that they're pleased for me.

We start to eat. It's everything I've ever wished for – turkey, pigs in blankets, carrots and roast potatoes, honey-sweet walnuts, puff pastry salmon and the pink and purple flowers. Theo is down the other end of the table, tucking in, and Maria is talking to Leroy about the plans for Power Squad next year.

I raise my eyes to the ceiling and watch the fairy lights shimmering above us. Something great happened today, something that I was part of.

The Giraffe gets to her feet and unfolds her very long legs. Then the Monkey scurries to the very top of her very long neck. He opens his mouth wide and serenades us with a Christmas tune. It's not Mariah Carey, but it's a song composed for a whole bunch of friends.

We saved the day, hip hip hurray,
No better could this be.
A scrumptious, delumptious, unctuous feast,
With our friends and family.

And though we'll soon all say goodnight,
It's been delightful company:
Our Christmas group, a fabulous troupe,
And the Giraffe, the Pelly, and me.

THE WITCHES' FESTIVE FLOP

Pamela Butchart

‘I am not, of course, telling you for one second that your teacher actually is a witch. All I am saying is that she *might* be one. It is most unlikely. But – and here comes the big “but” – *it is not impossible.’*

Roald Dahl, *The Witches*

CHAPTER 1
There's Something Wrong with Miss Marie

When the bell went on Friday, our teacher handed each of us our homework and told us to have a lovely weekend.

That was the last time we ever saw her.

My friend River said he saw her in Tesco working behind the fish counter and that she looked a bit confused when River waved. But no one knows for sure if it was her.

That's when we got a new teacher, called Miss Marie. And she had really ***SHINY*** hair and wore **FANCY** gloves and smelled like roses. Miss Marie was really keen to get to know us, so we spent the whole day making an all-about-us display with all of our hobbies and favourite things on it. That afternoon, we all went to rehearsals for the Christmas concert, but Miss Marie didn't come with us because she said she had a headache. When we got back to class, Miss Marie was standing with her hands on her hips staring at our display wall.

We waited for her to tell us what to do next. But Miss Marie just stood there staring at our display with a weird smile on her face. That's when Gray said, 'I think there might be something wrong with Miss Marie.'

Then, suddenly, she gasped and we all jumped in our seats. Miss Marie turned and stared at us and that's when I thought that her eyes looked a bit different than they had that morning. But I wasn't sure. And then she said, 'It's Christmas. Your favourite thing in the world is Christmas!' Miss Marie clapped her hands and laughed really **LOUD.** But none of us laughed. Because that's when we started to suspect that there was something odd about Miss Marie.

Something very odd.

But we didn't know yet that she was a **WITCH.**

CHAPTER 2
The Teachers Go MISSING

Things got even stranger on Tuesday. Two more teachers went missing and were replaced by new teachers. We asked Miss Marie what had happened to our teachers and she said, 'Nothing happened to them! They were just FAR too old to teach. They've retired.'

But that didn't make any sense because Mr Cunningham looked so young that one time the headteacher actually shouted at him for being out of class without a note – because he thought he was one of the Year Sixes! I looked at River and he looked at me and I could tell by the look on his face that he was thinking the same thing as I was.

Miss Marie was lying to us.

❄

Things were getting serious. And we knew it.

I mean, teachers lie about stuff all the time. Like how long it is until break time and what they did at the weekend and how much they **LOVE** school dinners (even though I have never seen even one teacher eat the toxic turkey pie!). But we all knew that this was different. Because this wasn't a normal teacher lie. This was **BIG.** And it was obvious that something strange was going on.

So that's when I said, 'We need to tell the headteacher.'

River shook his head loads because our headteacher is a bit scary. But then at break, when we were on our way to the head's office, Amal pointed out the window, and that's when we saw that three more teachers were leaving! And it was obvious they were leaving for good because they were all carrying BOXES of their stuff to their cars and they looked a bit shocked.

That's when one of the Year Sixes turned to us and said, 'The head just sacked them. Now the poor Year

Ones don't have a teacher!' But we just stared at the Year Six girl because Year Sixes never usually talk to us or even look at us. So we didn't really know what to do. Then everyone gasped and that's when we saw three figures marching in through the school gates, side by side. I heard River gulp and I knew he'd spotted the same thing I had. Their feet were moving at exactly the same time – like soldiers do.

It was more new teachers!

CHAPTER 3
The NEW Headteacher!

When we got to the headteacher's office, I took a deep breath and knocked on the door. We all stood there, frozen to the spot, waiting to be told to 'Come in!' in a really loud voice (because that's what usually happens).

But nothing happened.

Amal said that maybe I hadn't knocked loud enough, so I raised my hand and knocked again, a bit harder this time. But then I froze with my hand in mid air. Because I'd knocked so hard that the door had opened! I waited for the head to scream at me for knocking his door open.

But no one screamed.

And that's when Amal peeked inside and gasped. Then she pulled her head back out and said, 'I think we've got a problem, run!' I felt my stomach DROP down to my feet (which is what happens when you are in an emergency situation). And I was definitely going to run away because Amal does not scare easily. So if she said run, then I knew that whatever she saw must be bad.

But that's when we all heard a voice say, 'There's no need to run.'

❄

We gasped when we saw her. And it wasn't just because she looked a bit serious. It was because she was sitting at Mr Seith's desk. In Mr Seith's seat! I turned and looked at the door and she must have known I still really wanted to run because that's when she looked right at me and said, 'Sit.' But none of us moved.

The lady stared at us as she **SLOWLY** stood up.

And we all gasped.

Because she was so **TALL** that she was almost touching the ceiling!

She pointed to the chairs in front of the desk with her eyes. So we all sat down because it didn't really feel like we had a choice. River nudged me and pointed and I gasped because the little metal sign on Mr Seith's desk didn't say Mr Seith any more. It said **MISS STEEL.**

We watched as Miss Steel sat back down. But to be honest, even when she was sitting down it still felt like she was standing up. That's how tall she was.

'So I am the new headteacher. And I don't appreciate random visits to my office!' she said. 'I suppose you've come to ask about the missing Year Fours?'

We all looked at each other because we had no idea the Year Fours had gone missing!

'No need to worry. No one is missing. The Year Fours are on a school trip. The **LUCKY** critters were given a last-minute opportunity to go on a hike! Isn't that wonderful? They'll be back this evening . . .' Miss Steel got up and opened the window and started wafting fresh air at us, like there was a terrible smell in the room, although I couldn't smell anything.

We all looked at each other and then I took a deep breath and said, 'Our teachers. Where have they all gone? There's only a few left.'

Miss Steel leaned over her desk and stared at me. And that's when I noticed that her eyes looked a bit weird – the pupils were sort of **GLOWING.** I held my breath as she opened her mouth to say something.

But before she could say a word, we all heard a scream.

CHAPTER 4
The Accident

We raced out of the head's office and up the stairs to where the screaming was coming from. And that's when we saw it.

The Christmas tree was down!

We stared at the huge tree lying on the ground and all the smashed baubles **SCATTERED** everywhere. But then River gasped and pointed, and that's when we saw legs sticking out from under the tree! We all knew who the legs belonged to. They belonged to Mrs Moug because the legs had shoes on them. Mrs Moug is the only teacher who wears woollen shoes that she makes herself.

That's when I noticed that Miss Steel was smiling. Not a lot, just a tiny bit. But it was definitely a smile. She spotted me looking at her and stopped smiling and rushed over to Mrs Moug and yelled, 'Everyone! **LIFT!**' And the second she said that, all the new teachers lunged forward at the same time and lifted the tree off Mrs Moug in one move like they were super-strong robots or something!

I looked at River and he whispered, **'WOW!'**

I was worried that Mrs Moug was going to be totally **SQUISHED**. But she wasn't. And she was even able to stand up on her own.

But that's when Miss Steel swooped over and said, 'Mrs Moug. I think it's best to lie down until the ambulance arrives.' Mrs Moug said that she was fine and tried to get up again but Miss Steel said, 'Lie down.'

She sounded terrifying.

That's when I saw Mrs Moug's eyes go a bit weird. She lay back down on top of all the broken baubles and didn't move. That's when Amal whispered, 'You realize what this means, right?' And I shook my head because I didn't. Amal said, 'When Mrs Moug leaves in the ambulance there will only be one of our old teachers left!' And I gasped.

Because she was right.

CHAPTER 5
Christmas Jumper Chaos!

On Wednesday, when we turned up at school, the Christmas tree and all the decorations were gone. Instead there was a big sign that said:

> DUE TO THE SERIOUS INCIDENT THAT HAPPENED YESTERDAY, CHRISTMAS TREES HAVE BEEN **BANNED** AS A MARK OF RESPECT TO OUR DEAR MRS MOUG, WHO IS RECOVERING WELL OVERSEAS.

'Why is Mrs Moug recovering overseas?!' asked Amal. 'She seemed fine when the ambulance got here.'

I had no idea what overseas meant. Hoorain said she

thought it meant Mrs Moug was on a boat. But River said that it meant Mrs Moug was in another country across a sea. None of us knew why Mrs Moug had to go so far away to recover, but we all agreed it was a bit weird.

That's when April and Cohen (the twins) appeared wearing matching Christmas jumpers. You would never guess just by looking at them that they were twins (because they look completely different), but they're able to do this spooky thing where they say the exact same thing at the exact same time (and it freaks everyone out). The jumpers had **FLASHING** lights and music and Cohen and April kept pressing each other's jumpers and **LAUGHING** and it was really funny and it made us forget about the Christmas tree and terrifying Miss Steel for a while because it was Christmas jumper day.

We all showed each other our Christmas jumpers and then we took our Santa hats out of our bags and put those on too. We all loved **CHRISTMAS JUMPER DAY** (and our old teachers used to love it and wear Christmas jumpers too!), but when the new teachers saw our jumpers and hats, they tutted and shook their heads and said that they were not correct school uniform.

And I'm sure I even heard one of them call the jumpers ugly!

Then, just before assembly started, one of the new teachers yelled and dropped a box of scissors all over the floor and said that the flashing Rudolph nose on April's Christmas jumper had blinded her.

That's when Miss Steel said, 'Then it's decided. Christmas jumpers are **DANGEROUS** and are now banned. And those hats can go too. Please take them off right away!'

So we all had to take our jumpers and hats off, even though we only had our T-shirts on underneath and were all freezing. That's when Mr Cottage (the only original teacher left!) stood up and said, 'This is NONSENSE. You can't ban Christmas jumpers!'

We all watched as Miss Steel's eyes went a bit wide. 'Mr Cottage,' she said. 'Would you please join me on the stage?'

Mr Cottage looked a bit unsure. 'Well . . . I don't see why that's necessary. Um, I mean . . .'

Miss Steel stared at Mr Cottage, and that's when he started walking up on to the stage. He stood on the stage, staring out at us with a weird look on his face.

Amal WHISPERED, 'That's the exact same look Mrs Moug got when Miss Steel told her to stay down.'

I nodded – because I had noticed that too!

Miss Steel said, 'Mr Cottage doesn't think we should ban Christmas jumpers. He doesn't think they're dangerous. Is that right, Mr Cottage?' But Mr Cottage didn't say anything. He just stood there with the weird look on his face like he was frozen. Miss Steel smiled and said, 'What's this I see on your Christmas jumper, Mr Cottage? Is that a loose thread? Those can be as dangerous as an untied shoelace. Isn't that right, teachers?' All the new teachers agreed loudly.

River moved closer to me and said, 'I don't like this. Something's about to happen.' And he was right. We watched as Miss Steel began to pull at the **LOOSE** thread on Mr Cottage's jumper.

At first she just pulled a little bit. But then she started pulling a lot.

We all stared as Miss Steel kept **PULLING** at the thread until Mr Cottage started spinning around a bit.

Then Miss Steel started using both hands to pull at the thread.

We all stared as Mr Cottage started **SPINNING** round and round, getting faster and faster. Then Miss Steel smiled and gave a great big tug on the thread and Mr Cottage tripped and crashed into the drum kit that was on stage and everyone gasped.

Miss Steel stopped pulling and helped Mr Cottage to his feet. 'I am so sorry,' she said. 'Are you OK, Mr Cottage?'

But Mr Cottage didn't respond. So Miss Steel clicked her fingers and two of the new teachers rushed onto the stage and helped him back to his seat. And then she dropped the thread and dusted her hands off and said, 'You see? I told you Christmas jumpers were dangerous.'

CHAPTER 6

The School Dinners Are on FIRE!

That afternoon at school dinners, we were all sitting waiting for the dinner ladies to serve us Christmas pudding. And even though we really don't like most of the food they serve (like the lumpy custard and the **FIZZY** vegetable soup), everyone loves our Christmas pudding because it's filled with melted chocolate.

But all of a sudden the fire alarm went off and one of the dinner ladies came rushing out from behind the kitchen doors holding a giant Christmas pudding that was on fire! Within one second Miss Steel had appeared with a fire extinguisher and blasted the pudding! And even when the flames were obviously out, she just kept blasting the pudding and the dinner lady – until the pudding exploded everywhere.

We all sat there in shock (and pudding!), as Miss Steel put down the empty fire extinguisher and wiped her forehead. 'Setting fire to the school dinners is against the rules,' she said. The dinner lady tried to explain that they hadn't set fire to the school dinners and that they had just meant to light the tiny candle on top of the Christmas pudding and that it was a school Christmas tradition.

'I don't know how it caught fire! I just lit the candle on top and then the whole thing went up in flames! That's never happened before. I'm always careful. It's like someone tampered with it!' the dinner lady said.

That's when Miss Steel did her tiny smile thing again. Just for a second.

But I saw it.

And then she looked at the dinner lady and said, 'You're sacked! You're all sacked!'

CHAPTER 7
They're Not Teachers!

On Thursday, everyone brought a packed lunch because there were no dinner ladies left to cook.

After lunch, we tried to go to rehearsals for the Christmas concert (which we were all really **EXCITED** about!) but when we arrived at the music room, the music teacher who normally visits the school was nowhere to be seen and there was yellow tape all over the cupboard door where the musical instruments were kept!

That's when River said, 'It looks like a crime scene!' And it did because of all the tape and the signs that said **'NO ENTRY'** and **'OUT OF BOUNDS'** and **'DANGER'**.

We all looked at Gray because he plays loads of instruments and we knew that he had his guitar lesson on Thursday lunchtimes in the music room. But Gray said that the music teacher hadn't turned up for his lesson either and that he'd waited around for **AGES** before giving up. 'I thought maybe I'd got the day wrong, but it's definitely Thursday today, isn't it?'

And we all nodded because it was Thursday. River said that he thought we should peek inside the music cupboard to see why it was out of bounds – in case the music teacher had left a note or anything. But when we pulled the tape to one side and opened the door we all saw that the cupboard was empty.

Then Amal whispered, 'We need to have a chat about what's going on!' She looked around to make sure no one else was nearby. 'A secret chat.'

So we all **SQUEEZED** into the music cupboard and shut the door behind us, and Gray pulled the cord so the light came on. Amal took a deep breath. 'Something's going on. Our teachers have all disappeared and the new teachers are getting more and more weird. And the Year

Fours still aren't back. They were supposed to get back on Tuesday and now it's Thursday and there's still no sign of them!'

We all nodded.

'And they're banning everything to do with **CHRISTMAS!** What if the Christmas concert is next?!' Everyone gasped when Amal said that, and I jumped because it's a bit loud when you're squashed in a cupboard with twelve other people and they all do a dramatic gasp at the same time!

'Amal's right. They are weird. And what's with the gloves? Miss Marie wears hers all the time. Even in the classroom!' said River.

'And they're always touching their hair,' said Amal. 'It's weird. Have you noticed that?!' Loads of people nodded that they had.

And that's when we all heard laughing.

Everyone froze.

At first we thought it was coming from the music room but then we realized it was coming through the back wall of the music cupboard. And we all knew who it was.

It was them. They were in the staffroom next door and we could hear them through the wall!

And that's when we heard a voice say, 'I couldn't stand those smelly sprouts at dinner today!' We all looked at each other because there hadn't been any sprouts at dinner today!

Then another voice said, 'I almost miss those ugly Santa hats! At least when they were wearing them it contained some of their stink waves!' We looked at each other.

They were talking about us!

Then another voice said, 'I had to wash my hands **TEN** times to get the smell off after I helped that little rat with a plaster at breaktime.'

River gasped and held up his hand. He pointed to his plaster and whispered, 'Hey! That's me she's talking about! I don't smell!! And neither do my hands, look!' River shoved his hands in everyone's faces and we all **SNIFFED** them and shook our heads to confirm that they didn't smell.

Then we heard Miss Steel say, 'I'll never get the smell of Christmas pudding out my hair! But it was worth it to see how upset the little slime balls were that they didn't get their hands on it! And now we'll never have to worry about hearing those smelly little rats sing. It's a good thing I took care of that music teacher. Let's just say that she won't be coming back any time soon . . .'

We all stared at each other with our mouths **WIDE** open.

Miss Steel continued. 'And now that we've discovered what these little beasts love most, we can DESTROY IT. And by the time we've destroyed their precious Christmas, we will have destroyed them too!'

'They're planning to destroy **CHRISTMAS!'** Gray whispered.

'And US too!' I whispered back.

We stared at each other again in shock. Then River said, 'Aren't teachers supposed to like pupils?!'

And that's when Gray whispered, 'Um . . . they might not be teachers.' We all turned to Gray. He had his face pressed up against the cupboard wall. We watched as he pulled his face away and pointed to a little hole. I moved forward and looked through it. 'You can see right into the staffroom!' I whispered. Everyone gasped because we had never seen inside the staffroom before.

'What are they doing?!' asked Cohen.

'They're all just sitting around.' Then Gray said, 'That's not good. And they're all wearing gloves, aren't they? And they're not taking them off?'

I watched as one of the teachers opened her lunch box and took out a sandwich and started eating it. And she kept her gloves on the whole time. I looked at Gray and nodded. Gray took a deep breath and said, 'We're in deep trouble, people. I didn't want to say anything before because I wasn't sure and I didn't want to worry anyone. But I think I might be sure now.' I could feel my heart **THUMPING** in my chest because I didn't know what Gray was about to tell us, but I knew that it was going to be bad.

'My grandma told me something before she passed away. I thought she was joking at the time but now I'm not so sure. I mean, they all wear gloves. And they obviously hate children, so . . .'

We had NO IDEA what Gray was about to say. He

could have given us one thousand guesses and I don't think any of us would have got it right. Because that's when he said, 'I think they might be witches.'

CHAPTER 8
Witches!

Suddenly the laughing stopped. 'They couldn't have heard me! I whispered!' said Gray. But I wasn't so sure. We all sat in silence waiting for them to laugh again.

But they didn't.

Then we heard the staffroom door creak open and a voice outside said, 'The little **WORMS** must have run away. But they were here . . . I can still smell them!'

I peeked through the hole again even though my heart was racing – and that's when I saw Miss Steel stand up and hold something in the air.

'Any time you get a disgusting *WHIFF* of child, please remember to spray!' she said.

I watched as the teachers all nodded eagerly and began spraying themselves in the face with little bottles of perfume. I could smell roses. The bell went and the teachers rushed off to class. But we knew that we couldn't leave until everyone had gone or we might get caught. I looked at Gray and he looked as white as a sheet and he had his eyes closed. And I knew that he was in shock. So I took a Twix out of my bag, opened it and put it under his nose so he could smell it, because Gray loves chocolate. It worked – he opened his eyes and started eating it.

'Wait. They can't be witches. I don't think witches are real . . . are they?' asked April. But Gray nodded that they were.

'Are you sure?' said April. And Gray nodded again.

That's when Amal said, 'Gray . . . you're going to need to tell us more about what your grandma said.'

Gray looked at Amal with wide eyes. 'Grandma said the most important thing I need to know about witches is that they hate all children.' That's when I heard River gulp.

'She told me witches appear out of nowhere. And that they could be anyone.' I gave Amal a look and she gave me a look back. We all waited in silence while Gray took out the second finger of Twix and ate it. And when he was finished he said, 'Witches might have super hearing. That's probably how they heard me. And Grandma said they have dancing pupils that can change colour.' That's when I gasped because I knew Miss Marie's eyes had looked different the other day when she had been staring at our display board, but I didn't realize that they had changed colour.

'And they can sometimes **HYPNOTIZE** and control people with their eyes,' said Gray. Cohen and April gasped at the same time and said, 'Mr Cottage!' And then everyone else gasped too because we all remembered the weird look Mr Cottage got on his face when he was on stage. And how it seemed a bit like he was in a trance. Gray took a deep breath. 'The thing I remember MOST is my grandma said witches can **SMELL** children. And that to them, we smell like the most disgusting thing in the world!'

'Like the fizzy veg soup?!' asked River.

Gray shook his head. 'Worse,' he said. 'We smell like

dog poo to them!' I stared at Amal and I knew that we were both thinking about when we were in her office, how Miss Steel had been covering her nose and wafting air in from the window like there was a bad smell. We must have been the bad smell that was bothering her! I couldn't believe this was happening. Even though some teachers don't like children, and some teachers can hear you whisper even when you're at the back of the class and some teachers scratch their heads a lot . . . this was different. Because these teachers didn't like the smell of US.

Because they weren't teachers at all.

They were **WITCHES.**

That's when I said, 'What do you think they want?' Gray gulped and shook his head like he was too scared to even say it! So I looked in my bag and found an old biscuit and gave it to him and that calmed him down a bit. And then eventually he said, 'They want to get rid of EVERY SINGLE CHILD IN THE WORLD.'

And that's when we knew we were in deep trouble.

CHAPTER 9
Christmas Is CANCELLED

All of a sudden we heard five short bells. And everyone gasped. Because that's the signal for an emergency assembly. And it means that you have to drop whatever you're doing and get to the assembly hall ASAP (even if what you are doing is going to the toilet!). It's only happened twice since I started school. Once when the toilets flooded and we had to evacuate and another time when the headteacher couldn't find his car keys. When we got to the assembly hall, Miss Steel walked on to the stage and all the witches started clapping really loudly. We rushed in and Miss Steel said, 'Sit. NOW!' And all the other witches sat down at the exact same time – like soldiers.

That's when River leaned over and whispered, 'They act like she's famous or a **QUEEN** or something!'

Suddenly, Gray grabbed my hand and WHISPERED, 'This is worse than I thought!' I didn't know what Gray meant and I couldn't actually see how things could get any worse because we had a school full of witches who wanted to GET RID OF US ALL.

That's when Miss Steel said, 'I have a very important announcement.' All the witches smiled and giggled and started whispering excitedly to each other. Miss Steel took a deep breath and said, 'In light of all the dangerous incidents that have occurred, I have decided to place a ban on all Christmas activities . . . especially the Christmas concert.' A huge creepy smile started to spread across her face as she continued. 'CHRISTMAS IS OFFICIALLY CANCELLED!' And that's when all the witches **CLAPPED** really loud for ages and they were all grinning and nodding.

'I can't believe it's her.' We watched as Gray raised his finger and pointed at Miss Steel and said, 'She's no ordinary witch. She's The Grand High Witch! My grandma warned me about her. She's in charge of all the witches in the world. And she's here. At our school!'

We knew we were all doomed.

CHAPTER 10
RUN FOR YOUR LIFE!

We all tried to tell our parents about the new teachers being witches, but they just didn't believe us.

My mum said it wasn't nice to call people witches and that we shouldn't be spying on the staffroom and that the teachers were obviously just joking.

But we knew that they weren't joking.

Then on Friday, when we arrived at school, all of our parents were ushered into the assembly hall for an emergency parents' meeting, and the doors were closed behind them. We had no idea what the meeting was about, but I had a bad feeling about it. Then, just before lunch, I looked outside and saw that my mum's car was still parked in the car park with all the other parents' cars. I was going to tell River about the cars when the door flew open and The Grand High Witch appeared with an evil look on her face!

Amal stared at me with **WIDE** eyes and said, 'Something bad is about to happen.'

And she was right, because that's when The Grand High Witch yelled, 'It is my pleasure to inform you that as of today we are officially a boarding school. **CONGRATULATIONS,** girls and boys! I am delighted to say that you will not be going home for Christmas!' We all stared at The Grand High Witch with our mouths wide open. 'You will be staying here at school throughout the Christmas period, learning lots of new skills, such as how to make delicious cabbage soup and how to scrub a toilet with a toothbrush until it **SHINES!'**

That's when April and Cohen stood up and said, 'Our mum won't let us stay here! It's Christmas Eve tomorrow!' A smile slowly spread over The Grand High Witch's face and April and Cohen sat back down slowly.

'I am pleased to tell you that after a very productive meeting, all of your parents agreed that it was a wonderful idea!' That's when I looked outside again and saw that our parents were actually sitting inside their cars. Not moving, just staring straight ahead. And I realized that the witches had **HYPNOTIZED** them.

Everyone was starting to panic and April and Cohen actually got up and tried to run. But then they stopped and just sort of fell down.

The Grand High Witch said, 'Too weak to run, little ones? Hmm?'

I looked around. River was almost asleep. I nudged him and he opened his eyes wide and said, 'What? What?!' I looked at Amal and she looked just as worried as I felt. And that was probably because she was thinking the same thing as me.

The witches were doing something to us.

And we needed to find out what it was so we could stop them.

❄

I couldn't believe that we were back in the music cupboard. But we knew we needed to spy on the witches so we could find out how to stop them and save ourselves.

We took turns peeking through the hole. The Grand High Witch stood up and said, 'Those little slime balls have no idea what we're up to. Without their precious **CHRISTMAS,** they'll grow weaker by the day!' The witches nodded and grinned and rubbed their hands together. 'Yes, O Your Grandness!' they all said in unison.

'By Boxing Day we will have successfully tested our brilliant new plan to destroy children by destroying what they love most! Without their precious Christmas, they'll get weaker and weaker until **POOF** . . . they'll disappear altogether! Destroy Christmas . . . destroy the child.'

We listened in horror as all the witches chanted, **'DESTROY CHRISTMAS, DESTROY THE CHILD!'** and giggled and clapped excitedly.

'SILENCE!' screeched The Grand High Witch. The room fell silent. 'Our trial is working. Which means that once we successfully destroy the children at this school, we'll be able to visit more schools across the country.'

The witches all started clapping and cheering again. River whispered, 'Did they just say they we were going to make us disappear?!' I nodded and River did the loudest gulp I have ever heard.

That's when The Grand High Witch said, 'SHHHHH! I heard something!' I grabbed River and put my hand over his mouth so he couldn't make any more noise.

None of us moved.

Or even breathed.

We froze and waited for them to start talking again.

But they didn't start talking again.

They stayed silent.

And then the music room cupboard door flew open.

CHAPTER 11
Cabbage Soup

We shouldn't have tried to run.

It didn't take The Grand High Witch long to catch up with us. She was so **TALL** that for every six legs of running we did she only had to do one big leg of walking. The Grand High Witch cornered us next to the fire exit and waited for all the other witches to catch up with her.

She stared at us. 'So . . . you've been spying on us, have you?' We shook our heads. The Grand High Witch smiled and said, 'I would hate it if something happened to you all!'

That's when Amal stepped forward and said, 'And we

would hate it if something happened to YOU.' And even though it was just for a second, we all saw it. The Grand High Witch looked a bit surprised. And I knew that it was because she hadn't expected us to stand up for ourselves.

And I also knew that she'd better get used to it.

Because we weren't going anywhere without a fight.

❄

We got sent to detention and had to put on the dinner ladies' old aprons and hair nets and were told to make cabbage soup.

None of us ate the soup. But the witches did. And they loved it.

And as soon as they were finished, The Grand High Witch yelled, 'LIGHTS OUT! IT'S BEDTIME!'

We couldn't believe what we were hearing. It was only five o'clock! But we all lay down on the bare floor of the dining hall without any pillows or covers and listened as the witches padlocked the doors shut.

Even though it was really uncomfortable, loads of people fell asleep right away. I almost fell asleep too! That's when I realized I was starting to feel a bit weak. We needed to do something, and fast. So as soon as I was sure the witches were gone, I pulled myself up and said, 'It's time to get our **CHRISTMAS** jumpers back. I've got a plan!'

And I did.

CHAPTER 12
The RETURN of the Christmas Jumpers!

We waited until the witches thought we were asleep and then a group of us sneaked out through the canteen window and ran around the back of the school to the bins. And that's where we found our Christmas jumpers. And even though they did smell a bit like old cabbage, it felt GOOD to put them back on.

'It feels a bit like Christmas again,' said River, yawning.

Then Cohen and April switched each other's jumper lights and music on and said, 'It is **CHRISTMAS!'** And I know it sounds weird, but when I saw everyone in their jumpers, I stopped feeling weak. I actually started to feel **STRONG.**

Because it was **CHRISTMAS!**

I stood on top of the bins and looked down at everyone with my hands on my hips to show them that I wasn't scared (even though I was a bit!). Then River climbed up too and stood next to me and did the same. And I said, 'First they got rid of the Christmas tree, then they banned our Christmas jumpers and took our Christmas pudding away! And now they've locked us in here and CANCELLED CHRISTMAS! They say cancelling Christmas will destroy us. So we need to fight back. We need to destroy THEM before they can destroy US!'

And everyone yelled, 'Yeah!'

❄

One of the witches spotted us from the window.

But we were too fast for them.

We headed full speed all the way to the staffroom and when we got there Amal kicked the door open with one **GIANT** kick. The witches gasped when they saw us standing there and then one of them shouted, 'THEY'RE

STINKING! WHAT ARE THEY DOING HERE?' And even though my heart was pounding in my chest and my hands had gone all sweaty, I stepped into the staffroom.

That's when The Grand High Witch said, 'I'd stop right there if I were you!'

And I said, 'But we're NOT you. Because we're not ancient witches with terrible hair!'

The Grand High Witch gasped. 'How dare you! I do not have terrible hair!!'

But before she could say another word, Amal shouted, **'GO! GO! GO!'** and everyone raced into the staffroom and formed a circle around the witches.

River yelled, 'FIVE, SIX, SEVEN, EIGHT –'

And that's when we all burst out **SINGING!**

Because that was the plan.

To sing Christmas carols as loudly as we could.

My heart was thumping and my ears were ringing because of how loud we were singing.

But we were all loving IT.

I wasn't sure if the plan was going to work, but

suddenly all the witches clasped their hands over their ears and began shouting, 'NOOOOO!' and 'MAKE IT STOP!' and 'MY EARS ARE BLEEDING!!'

Then one by one they started falling to their knees.

Because I'd remembered what I'd overheard in the music cupboard. Miss Steel had said that singing was repulsive to them. That was why Miss Marie hadn't come to rehearsal and had pretended to have a headache. They were scared of our singing!

We kept singing **LOUDLY,** and that's when the witches started shaking violently. 'It's working,' I shouted. 'Keep singing!' So we kept singing as one by one the witches collapsed to the ground, until there was only ONE witch left standing.

The Grand High Witch.

That's when I looked at River and nodded and River raised his hands in the air and everyone took a deep breath. The Grand High Witch wobbled on her feet. And then she said, 'Don't do it. I'm warning you!'

But we did do it!

Because that's when River shouted, 'KEY CHANGE!'

A TODD

And we all started singing really high, like they do in those TV singing competitions when fireworks explode around them and the crowd goes wild.

Except it wasn't fireworks exploding around us. It was witches. They were exploding into dust in front of our eyes! Our joyous singing and Christmas happiness was destroying them. The Grand High Witch clasped her ears and screamed one big long scream for ages.

And then all of a sudden her HAIR stood RIGHT up in the air.

And then she dropped to the floor.

❄

When the police and ambulance arrived the paramedics looked a bit shocked. And I wasn't surprised because the witches had exploded into thin air leaving only dust and their clothes behind!

'Your parents are in the car park, waiting,' said a police officer. She took her glasses off. 'What happened here?' she asked, peering down at me.

But I didn't say anything. Because I'd spotted that she had glowing, dancing eyes.

'I think he's in shock,' said a paramedic.

But I wasn't in shock. I mean, I was, obviously, because a bunch of witches had just taken over our school and tried to destroy us!

River must have noticed her eyes too because he said, 'Um . . . I think it was something they ate.'

The police officer stared at River. Then back at me. And then she did a tiny smirk, just like the one Miss Steel had done. 'Well, thank goodness none of you ate whatever they ate,' she said. 'Maybe you should all bring a packed lunch from now on.'

We nodded and tried to walk away.

But that's when she reached out and gripped my shoulder and asked, 'What's your name?'

I looked up at her. She was tall. Really tall.

'My name's Albie,' I said.

'Well, Albie, are you sure there isn't anything else you'd like to tell me?'

But I just shook my head. We had to keep quiet.

Because we knew there were more witches out there.

And we didn't want them to know that we knew how to stop them.

Because we had work to do.

Sammy, Lisa and Danya, Champions of Christmas

Konnie Huq

'I need the loo!'

'Me too!'

It wasn't that there was a psychic connection between twins Sammy and Lisa – they had just been in the car for (what felt like) an awfully long time and they both now needed the loo. They didn't have that telepathy thing that people think twins have. In fact, in many ways, they were pretty much total opposites. Sammy was always on the go – he loved nature, creepy-crawlies and all things outdoors. When not googling questions such as 'How many years have dragonflies been on Earth?' (answer: 300 million) or 'What is the most endangered species in the world?' (answer: the vaquita, a porpoise found in Mexico), he would be up a tree or down a pothole.

Lisa, meanwhile, was much calmer and loved problem-solving and thinking things over. She was often to be found curled up on the sofa reading, or googling issues such as 'How to solve world poverty' or 'How long has climate change been a thing?'

Although very different, the twins complemented each other and got on extremely well, making a great team. Something that would certainly come in handy that Christmas . . .

'We're nearly at the services. Hang on, guys!' their dad, Danny, said.

'Deep breathing, gang – you can do it!' said their mum, Heather, as Dad pulled off the motorway.

It was the briefest of stops and they were soon back on the road.

The family were off down south for the Christmas break, to the small Buckinghamshire village where their dad had grown up. Although they'd never actually been before, they felt like they knew the place inside out. Their dad had told them about it dozens of times. They'd heard stories about their late grandad, William, about Dad working at the local petrol station as a child, and all about the famous pheasants of Hazell's Wood – but more on that later.

They'd also heard all about the awful Victor Hazell. Back then, Victor had owned the poshest pad for miles around – a huge manor house surrounded by acres of woodland, teeming with all sorts of greenery and wildlife, known as Hazell's Wood.

Their dad hadn't been back to the village in over TWENTY YEARS. After his beloved dad (the twins' grandad, William) had died, he had found it hard to go back. He'd kept up with all his village friends, but only on the phone or if they ventured up north and visited him. Now, at last, his old school friend, Sidney Morgan, had enticed him back because there was a cause, a need, something that Dad and Mum could hopefully help with. And besides, what better time to show the family the picture-box village he had grown up in than Christmas?

The drive to the village took several boring hours. Much to the twins' utter annoyance, their mum had confiscated their iPads before the trip had even begun.

Dad had grinned. 'You know, when we were growing up, we didn't have mobile phones – they weren't even invented! I didn't even have a telly. I made –'

'We know,' the twins had interrupted in unison. 'You made your own fun!'

'Correct. And that's exactly what you'll do on this holiday. You're going to have some screen-free **ADVENTURES!'**

I-spy became repetitive after a while, so Lisa read her book curled up on the back seat, and Sammy began daydreaming, head bobbing against the back rest as the car drove along. His mind was awash with the tales his dad had told him about growing up in the village. He SMILED, thinking about the time when his dad and grandad, William, added crushed-up sleeping tablets to raisins so that the pheasants from Hazell's Wood (who gobbled them up) could be saved from Victor's evil annual pheasant shoot. He giggled at the thought of dazed and confused pheasants staggering about and an angry and confused Victor Hazell stomping around. Hunting pheasants indeed, how awful. He shuddered at the thought.

Sammy stared out of the window as they finally turned off the motorway and began making their way down beautiful country lanes, banked by lush green fields and hedgerows. Their dad had always said how stunning it was out here – but it had to be seen to be believed. This place felt a world away from their house on the outskirts of the busy city, and Sammy couldn't wait to explore the undergrowth of the Buckinghamshire countryside.

'We're here!' Dad said, as they drove into a small village.

The houses that lined the main street looked different from one other, each with its own character, quirks and individuality – unlike the identical rows of houses crammed into the streets back home. As they neared the end of the main stretch, Dad turned into a small driveway that led up to a charming, **HIGGLEDY-PIGGLEDY** cottage covered in ivy. Posters displayed in the upstairs bedroom windows declared, **'NO TO THE BUILD'.**

'What does "No to the build" mean?' asked Sammy.

'There's a development that the villagers are protesting against that your mother and I are going to try and help the village council navigate. You'll find out all about it, I'm sure – it's a big issue here.'

'OK, troops, dismount; we have arrived!' Mum announced.

'Cute cottage!' said Lisa.

'You'll definitely find it more comfortable than the old wagon your grandpa and I lived in!' Dad said, laughing.

They were staying at the home of Dad's old friend Doc Spencer, who was away over Christmas. He had left his keys under a garden gnome with an extremely **LARGE** pair of flashy sunglasses and baseball cap, and they were thankfully still there when the family arrived – the keys, that is, not the glasses and cap, though they were there too!

'Gnome sweet gnome!' Dad said, grinning. 'You could leave your front door unlocked around here and you wouldn't be burgled. Safe as houses!'

Before they'd even unpacked, the twins and their parents wasted no time in having a little wander around the area. It was a CRISP, sunny winter's day, and Dad wanted to make the most of the daylight and good weather by giving the kids a tour.

The village really was the most perfect setting for Christmas. The buildings oozed character and ranged from Tudor cottages to Victorian villas and everything in between. Thatched roofs, stained-glass windows and a multitude of original, unique features all clamouring for attention. Though it was not dark yet, multicoloured fairy lights twinkled from a **MAJESTIC** Norwegian spruce tree proudly boasting a gold star emblazoned with the village shield. At the far end of the road was a small row of shops with a grocer, butcher, newsagent's and, on the corner, the local pub. The shop windows looked friendly and inviting, decked out in evergreen garlands, shiny baubles, tinsel, twinkly stars and all manner of festive decorations. It was like a little oasis in the middle of the wilderness of the countryside, with its sprawling lanes, fields and undergrowth stretching out beyond the village as far as the eye could see.

'Well, if it isn't Danny, Champion of the World!' boomed a friendly voice from behind them.

Dad spun round. 'Sidney Morgan! Good to see you!' he said, playfully wrestling the large man into a bear hug.

'And the lovely Heather,' Sidney said, beaming at Mum. 'I must say, we are just so grateful you're both going to lend a hand to help – see if we can somehow get this hotel a bit more environmentally friendly. Most of the village is up in arms about it. Plus –' he raised his eyebrows, '– it felt like the only way to get you back here, Danny!'

'Yeah, well, it certainly worked.' Dad smiled. 'It's been a while . . . but you know what? It's good to be back.'

He had been unsure about this until the words came tumbling out of his mouth. But now he knew he meant it. It was good to be back. For him this place held what he thought were painful memories of his father. His dad, William, had brought him up single- handedly and they had had so much **FUN** together along the way. When William passed away, Danny had moved from the village to make a fresh start. He had resisted returning for years. But, as with many things you fear, you realize when you face them head on, actually, you have built up something in your head that perhaps doesn't exist. He saw now that he didn't feel pain or sorrow at returning, only a fondness. A very deep-seated fondness. It was as though all his worries had melted away. Being here actually made him feel close to his father, which was a lovely warm feeling that he liked very much.

Dad glanced around and smiled. 'It really is good to be back,' he repeated, nodding appreciatively. The village was definitely well-to-do now. It had come a long way since his boyhood days of living in an old wooden caravan, but he could see it was still the same old place at its core. The cosy familiarity struck a chord with him – it always would. He cherished the memories it held for him, for the upbringing he'd had here with his dad that had shaped the man he was now. He realized he was truly happy to be back and wondered why he had resisted returning for so long.

Mum and Dad worked as eco-consultants, which meant they advised companies on how to protect the environment. The reason they were visiting Dad's childhood village now, after all these years, was that they had been asked to advise the village council on the plans for a brand-new building – a hotel – and how to make it as green as possible. The proposed site for the build was Hazell's Wood, which was to be sold to developers, who would knock down the manor house situated at one end of the site to make way for a fancy complex.

'Can't say I'm a fan of all this, but it's not our land, so it's not up to us,' continued Sidney.

'Eugene Hazell is pretty ruthless – it's all about money to him. There's a New Year's Eve deadline for the sale to go through to the hotel chain, and he's determined to meet it. Oh, and get this, the company now also want an access road, which would mean loads of homes would be bulldozed too.'

'Ugh. Doc Spencer told me the pressure of it all was really getting to everyone. All the disputes and protests over it are why he felt he needed a short break away this Christmas.' Dad sighed.

Sidney nodded with a wolfish grin. 'Fingers crossed you two are our saviours! No pressure!' The large man playfully slapped Dad on the back, then turned to Sammy and Lisa, bending down to shake each of them by the hand.

'Sorry about all our boring grown-up chat. Major yawn, huh?' He grinned. 'Pleased to meet you, by the way. I'm Sidney – I was at school with your dad in this very village. He made it out of here to the big smoke, but I've stuck around even after all these years!'

'Sidney is in charge of the local council,' Dad cut in. 'He's the one who makes all the decisions around here

– the most important person in the village! He was always destined to go far.'

'What your dad's trying to say is that I was bossy then, and I still am now,' Sidney said to the twins with a wink. 'Right, I'd best be off, but Heather, Danny, I'll see you both at the council meeting tomorrow afternoon. Sammy and Lisa, be good and stay out of trouble. If you can, that is – troublemaking might run in the family!' He laughed. 'Me and your dad had all sorts of scrapes when we were your age! No pheasants in my **SHENANIGANS** though. You should get your dad to tell you about the time when –'

'Oh no, stop!' Lisa laughed. 'We already know!'

'We've only heard it about a million times!' said Sammy, rolling his eyes.

Chuckling to himself, Sidney headed off down the road, leaving Dad to continue the family's tour.

'This red telephone box is where we used to make calls from – with coins! No mobiles, no internet data allowance!'

The family walked on. A number of buildings and dwellings had posters in their windows, like those at Doc Spencer's. Slogans like **'NO HOTEL HERE',**

'PROTECT OUR VILLAGE' and **'DEVELOPERS OUT'.** There were even signs on trees.

'Wow! People are really resisting the development, aren't they?' said Lisa.

'People-power can go a long way!' replied Mum. 'It can change government policy, win rights and protect the environment!'

'Like when our class pressured the school to stop single-use plastic in the dinner hall,' said Sammy.

'Exactly that. Power to the people!' Mum exclaimed, flinging her fist in the air as they laughed.

Across the way, a shifty-looking man with a loud, wheezy cough got into a shiny black convertible car with a private number plate – EH1. He sped off down the road, revving his engine noisily as though mistaking the village for a Formula 1 racetrack.

'Ewww. That man was totally creepy – he stared right at me with a mean look on his face.' Sammy shuddered.

'He did, didn't he?' Lisa agreed. 'What a weirdo.'

'EH1 indeed,' Dad scoffed. 'That's got to be Eugene Hazell. I can one hundred per cent see the family resemblance with Victor. They both have the exact same jawline and eyes, not to mention the same posture. Ugh, it brings back memories. If he has anything to do with it, this place will be a shadow of its former self.'

'He reminds me of a villain in a Bond movie or something!' Sammy said.

'He's just like that!' agreed Mum. 'The evil baron about to make villagers homeless and jobless.'

'MWAH-HA-HA-**HA!'** Sammy laughed in a menacing, maniacal manner. 'I will step over anyone and everyone to become richer and meaner!'

'Just like Victor,' Dad joined in.

'What happened to Victor?' asked Sammy.

'He was being investigated for some sort of money fraud and fled the country, apparently to South America, never to be seen again. Then Eugene appeared on the scene, and the next thing we know is that the house and grounds are up for sale and this hotel is being proposed.'

Lisa turned to her parents with a serious look on her face. 'The village will be OK, won't it?'

'Fingers crossed we can help,' Mum replied.

'Can't we just stop the construction from happening?' asked Sammy.

'I wish we *could* block it somehow, but all we can do is advise the council on what can and can't be done lawfully when it comes to building a hotel. Unfortunately, that's it. You can't stop anything if it's within the law.'

'As long as it's legal, someone could put up a space station if they wanted,' Dad explained.

Lisa pictured a rocket launching from behind a nearby row of cottages. *Now that would be weird*, she thought to herself. Weird but kinda cool.

'We need to find any reasons that the development isn't compliant with environmental law. If we find a really good one, maybe the build will become too difficult for the developers to go ahead,' said Mum.

'Here's hoping,' Lisa sighed as they walked on.

Nearby, a girl was sitting on a wall, swinging her legs, with her bike propped up next to her.

'Hello!' Mum called out as they walked past.

'Hiya!' the girl called back breezily.

'Do you know her?' asked Lisa, confused.

'People often say hi to each other in small villages,' Dad told them. 'It's friendly and polite. Part of the community feel. You know –' he turned to Mum with a twinkle in his eye, '– we really should teach our children about the concept of being friendly and polite.'

'Hmmm, yes, good idea – we really should,' Mum said, giggling. 'Do you think they'd grasp something so alien to them though?!'

'F-u-n-n-y,' said Lisa in a slow, sarcastic voice.

'We are indeed! We know,' came Dad's cheeky reply.

'Hey, where did you used to live, Dad?' asked Sammy.

'In the other direction, so that's probably best saved for tomorrow. You two could take your bikes out and explore – go wild! This village is great for romping around in and gaining a bit of independence. I used to roam about, up to no good, all the hours of the day in my summer holidays, often by myself. The main hub is really only this road and a dozen roads off it with shops, houses and businesses. After that all you have is fields, scrubland, woods and lone houses on all sides, and all manner of footpaths, country lanes and cut-throughs linking it all up. It really is glorious exploration territory!'

❄

The next morning, Lisa found a map of the village. Doc Spencer had left it for them pinned to the kitchen noticeboard.

'According to this, Dad, your petrol station now has a convenience store attached to it!' she said, scrutinizing the map.

'Yeah, that's right,' said their dad. 'Loads of villages have had local businesses taken over by bigger ones. It can be a shame. Back in the day, it felt more personal – everyone knew each other and helped each other. I'm hoping that won't be lost.'

In the afternoon, Sammy and Lisa would be on their own while their parents attended meetings about the hotel. So, in the morning, while their dad went off to do some catching-up with old friends, the twins and their mum went out on their bikes to get to know the place. Riding around the village was brilliant! They found loads of the alleys and cut-throughs and soon, with the help of the map, they pretty much knew their way around the place, how to get to the woods, the fields, the scrubland and of course the old manor house. After a while, they decided to stop for a break, and found Dad's old petrol station was now indeed owned by a big petrol company chain with a small Tesco attached. Mum decided to pick up some bits and pieces for a picnic lunch.

'Can we get an ice-lolly, Mum?' Sammy asked.

'Go for it! A bit of brain-freeze will really wake you up and get your circulation going. Why not?!'

The twins never seemed to feel the cold; even in midwinter they would happily run around in T-shirts, without a jumper in sight.

By now the iPads were a distant memory, as they biked to the park, ready to get stuck into their food.

'Hey, there's that girl who Mum said hi to yesterday,' said Lisa as they settled on a picnic bench and began tucking into sandwiches and munching on crisps.

Sammy looked up. 'Oh yeah!'

The dark-haired girl was sitting on one end of the see-saw, bobbing it up and down on her own.

'Why don't you go and say hi?' Mum suggested. 'Do some "good PR for us out-of-towners". And it'd be nice for you to have a friend your own age to hang out with while we're here.'

'OK, I'll do some "good PR for us out-of-towners". I'll see if she wants me to get on the other side of the see-saw!' said Lisa, walking over to the play area. 'Hi!' she said to the girl. 'I'm Lisa. We saw you at the shops yesterday.'

'Hi!' said the girl warmly. 'Yeah, I remember. I'm Danya.'

'We're about the same size,' Lisa carried on. 'I reckon we'd make good see-saw buddies!'

Danya paused for thought before breaking into a big GRIN. 'Perfect!' She gestured towards the empty seat.

Lisa clambered on, and the girls began bobbing up and down, chatting away as if they had known each other for years. Lisa ran back over to the picnic bench. 'Hey, Mum – can me and Sammy go biking round with Danya till teatime? She lives in a cottage on the grounds of Victor Hazell's old place. Her dad's the caretaker. It would be so fun! Pleeeaaase!!'

'That sounds like a plan! I have to go off to the council now with your dad anyway,' said Mum. She turned to Danya. 'As long as that will be OK with your parents?'

'It's just me and my dad. But he'll be totally fine with it – he likes me to have kids my age to play with.'

'Well then, off you go, guys. Make mayhem and enjoy!'

'Thanks, Mrs Lisa's-mum, we will!' Danya giggled.

'No problem. Be safe, have fun,' she called out as she walked off, turning back to add, 'and call me Heather!'

❄

The manor house and its estate were pretty **MAGNIFICENT.** The grounds were perfect for biking, almost like an assault course with hilly bits, narrow bits, bumpy bits, twists, turns, slopes and ditches. There was a hedge maze, a stream through the woods and even a lake.

'Come on, I'll show you my house!' Danya said to the twins.

She cycled off with Sammy and Lisa hot on her heels. They soon came across an incredible-looking area, lovingly planted with various crops and produce, all in neat little labelled sections. A sweet scarecrow smiled up at them bashfully from his perch as if to show he was not scary at all.

'This is our kitchen garden. We grow our own fruit and veg here,' Danya yelled to the twins as the three of them whizzed past. 'We get heaps of marrows, carrots, potatoes, squash, tomatoes and all sorts throughout the year. My dad loves growing stuff.'

A short while later they arrived at Danya and her dad's little cottage. It was near enough to the manor for Sammy to spot it in the distance as they dumped their bikes out the front, but far enough away for it to feel as though these gardens and grounds were all Danya's.

'Well, hello there, young people!' Danya's dad was just leaving, pushing a wheelbarrow full of garden tools.

Danya introduced the twins to him. He had a

weathered, friendly face with a permanent smile in his eyes.

'Make yourselves at home!' he grinned. 'Would love to stay and make mischief with you tinkers, but my purple potatoes aren't going to dig themselves.'

'Purple?!' exclaimed Sammy, wide-eyed.

'Purple indeed,' Danya's dad confirmed. 'High in nutrients and antioxidants, and better for your blood sugar! Danya will give you some to take home – you won't look back. Lovely, nutty taste. Yellow potatoes will never be the same again – they'll seem boring in comparison!' He laughed – and off he went, whistling to himself.

Danya led Sammy and Lisa inside and up to her bedroom, where they flopped down on beanbags. She chucked some purple potatoes to Sammy, which she had picked up in the kitchen on the way through.

Sammy studied them. 'Ha-ha, this one looks like Eugene Hazell!'

'Let's see!' his sister requested.

He held it up to show the others.

The potato had a little sticky-out bit that looked like a

nose and two marks for eyes. It was indeed shaped a bit like Hazell's face. The others laughed. Danya got a felt-tip out and drew on a mouth. They acted out a little scene with the Hazell potato telling the other potatoes he would take their homes and jobs, and fell about laughing.

'Purple potatoes! Who knew?' said Sammy.

'We've had loads of crazy veg in our time, even purple carrots! Check out the pictures up there.' Danya pointed to the wall where there was a noticeboard filled with photos of Danya and her dad out in the gardens – among greenery, animals and nature. It was obvious this place held loads of happy memories.

'Wow! Is that a pet bat you're holding?' Sammy asked, pointing at one of the pictures on the board.

'Yeah. I called him Archie! We found the poor thing struggling with an injured leg, so we looked after him till he got better and then returned him to the wild.'

'So cool!' said Sammy.

'You're really lucky to live here,' said Lisa, gazing out of the bedroom window, taking it all in, as if inhaling the beautiful surroundings.

'Yeah.' Danya's voice faltered, and she looked down at the floor and swallowed. 'Not for much longer though. We're going to have to move soon. When they knock the main house down for the hotel, ours will be knocked down too. We have to move out as soon as they've sold it.'

'That's awful! Surely they'll need a caretaker?' said Lisa. 'Ugh! It's just so annoying! Everything about this hotel feels wrong.'

'I know. It's been the talk of the village for months now. No one seems happy with it,' Danya replied.

'We need to do something!' Lisa declared.

'I wish,' sighed Danya.

'No, seriously, Lisa's right. We should find a way to stop the hotel and save this cottage!' said Sammy.

'Totally,' agreed Lisa. 'We'll make it our **MISSION!'**

'Really? I don't know what to say. Well . . . what I mean is, that would be great!' Danya gulped, tearing up. 'My dad has been putting on a brave face, but he's been really worried about it all. If we even just tried to help it would be amazing.' She smiled.

Lisa put her arm round Danya.

'We can definitely give it our best shot,' Sammy said reassuringly.

❄

At dinner in Doc's cottage, Dad was in full storytelling mode, recounting his morning. '. . . and after that I met some of the Clipstones, always a big fun family. There's so many of them now, and they all still live here. So does Sergeant Samways, now retired and, oh yes, I also had a cup of tea with Doc Spencer . . .'

'Huh? Isn't he away? Aren't we in his house right now?' Lisa asked, confused.

'I met the *original* Doc Spencer – Doc Spencer senior, not Doc Spencer junior,' Dad replied. 'We're staying in his nephew's house, who I was at school with. He's a doctor now too, so he's also called Doc Spencer!'

'Doc Spencer the second!' Mum laughed. 'So how is Doc Spencer the first?'

'He's an old soul these days, but he's as SHARP as anything. His house will be demolished if the build goes ahead, and he's having none of it. He's made a petition and has already got hundreds of signatures, including mine, and you'll all have to sign it too. You should get involved.'

'Definitely!' said Lisa. 'We could get loads of signatures. Who could resist charming children like us!?'

'Yeah, don't I know it – you two could convince the Pope to be an atheist if you put your minds to it!' Mum teased.

'If only we had our iPads, we could put up an online petition and get it to go viral. It could be massive!' grinned Sammy with a glint in his eye.

'Nice try, mister,' said Mum. 'I'm not sure we need 100,000 signatures and to get it debated in Parliament!'

'Although if we did, we'd definitely win!' Sammy jumped up. 'Seriously though, we do want to help. We were there today with our new friend, Danya. We had such fun.'

'It would be really sad if they knocked it down – Danya and her dad would lose their home. I can't imagine a hotel there . . .' Lisa looked at her parents.

'Oh my gosh, you should see the plans.' Mum pulled a face. 'The new building looks really ugly.'

Dad agreed. 'Yeah, and they don't want to stop at a hotel. They want a nearby shopping complex and leisure facilities as well. Hazell's Wood is a **BIG** bit of land. Not only would it threaten local homes but lots of the lovely little shops and businesses around the village too. Some have been up and running for years.'

'What? A hotel isn't enough? No way! The manor house and grounds are too nice to get rid of,' said Lisa.

'Yeah!' Sammy chimed in. 'We're going back tomorrow to explore some more. The gardens are amazing for playing in. We even saw the pheasants.'

'Good to hear they're still knocking about,' said Dad, laughing.

Sammy continued, 'There's all sorts of other wildlife too. They can't get rid of it all!'

'Well, we'll see it for ourselves tomorrow,' said Mum. 'We'll be doing a site visit. The hotel buyers will be looking around, led by the person in charge, Monty Postlethwaite, and that awful Eugene Hazell. You wouldn't believe it – it's like the two of them were separated at birth. When they aren't sucking up to one another and hanging on each other's every word, they seem to be competing in a bid to be the more superior and powerful. They're like a love–hate comedy double act!'

'Nothing about Eugene makes me want to laugh,' said Sammy.

'He's an odd one. On the surface, he can actually seem very charming and almost friendly if he wants to – but, underneath, he's not a very nice man. All he can see is pound signs. He doesn't want anything getting in the way of all the money he'll make from selling the hotel before the deadline of New Year's Eve,' said Mum.

'That really doesn't leave us long,' Sammy whispered to Lisa. 'Everything stops for Christmas – we need to think fast.'

'What was that?' asked Mum.

'Oh, nothing,' said Sammy. 'Nothing important.' He exchanged glances with Lisa. They'd agreed with Danya that it was probably best to keep their little scheme to themselves for now.

❄

The twins spent nearly all the next morning in the gardens at Danya's place. They rode their bikes around the grounds, climbed trees in the woodland, skimmed stones on the lake and immersed themselves in the wonders of nature.

'It'll be so sad if you have to leave,' said Lisa.

'I know, I can't bear the thought of going,' Danya said sadly. 'We'll have to find a new place to live, and Dad will need to get a new job. He reckons it'll be hard to stay in the village as it's too expensive for us. The caretaker's cottage comes with his current job, you see, which will mean I'll have to leave my school as well. There are so many knock-on effects.'

'That sucks,' said Sammy. 'All because some rich person wants to get even richer! But we're not gonna let it happen. We will find a way.'

'I hope so! My mum really loved it here. When I was just a baby our family fled here from troubles back home in their country, and this was the one place she said actually felt like home.'

Lisa was tempted to ask Danya more about her mother and her life before, but thought it might be too upsetting so she bit her tongue and tried to change the mood. 'Well, we'll make sure you guys don't have to leave your home again in that case.'

'Hey!' Sammy's eyes lit up. 'I have an idea. The people who want to buy the hotel are visiting it this afternoon. Maybe we could put them off wanting it? We could pretend the house is haunted or something. Make noises or move stuff around – freak them out!'

'Hmmm. It's a crazy idea but it might just work!' Danya declared in a spooky voice.

Lisa giggled and began pretending to be a zombie, chasing Danya round the room. 'Yeah, it's definitely worth a try,' she agreed. 'If we can give them a bad feeling about the place then they might want to find somewhere else.'

The three children got ready to put their plan into action before heading over to the manor house. Danya pulled out a dressing-up box with Halloween costumes, scraps of material, fake moustaches and all sorts of other bits and pieces. Lisa began scrawling notes: plans of the locations they would be at, who would be in charge of what, and how they would orchestrate the whole thing. Sammy devised different ideas for scare tactics: some more complicated, involving buckets of water, fans and different props and set-ups; others more simple, involving weird noises and mind games. After disagreeing and agreeing on various details and going round the houses a few times, they finally settled on a simple but effective strategy. Excitedly, they practised their moves and rehearsed the scene for the rest of the afternoon . . . until it was time to go to the manor house.

❄

Danya had taken her dad's spare set of keys for the main house and, when the coast was clear, the three children snuck in through the front door in broad daylight. Riding on the high of how easy it was to get in, Sammy and Lisa took in their surroundings. They couldn't believe how stunning the building was, with a huge, imposing hallway, ornate plasterwork, high ceilings and beautiful period fireplaces in almost all the rooms.

It was PERFECT for a haunting.

They had each taken on a role. Danya would stay hidden and make strange noises and clatter things about when people were nearby. Lisa was to move things around to confuse people as they went from room to room – furniture, ornaments and the like. Sammy had donned a dust sheet and was going to creep about in the shadows and act all ghostly! Everyone got ready. There was a palpable sense of excitement between them.

They heard a wheezy cough from downstairs, signalling the arrival of Eugene Hazell with his cronies.

'The footprint is really vast. According to the plans, 10,000 square feet. Mammoth footprint.' Head buyer Monty Postlethwaite's voice could be heard echoing around the cavernous hall downstairs.

'Yes, I did see from the plans,' came the reply from his nondescript colleague, suitably clad in grey.

'Mammoth footprint. Huge shoes!! HUGE SHOES!!'

cackled Postlethwaite as though he had cracked the most hilariously witty joke, even though what he said didn't make sense. The rest of his party looked a little perplexed, and an awkward silence ensued, before Hazell rescued him by offering some fake, over-the-top laughter.

'Huge shoes!' he repeated, also cackling.

Danya and the twins exchanged glances. This was going to be interesting.

Voices continued downstairs in the front doorway as the three children peeked through the upstairs banisters. The stiff, suited group of people were clutching clipboards. They wore hard hats, high-visibility jackets and stern looks on their faces. They had now all fully entered the main hallway and were looking around while jotting things down on their clipboards. They chatted at the bottom of the stairs for what felt like ages before peeling off into smaller groups to look around some more.

The children got to work.

'That's odd – this vase wasn't in the doorway just now.' Postlethwaite's confused voice could be heard speaking to one of the buyers.

Lisa grinned from her hiding-place in a musty cupboard – she had deposited the vase on the floor and scuttled back undercover in the nick of time, undetected by the perplexed, portly man. Meanwhile, Danya was doing a sterling job of stomping about in the loft. The banging noise was quite disconcerting and a tad eerie, as the eaves were extremely creaky.

'What on earth . . .?' Postlethwaite looked upwards. He did not like this one bit. 'Is this place **HAUNTED** or something?'

'You don't believe in all that, surely?' Hazell said dismissively.

'My late, great-aunt and I discuss philosophy every night, I'll have you know. My dear, dear great-aunt Lily.' His eyes looked dreamy. 'So yes, I believe in all that. In fact, I *know* of all that. It's not a belief!'

The stomping got louder.

'Er . . . someone must have left a window open in the attic. It's just a bit noisy and draughty is all!' Hazell offered in a conciliatory manner, trying to walk quickly away from the din before tripping over a piece of cabling the children had strategically placed, and whacking his head on the doorframe.

Next it was Postlethwaite's turn. Agitated by the incident, he too lost his footing, stumbled and hit the landing with a thump, crumpling his pristine new suit. He had fallen over Sammy, who was lying on the floor under a dust sheet.

'You see! The sooner this place is ripped down, the better. Uneven floorboards!' Hazell blustered to his bemused buyers. He tried to help Postlethwaite up, but he became annoyed at being offered assistance and tried to get up on his own, falling back down in the process. Trying to get back in favour, Hazell attempted to smooth down Postlethwaite's suit, further exasperating him.

'Duh, get off me!' He brushed Hazell away, irritated.

Lisa giggled on hearing this comedic exchange – but then noticed her parents enter the vast, empty spare bedroom she was hiding in.

'Psssst, it's me!' She grabbed a dust sheet to put over herself in case anyone else walked in.

'What on earth are you doing in the cupboard

under a dust sheet?' Mum asked.

Lisa explained the plan to her parents.

'Seriously, Lisa? You should know better than behaving like this and interfering with serious matters. You could get us all in trouble. This isn't *Scooby-Doo*! Though if it was, you lot are definitely more Scooby than Velma!'

Her parents looked disappointed and almost cross. Lisa suddenly felt bad and a bit silly about their cunning plan, which had seemed so foolproof and BRILLIANT at the time. Seeing her face drop, Dad softened and tried to ease the situation.

'Besides, pumpkin, it'll take a lot more than that to put them off. This deal is worth millions and millions. To be honest, it wouldn't matter if the house *was* haunted – it's due to be demolished anyway.'

'Oh yeah, I, er . . . didn't think of that!' said Lisa.

'What we need to find is a problem with the surroundings. An ancient, valuable burial site under the ground so it can't be built on, or something else big and obstructive,' Mum added. 'You think you can find one of those for us?'

'Exactly that,' said Dad with a GLINT in his eye. 'That is your mission, should you choose to accept it.'

'A problem with the surroundings? Not exactly easy,' said Lisa, wondering if there was realistically anything they could do.

Just then, Hazell walked in, and Lisa tried to duck back under her sheet as fast as possible, falling over in the process. A big **'CLONK!'** was followed by a muffled, **'OW!'**

It seemed the game was up – but then . . .

'Huh?' Hazell wheezed. Now it was his turn to get nervous and panicky. 'What was that? I saw something. It moved. W-w-what is going on? Who else saw that?' He looked distressed and turned to Lisa's parents.

'Well, the thing is . . .' began Lisa's mother, pausing to choose her words carefully. 'Well, you see, the house isn't haunted as such. It's just . . .'

Lisa knew she had to come clean. Sheepishly she ventured forth from undercover. She laughed nervously but looked as though she was about to cry.

'I knew it – pesky children!' He scowled. 'I thought I

saw one earlier.' Hazell was not at all amused.

Lisa turned as white as the sheet she had been hiding under. Hazell narrowed his eyes and looked straight at her. This was going to take some explaining.

❄

A crestfallen Danya slumped down on to one of the beanbags in her bedroom.

'Well, it was worth a try, I guess,' she said, trying to lift the mood.

'Did you see the way Eugene was looking at us when we all came out? He is one scary man,' said Sammy. 'Ugh! We're never gonna stop them now.'

'Mum and Dad said we need to find a problem with the surroundings,' Lisa informed them matter-of-factly. 'Something that will actively obstruct the developers from going ahead with their stupid build.'

The frustrated children sat in silence, having a think and mulling over the situation.

'It's no good,' said Sammy, getting up and breaking

the silence. 'We don't have enough time.'

Lisa looked over at him and then did a double take at Danya's photos on the noticeboard, realizing something. 'Hmmm . . . hey, Danya, is Archie's nest in Hazell's Wood?'

'Yeah, there are loads of nesting bats there,' Danya replied.

'Well, that's just brilliant!' Lisa exclaimed unexpectedly.

'Is it? Oh, wow, yes . . . it is, isn't it? said Sammy slowly, punching the air as the penny dropped. 'Yesss! Lisa, are you thinking what I'm thinking?'

She turned to her brother, grinning. 'I hope so! Didn't you once tell me that bats are a protected species?'

Sammy grinned back. 'They totally are! In fact, there's no way people will be allowed to build on Hazell's Wood if there are *any* nesting bats there.'

Now it was Danya's turn to **GRIN.** 'Well, it gives me great pleasure to tell you there are *loads* of them!'

'We've got to let everyone know,' said Lisa, jumping up. 'They might still be on the site visit.'

'Yeah!' agreed Danya, 'we need to hurry. Let's go!'

The kids got on their bikes and raced back over to the manor house. But there was no sign of the adults.

'Oh no, where are they?' asked Sammy.

'Ugh, we're running out of time!' said Lisa. 'It's Christmas next week. No one works at Christmas, and the deadline is New Year's Eve, which is the week after.'

'We really need to tell them right now!' Danya agreed.

'Tell who what?'

A wheezy cough and a smarmy voice came out from behind them. Eugene Hazell had emerged from the main house.

'There are bats nesting in the woods and they cannot be disrupted. They are a protected species,' declared Sammy.

'So it looks like your deal is dead, Mr Hazell!' Lisa added jubilantly.

'Yeah! Just wait, we're gonna tell everyone!' Danya said confidently.

'Don't be ridiculous! No one's going to believe some scrawny little kids!' Hazell drew himself up to his full height, all five foot two of him, and squared up to the kids in an attempt to be intimidating.

'They don't need to believe us, Mr Hazell,' said Danya. 'There are loads of roosting bats, they can see for themselves.'

For a moment Hazell seemed genuinely worried. The three children looked at each other **TRIUMPHANTLY** – his face said it all. They had got him.

'The bats won't come out though, will they?' Hazell asked nervously.

'Well, it's gonna be dark soon so they could well do...' taunted Danya, knowing full well that actually bats hibernate in winter.

'Not so confident now, Mr Hazell, are you?' said Sammy. 'You are not a nice man and I don't know how you sleep at night.'

Hazell paused, but then his worried demeanour changed and he smiled maniacally. 'I sleep extremely well, thank you. Extremely well.' An evil glint flashed in his eye as though he had just thought of something, leaving Sammy, Lisa and Danya a little confused. 'No one will be seeing any bats on my watch, I'm pleased to inform you. Anyway, the group have probably left by now. What a crying shame. Boo-hoo-hoo! Now, get off my land!' he yelled forcefully, sending the kids biking away in fright.

'What did he mean?' asked Lisa.

'Dunno. Anyway, we need to get to the main gate before we're too late!' Danya cried to the others as they furiously pedalled. 'I know a short cut – follow me!' She took charge with the twins hot on her tail.

The cold air whipped against the three children as they sped along as though their lives depended on it. Crunching gravel as they went, zooming over bumps and crags, they didn't let up until the grown-ups were in sight ahead.

Just as they were in spitting distance – ***THUNK!*** Sammy's bike went flying as it hit a bump and crashed down!

'Oops! Don't worry, I'm OK,' he reassured the others, in a daze. The wheels of the bike continued to *WHIZZ* round even after he had let go of it. Everyone looked concerned. The children had caught up with the main group by the car park near the exit of the main house and grounds. The party was just about to leave.

'Well, that was dramatic! Are you OK, young man?' Sidney asked.

'More than OK – I'm great, we all are!' Sammy said, still lying on the ground where he had fallen.

'That's quite a statement for someone who's just had a bike crash and is in a heap on the ground,' said Dad. 'Why so great?'

Sammy got up and brushed himself down. Gasping for breath and extremely excited, the twins and Danya explained their revelations to the grown-ups.

'Is this really true?' asked Sidney.

'Yes! Bats! Tons of them,' Danya exclaimed. You could've seen for yourself if it wasn't winter!'

'What do you mean?' asked Sidney.

'They hibernate during winter but in summer my dad and I love watching them fly at sunset. And my mum used to as well.'

Just then, the group heard a voice calling over. It was Danya's dad, on his way to the manor, and he appeared quite perturbed.

'Ahhh, there you all are. Well I must say, I'm a bit confused. Eugene Hazell seems to have lost his wits. He's in the woods, shouting to himself. I left him halfway up a ladder, trying to put these in a bat's nest.' He held up a small bottle. 'Sleeping pills! He has **LOADS** of bottles of the stuff. I had to wrestle this one from him. I'm not exactly sure what is going on . . .'

'You don't think he's actually trying to drug the bats, do you?' Sammy asked in disbelief, wide-eyed and innocent.

'That's exactly what he's trying to do!' said Lisa. 'You heard him, he thinks they're gonna fly out. He doesn't realize they're hibernating.'

'Yep! I would agree – we all know how desperate he is. Desperate enough to harm an endangered species,' Dad added.

A gasp of realization spread among the group as everyone began to understand exactly what was going on. Much murmuring and nodding in agreement followed.

Then Postlethwaite spoke out. 'Surely not? What do you mean?'

'He's hoping that the bats will fall asleep, so we don't see them. He doesn't realize they're hibernating. He doesn't want anything getting in the way of this sale,' Dad explained.

'If the sale goes through, you'd be left with land you can't build on,' Mum chipped in.

The children nodded.

'We raced to tell you as fast as we could,' Danya reassured him.

'R-r-really?' Postlethwaite stammered. Mildly shocked, he began to turn an odd shade of dark red. He looked angry and as though he might explode. His nervous assistant quickly came forward and handed him a bottle of water, which he eagerly glugged down. Thankfully it seemed to help calm him somewhat. He slumped against a wall, taking everything in, and slowly the deep-red colour drained from his face as he recomposed himself.

'Sleeping tablets? Bats? Where on earth would he come up with an idea like that?' Postlethwaite asked, confused. Then, becoming angry again, he added, 'How dare he think he could get away with it?' His assistant quickly handed him another bottle of water.

'We know exactly where he'd come up with an idea like that,' Sidney declared.

'Yes, it's all to do with the annual pheasant shoot that used to be held at Hazell's Wood a long time ago, but that's a whole other story for another time,' said Dad.

'It's such a shame you guys won't get to see them,' added Danya. 'It really is breathtaking. If only it was summer.'

It was getting chilly now and the sky was turning an amazing array of colours – all smears and stripes, merging into one another like an artist's landscape painted in streaky watercolours. Light blue gave way to stunning shades of yellow, russet, auburn and an underlying most beautiful pinky orange. In the distance, a soft squeaking noise could be heard – a chorus of clicking, chirping and very quiet high-pitched friendly squeals. It grew closer, filling the sky and echoing about.

The group slowly looked up, taking it all in as hundreds of tiny bats, emerging from the woods, flew overhead. The minute black dots swarmed over, getting a little bigger as they neared, gliding, gracefully flapping and swooping up high. It was epic.

'It's like they knew . . .' gasped Danya. 'They would never normally come out in winter.'

Everyone stared in awe, wide-eyed at this magical appearance. It was jaw-dropping.

Dad's eyes began to tear up as he looked overhead. Here he was with his children in Hazell's Wood, after all these years. He had been here so many times before with his own father. His childhood, and all the memorable moments, people, places and experiences he'd had, flashed before his eyes. It really was a special place and he knew he'd never leave it so long again to return.

In silence, everyone watched the visual spectacle in utter awe, as though at their own private viewing of a very special event. It was like a beautifully choreographed dance routine performed by bats against a stunning multicoloured ever-changing backdrop, to which the group had front-row seats. Within ten minutes or so the whole display was over. It had got dark. There was a moment of silence. Everyone felt as though they had a shared understanding now.

'I can't believe these hibernating bats came out for us. UNBELIEVABLE. **MOMENTOUS.** Nothing short of **MIRACULOUS.** Well, we certainly won't be building here,' Postlethwaite declared. 'That's for sure.' He and his team marched off to their cars and left.

'It seems this will be the best Christmas present the village has ever had.' Sidney turned to Danya's dad, beaming. 'Looks like the development will not be going ahead! It appears it is in breach of environmental regulations after all.'

Danya and her dad exchanged glances of utter glee and he gave her hand a little squeeze. 'Your mother would be so proud of you.' He looked at the twins. 'And both of you as well, even though she didn't know you . . . but if she did, she would!'

The group laughed.

'We did it!' Sammy cried, jumping up and down with Lisa and Danya, as they hugged and cheered.

'You certainly did.' Dad grinned. 'Champions of Christmas!'

❄

Christmas Day came and went as though the whole village and villagers alike were in a dream sequence. A **BLISSFUL** dream sequence. After months and months of anger, conflict and frustration, the place felt cloaked in a veil of utter happiness. The protest signs had come down and more decorations had gone up. Just as Dad had envisaged, this was the most idyllic setting for festivities. Carols were sung around the huge Norwegian spruce, mulled wine and hot fruity spiced apple juice were ladled out in paper cups, along with mince pies. Residents and visitors alike were in tremendous spirits.

Danya and her dad joined the twins' family for a hearty Christmas evening meal, exchanging presents, pulling crackers and playing games into the night. Sammy, Lisa and Danya were delighted to stay up after bedtime, although they hadn't seen anything yet . . .

That New Year's Eve, the villagers decided to have a huge party because there was so much to celebrate. The divisions and disputes between residents had all dissolved, paving the way for the best knees-up the locals had ever seen. Danya's dad had convinced Eugene Hazell to let it be held in the Great Ballroom, saying that it would be a brilliant way to get the council to agree to buy the manor house. Hazell, who was desperate to sell to anyone now, agreed. (Development buyers don't tend to want land they can't build on. Funny, that!)

Everyone brought delicious home-made food and drink. Doc Spencer senior made his famous meat pie (much to Dad's delight). Danya's dad's organic fruit and veg – plucked fresh from his garden and harvest stores – went down a storm. And even the kids donated three massive bowls of cranberries that had been picked in the gardens.

Dad wore a permanent **GRIN.** He was surrounded by all his old friends and neighbours. Even Doc Spencer junior was there – he'd returned early from his trip after hearing the good news about the hotel. Danya and the twins couldn't believe their luck when they were allowed to stay up later than they ever had before, to see in the New Year. Better still, they even got a mention from Sidney in the speeches! They hadn't been expecting it at all.

Sidney was recounting the saga of the hotel build. Just as they thought he was finishing, he cleared his throat and said, 'I'd like to give a special mention to three children who really were the saviours of the manor house after their revelations about the nesting bats. Ladies and gentlemen, a huge round of applause for Sammy, Lisa and Danya, our champions of Christmas!'

Everyone **CHEERED** as the children blushed and smiled bashfully with embarrassment.

Then Sidney held his glass aloft and proposed a toast. 'Now then, I'd like you all to join me and raise your glasses to the village . . . and to the manor house and its grounds. Long may they stand!'

'Long may they stand!' Everyone joined in. There was much celebration and merriment.

Only one key villager was notably absent: Eugene Hazell. Grumpy and livid at the whole situation, he had had an early night after deciding not to welcome in the New Year. With the help of a sleeping pill, he slept solidly through the whole thing.

On the stroke of midnight, the villagers cheered like

they'd never cheered before. It was as if they all knew the New Year was going to be a good one . . .

And they were not disappointed.

WHAT HAPPENED AFTER . . .

Eugene Hazell was never seen in the village again. Unable to sell the manor house and grounds for lots of money due to the nesting bats, he ended up selling it to the village council for not very much money at all. It became a successful visitor attraction and cafe. The council and other members of the village community were allowed to use the rooms for village get-togethers, meetings – and the odd party!

Danya and her father still live in their cottage on the grounds of the estate. And as well as keeping his job as caretaker, Danya's dad also runs the cafe, where he makes the most delicious home-made food, with fruit and vegetables from his ever-flourishing kitchen garden.

Archie the bat and all his friends continue to live in the trees at Hazell's Wood. Archie is now the proud father of bat triplets, Sammy, Lisa and Danya, born last New Year's Eve. Mother and babies are doing well.

Dad, Mum and the twins visit the village every Christmas (always without their iPads) and the family never fail to attend the now legendary annual village New Year's Eve party – always held at the thriving manor house and grounds.

Sammy, Lisa and Danya remain the **GREATEST** of friends and are often found exploring, biking and having great adventures in and around the village and the glorious Hazell's Wood, manor house and grounds. Long may they stand.

THE TWITS IN THE GREAT CARROT CAPER

Greg James and Chris Smith

CHAPTER 1
The Worst Beard in the Whole World

Did you know that after you fall asleep each Christmas Eve, something truly **MAGICAL** happens? A man comes sliding down your chimney. A man with a large tummy and a great big beard. And do you know what that man's name is?

That's right, his name is Mr Twit.

What's that? You thought we were talking about Father Christmas? Don't be ridiculous. What do you think this is, some kind of heart-warming seasonal story? Get real.

Here's Father Christmas, look:

And here's Mr Twit:

Quite different, aren't they? Well, they have both got beards, to be fair. Maybe that's where the confusion came from. But they are very, very different beards. If you need some help telling them apart, you can use this handy **BEARD COMPARISON CHART.**

	FATHER CHRISTMAS	**MR TWIT**
COLOUR OF BEARD	White as pristine, new-fallen snow at the North Pole on Christmas morning.	As black as a gigantic heap of burning tyres.
SCENT OF BEARD	Pine needles, cinnamon, crackling log fires and wrapping paper.	Year-old sardine tails, rotten sprouts, licked handkerchiefs and betrayal.
CONTENTS OF BEARD	Fresh air and Christmas spirit.	Year-old sardine tails, rotten sprouts, cornflakes (8) and several splashes of asparagus soup from the Tuesday before last.
CLEANLINESS OF BEARD	Shampooed, conditioned and combed each morning before breakfast.	Has never been washed. Ever. Except maybe once, by accident, when it rained.
TEXTURE OF BEARD	As fluffy as cotton wool that has been freshly washed in the tears of a baby reindeer.	As harsh and prickly as a pickled hedgehog sprinkled with actual nails.
CONCLUSION	Best beard in world.	Worst beard in world.

On the morning this story starts – which was **CHRISTMAS EVE** – Mr Twit was coming through the front door of his house laden down with a **HUGE** armful of holly. He was in an excellent mood, and Mr Twit was only ever in an excellent mood when he was about to do something truly horrible to his wife, Mrs Twit. He was in such high spirits that he was actually singing a song.

'On the twelfth day of Christmas, I sent to Mrs T,' sang Mr Twit in his foul croaky voice, 'twelve donkeys dribbling, eleven ponies pooping, ten lousy lemons, nine knotty knickers, eight mops a-minging, seven swans a-sinking, six greasy lions, fiiiiiive smelly bins . . .'

He lugged the holly through the sitting room and towards the staircase as he continued his festive tune.

'Four crawling bugs, three stenchy wrens, two purple clogs, and a badger with a bad knee.'

Mr Twit's big black boots stomped up the stairs, leaving behind a trail of muddy footprints and dropped red berries. Once in the bedroom (which smelled like mushrooms) he dumped the holly on the floor and got to work.

At this point we should probably mention that one of Mr Twit's favourite hobbies was playing tricks on his horrible wife. You're about to meet Mrs Twit in the next chapter and you'd better prepare yourself because she's really very nasty indeed. We're not sure how these two total twits ever got together in the first place, frankly. A lot of couples meet each other, fall in love and don't start hating each other until much later. For Mr and Mrs Twit, it was hate at first sight. They had met, fallen deeply in hate, got married and settled down to make each other's lives as miserable as they possibly could.

'Fill the bed with lots of holly, **FA LA LA LA LA, HA HAAAA HAAAA HAAAA,**' croaked Mr Twit as he pulled the mattress off his wife's bed. We won't spend too much time looking at the mattress because it was really very foul indeed. It was several colours, not one of which was the usual colour a mattress is supposed to be. Mr Twit rolled it up tightly like a giant but highly revolting sausage and stuffed it up the chimney. Then Mr Twit proceeded to pack the holly down tightly in a square shape where the mattress had been. He got quite badly pricked during this process but he didn't care because he was so excited about his horrible trick. The only part that really upset him was when an unusually prickly leaf accidentally combed a bit of his beard, leaving it fairly **CLEAN** and **TIDY**. A fragment of boiled parsnip was prised out of the filthy bristles and pinged away to disappear down a crack in the floorboards.

'I was saving that for my afternoon snack,' grumbled Mr Twit, adding one last piece of holly and fastening a sheet over the top. Once his holly mattress was complete, he carefully placed a pillow and bedspread on the top and smoothed everything down with an evil chuckle. At that exact moment he heard the front door open. Mrs Twit was home.

Brace yourselves, this isn't going to be pleasant.

CHAPTER 2
The Holly and the Ouch-y

You may have heard about the Seven Wonders of the World. It is a list of the most breathtaking, amazing, brain-bazoggling things ever created. You might not be aware, however, of the Seven Blunders of the World. This is a list of the things that should never, ever have existed because they make our small planet a much more unpleasant place. Here is the list, in reverse order:

7. Those pink wafer biscuits that coat all the other biscuits in the tin with a pink dust that looks and tastes like unicorn's dandruff.

6. Uncles who ruffle your hair.

5. Thinking you might sneeze, then not sneezing.

4. The Adam's apples of maths teachers.

3. When butter is too hard and it tears the bread.

2. Accidentally letting go of a balloon.

1. Mrs Twit first thing in the morning.

Mrs Twit constantly has rotten thoughts, just like her husband. This means she is a horrific sight at any time of the day, but it's particularly bad in the morning before her brain has had a chance to get properly warmed up. Here she is, look:

That stick is not used to help her walk. Instead, she uses it to hit people and – when she can catch them – kittens. And she's holding a bag of Brussels sprouts, which she likes to eat at Christmas time in the same way that you and I eat sweets. This means she smells extremely bad at both ends – not that she smells particularly fragrant in the middle section either, if you're interested.

'Where are you, you useless old twerp?' screeched Mrs Twit, hanging her stick over the back of a chair and peering around the sitting room.

'I'm here, aren't I, you beady old blobfish!' yelled Mr Twit in reply, stomping down the stairs . . . and wearing a crafty expression behind his beard. You might have expected these two twits to be a bit nicer to each other than usual, considering it was Christmas Eve and Christmas can bring out the best in almost anybody. But some people, sad to say, have no best to bring out.

'I've been out to get more sprouts,' announced Mrs Twit. 'Only good thing about this whole 'orrible time of year, sprouts. Everyone walking about smiling and buying presents for each other. Faugh!' At this point, a sprout she'd been chewing flew out of her mouth and landed with a moist plop in a bowl of dog food that was on the table nearby.

Ooh, you might be thinking to yourself at this point, *I didn't know the Twits had a dog. That's a plot twist.* Well, it isn't. Because the Twits don't have a dog. They're far too nasty and selfish to look after a dog. The reason there was a bowl of dog food on the table was because Mr Twit liked to eat dog food for his lunch. Sorry, but there it is.

'Oi! That's my lunch!' protested Mr Twit as his wife retrieved her sprout from the dog food and replaced it in her mouth, sucking noisily at the meaty chunks.

'Oh, stop moaning, you bristly old boot brush,' she scolded him through a mouthful of dog food. 'I'm in a bad enough mood as it is. I had to **SQUEEZE** through a whole crowd of CHILDREN on my way home from the greengrocer's.' Mrs Twit said the word 'children' in the same tone of voice that you or I would say the phrase 'a pigeon pecking up sick off the pavement'.

'Euuurgh,' replied Mr Twit, disgusted. The Twits hated children almost as much as they hated washing. And they hated that a very great deal.

'All **HAPPY** and **EXCITED,'** Mrs Twit went on, her face scrunching up in disgust, like a dirty dishcloth being wrung out. 'Talking about leaving a carrot and a glass of milk in the fireplace tonight.' With a slurp, she dislodged a final lump of dog food from the sprout and swallowed them both down with a giant gulp. 'Right,' she told Mr Twit, 'get out of my way, you useless, sodden bag of chicken gizzards. I'm going upstairs for my nap.'

'Enjoy your nap, Mrs Twit,' said Mr Twit with a sly smile, sitting down in his favourite chair and reaching for a mug of beer. 'Not that it's going to be very enjoyable, you wizened old hedge badger,' he added under his breath.

Upstairs, Mrs Twit pulled back the bedcover and prepared for her nap. She placed her bag of sprouts on the bedside table in case she fancied a mid-nap snack. Mrs Twit leaped into bed and pulled the cover across her, preparing herself for a delicious sleep (possibly involving a dream about running a baby otter over with a steam roller – this was the kind of dream Mrs Twit really enjoyed).

It took Mrs Twit's brain a few seconds to register that something was very, very wrong with her bed. But when her brain finally creaked into action, it realized that instead of lying on her lovely squashy mattress with its nice familiar collection of stains and smells, she was in fact lying on a large pile of extremely prickly holly.

Mrs Twit leaped several feet straight UP into the air, with a shriek like the whistle of a steam train. She hung suspended near the bedroom ceiling for a moment, bicycling her warty legs, before FALLING back onto the holly once again. This process was repeated five or six times before she finally managed to roll herself off the edge of the bed. She sat on the floor panting, feeling as if her whole body was on fire. Downstairs, Mr Twit was laughing so hard at the commotion that he almost choked on his beer. 'Having a nice rest, my dear?' he called, gurgling with delight.

'I'll show you, you mucky old goat,' muttered Mrs Twit.

CHAPTER 3
Creep-filled Wince Pies

Later that day, Mrs Twit was baking in the kitchen. For a lot of people this wouldn't be a very unusual thing on Christmas Eve. Many people like to spend the day making **DELICIOUS** food to share with their friends. But Mrs Twit disliked sharing, and she had no friends. Her oven was never turned on at Christmas time - apart from once when she'd switched it on by accident with her bottom while she was bending over to tie Mr Twit's shoelaces together. Today, however, Mrs Twit was cooking up a very special **FESTIVE** surprise.

RECIPE FOR MRS TWIT'S FESTIVE SURPRISE:

STEP 1: Make a shortcrust pastry. For this, you will need flour, sugar and butter. Blend the butter into the dry ingredients until the mixture is the same texture as the flaky skin that comes off Mrs Twit's hands when she rubs them together. Then add enough water to make a smooth dough. Roll out the dough, cut circles and use them to line an 8-cup pie tin.

STEP 2: Now you need to make your filling. For this, you will need to go out into the garden and find a large, rotten log - the damper and crumblier, the better. Turn the log over and look underneath. You will find a rich, dark mud filled with wriggling creepy-crawlies: cheesy bobs, skillywigglers, granfy-croogers, chiggy-wigs, granny grunters, chucky-pigs, curly-bakers and monkey peas. Scoop a generous portion of this rich wiggly goo into a bucket and return to the kitchen.

STEP 3: Bake the pastry cases until golden brown. Fill each one with two heaped tablespoons of under-log insect mixture and top with a pastry lid.

Mrs Twit finished her recipe, adding festive white **SPRINKLES** to her pies. She did this by leaning over the kitchen table and scratching her head so that flakes of dried skin fell across it, like the worst snow you could imagine. Then she marched proudly into the sitting room, bearing her creep-filled wince pies on a tray.

'Woss this?' grunted Mr Twit, looking up grumpily from his fifth mug of beer. The good mood that filled his tummy when Mrs Twit had laid down in the holly had thoroughly disappeared. This is the thing that horrible people never really understand. Doing a mean, nasty thing might bring you a moment of wicked satisfaction. But it soon floats away, leaving you looking for your next moment of evil joy. Good deeds last far longer – just one of those is generally enough to keep you going for a week or more. But there's just no telling some people, is there?

'It's pies,' spat Mrs Twit. 'And you can't have any.' She knew perfectly well that this would make her horrible husband want one more than anything.

'Oh, go on, give us a pie,' wheedled Mr Twit. 'The holly was just my little joke. Come on, it's Christmas. Just one pie. P– pie.' He had been about to say 'please' before stopping himself. But truly foul people never, ever say please. It's a good way of spotting them.

'No. I made these delicious pies, and I'm going to eat them,' snapped Mrs Twit, placing the tray on the table and flumping into her favourite chair. 'Every last one.'

There was silence for a moment. The only sound was the faint ticking noise made by horrible brains thinking horrible thoughts. Then Mr Twit lurched forward in his chair. 'Look!' he shouted, pointing. 'Behind you! It's Father Christmas! And he's brought you an enormous present!'

'Oooh!' Mrs Twit looked excitedly over her shoulder. Father Christmas had never brought her anything for the last fifty years. When she had been young, she had actually been quite a nice person. But as the years had gone by, and she had grown nastier and meaner and uglier, she had slipped onto the Naughty List. 'There's nobody there,' she said in a disappointed tone.

'HA HA!' Mr Twit was clutching the tray of pies. With his wife's back turned, he had darted out of his chair and grabbed them, as quick and crafty as a crab. Only even faster. Maybe like a crab if one of its grandparents was a cheetah.

'Give them pies back, you mangy old bog snorkeller!' screamed Mrs Twit. Secretly, of course, she wasn't in the least angry. This was exactly her plan. 'Those are my pies!' she went on. 'You're not allowed any!'

'Well, that's a shame,' gloated Mr Twit, his eyes gleaming with triumph. 'Because I'm going to eat them. Right now. Every last one!' And without hesitation, he began cramming the pies into his mouth, chomping on them with great satisfaction. An avalanche of pastry crumbs tumbled down his dirty old brown jumper and into his lap, and a cavalcade of wriggling insects began crawling across his beard and over his shoulders. Mr Twit – like all twits – chewed with his mouth wide open, and so his wife had a fine view of the squirming, wriggling, writhing mass of creepy-crawlies that now filled his mouth. Still unaware of what he was eating, Mr Twit pointed to his open mouth, waggling his hairy eyebrows in a dance of victory. It was only when he began to chew and swallow (after he had crammed no fewer than six wince pies into his mouth) that he registered something was awry.

'What flavour are these?' mumbled Mr Twit through a gigantic mouthful of buttery shortcrust pastry, garden insects and wet soil. 'They've got a funny sort of taste. Are they mince pies?'

'These are not just mince pies,' cooed Mrs Twit in her best TV advertisement voice, 'these are hand-filled, all-butter, creep-filled wince pies. And they're **FULL OF CREEPY-CRAWLIES FROM THE GARDEN!** You're eating a big mouthful of chiggy-wigs, Mr Twit, you silly old manatee! Ha ha haaaaa!' Mrs Twit leaned forward and thumped her knees in evil delight as her husband ran upstairs to the bathroom and began scrubbing his tongue with a nail brush.

CHAPTER 4
The Great Carrot Heist

Later that Christmas Eve, Mr and Mrs Twit were sitting in their front room as usual, thinking mean thoughts. Outside it had started to snow.

'What was that thing you said earlier?' said Mr Twit suddenly. 'You said something earlier that gave me an evil thought, but I can't remember what it was.'

Mrs Twit thought for a moment. 'Why don't you disappear, you useless old stoat?' she suggested.

'No, it wasn't that.'

'Well, you were out of the room when I said that, to be fair,' admitted Mrs Twit, peering at him.

'It was something about carrots,' Mr Twit

remembered, clicking his fingers. 'What did you say about carrots?'

'Oh yes,' she replied. 'I heard those horrible children going on about leaving a glass of milk and a carrot in the fireplace tonight when they go to bed.'

'Why?' demanded Mr Twit suspiciously.

'For Father Christmas, isn't it, you daft old hairbrush.'

'Why does he get free carrots and milk?' Mr Twit was outraged. 'What's he ever done for us?' Mrs Twit shrugged. Father Christmas, it's true, had done nothing for either of the Twits for many years, and rightly so.

At this moment Mr Twit hit on a really, really horrible idea. It was as if a small lightbulb had illuminated above his head – only more unpleasant than a lightbulb. A bunch of burning flowers, perhaps. 'I've just thought of a **SPLENDIDLY** evil plan,' declared Mr Twit, gurning and cracking his knuckles. 'If there's free carrots and free milk on offer, then what's to stop me climbing down the chimbley and getting it first, before **HE** arrives?'

Mrs Twit rarely agreed with her husband, but this scheme was too horrible to resist. She clapped her wrinkled hands together with delight. 'I'll get the ladder!' she declared. 'And you fetch your biggest sack to carry them carrots away in.'

And so, after dark had fallen, two figures could be seen flitting between the houses in the town. One carried a ladder and a walking stick, the other a large brown sack. Silently they crept into the first garden they reached. The house was in darkness, and flakes of snow fell softly from the dark sky. With a faint clunk the ladder was placed against the wall, and the figures began to climb.

Inside, all was peaceful. The last embers of a fire smouldered in the grate. A cat dozed on the hearthrug. A clock ticked on the mantelpiece. And next to the clock, a long-legged elf looked out across the room with bright, watchful eyes that reflected the twinkling coloured lights on the tall Christmas tree.

Suddenly, there was a scuffling from the chimney, and a shower of soot FELL into the fireplace. A foot appeared, followed by an ankle clad in a dirty grey sock. Then, with a ***WHUMP,*** Mr Twit plummeted into the grate, right onto the fire. For a few seconds he sat there silently before his twittish brain registered that he was sitting on red-hot embers. Then he began to say **'WAAAAARGH!'** at the top of his voice, until he remembered at the last minute that he was supposed to be creeping about silently and stealthily. So he jammed one of his fists into his mouth before leaping out of the fireplace and hopping about the room with smoke coming from his bottom. The cat, with a brief disgusted shake of its head, left the room to find a more peaceful place to sleep.

When Mr Twit had managed to put out his bottom by patting it, he turned back to the fireplace with a greedy expression. Sure enough, there on the hearth was a glass of milk and a carrot.

''Tis the night before Christmas,'

recited Mr Twit in a satisfied tone,

'and men of my ilk,
Are dreaming of stealing some carrots and milk.
The idiots have left them right here in the fireplace.
So I'm going to pinch 'em and take 'em to my place.'

'Oo are you talking to?' hissed the voice of Mrs Twit, who was listening from the roof.

'I'm reciting a festulant poem, you daft old mongoose,' whispered Mr Twit into the hearth. 'Shut up. I'm going to put the carrot in my sack and scramble back up the chimbley. The Great Carrot Heist has begun.'

'What about the milk?' came the reply. Mr Twit hadn't thought of that. He couldn't very well pour a glass of milk into his sack. He thought for a moment.

'I shall drink the milk and steal the carrot,' he announced quietly. 'Stand by while I execute my cunning plan.' And, with that, he picked up the glass of milk and sniffed at it. By this time, in the early hours of the morning, the milk had been sitting out for several hours and had started to turn slightly. It smelled very faintly of cheese.

'PERFECT,' said Mr Twit, 'just the way I like it. With any luck, it's gone nice and sour and there'll be some blobules in it.' When milk really starts to go off, it gets bits in it which Mr Twit calls 'blobules'. He insists that this is where the flavour is. The milk had indeed gone quite sour, and there were indeed several spongy globes forming in it. Mr Twit sucked these down greedily, smacking his lips with relish. Then he picked up the carrot - which was also not quite in its prime – and placed it in his sack before scrambling back into the grate.

'Prepare yourself, Mrs Twit,' he hissed, 'I'm ASCENDING the chimbley!'

And with that, Mr Twit disappeared from the room. He thought he had stolen the milk and carrots without anybody seeing him. But Mr Twit was wrong.

CHAPTER 5
The Elf on the Shelf

You might have noticed in the previous chapter that we mentioned an elf sitting on the mantelpiece. At the time, you may just have thought that this was simply a little detail put there to make things feel all Christmassy. But you would have been wrong. If you thought: *Aha! I bet that elf features later on in the story,* then award yourself an extra twelve Yule Points and a double helping of bread sauce. Because she does indeed feature in the story, and it starts right here, in the next paragraph.

The elf's name was Astrid and she was visiting from the North Pole to keep an eye on things. During her time as an elf on various shelves, Astrid had witnessed a great deal of bad behaviour. She had seen children refuse to go to bed at night. She had seen them have tantrums and kick the furniture. She had seen them throw food, go looking around the house for Christmas presents, try to put baubles up their noses . . . you name it. But she had never, ever seen anyone break into a house through the chimney, for the sole purpose of stealing carrots and milk. It almost took her breath away. Astrid immediately decided that she should follow this intruder and keep him under close elf surveillance.

She got to her feet and, with a POP like the cork coming out of a bottle, vanished. She reappeared in the house next door, where she hid in the branches of the Christmas tree and waited. Sure enough, before long there was a scuffling and an unpleasant smell from the fireplace, and Mr Twit skulked into the room, downed the glass of milk that had been left on the hearth and put the carrot in his sack. Astrid shook her head in disbelief. What was Father Christmas going to make of this? He was due here any minute, her elf senses told her. In fact, this particular town was the last stop on his long journey around the world. Delivering presents was thirsty work – he was not going to be impressed when, instead of some milk, all he found in each house was an empty glass. And how the reindeer were supposed to get by with no carrots . . . well, Astrid just couldn't imagine.

Using her **ELF MAGIC,** she followed Mr Twit from house to house until, in the very last house right at the edge of the town, she decided it was time to act. Mr Twit, she saw, was sitting down in a comfortable chair, gloating over his crimes. By now, his sack was full of carrots and his stomach was full of milk. So much so, in fact, that he made a sloshing noise wherever he went and was beginning to find it slightly difficult to squeeze down the chimneys. But that didn't matter, he thought to himself as he sat back in the chair and chugged his last room-temperature milk of the night. He had robbed every single house in the town – and he'd got away with it scot-free. It was the perfect crime.

Of course, it wasn't the perfect crime for two very excellent reasons. Firstly, Mr Twit had been in every house in the entire town and stolen nothing but carrots and milk. Secondly, his crime had been witnessed by an elf named Astrid. But Mr Twit did not realize any of this because, as you may have noticed by now, he was a twit.

'Hurry up!' hissed Mrs Twit from the roof. She was getting extremely cold standing up there in the snow – mainly because she was only wearing carpet slippers.

'I'm coming, ain't I?' grumbled Mr Twit, hauling his milk-filled tummy out of the armchair and bundling towards the fireplace. But, before he got there, he was surprised by a SMALL voice from behind.

'Not so fast!' said the small voice.

'Who said that?' snapped Mr Twit, spinning round on the spot and scanning the room. He could see nothing except an angel on the top of the tree.

'What's going on down there?' said Mrs Twit, stamping her wet feet impatiently.

'I'm being menaced by an angel,' said Mr Twit.

'You're going to pay for your horrible crimes, you big milk-thieving twit,' said the voice. 'And by the way, that is the filthiest, most disgusting beard I have ever seen in my entire life.' Having spent most of her life at the North Pole, Astrid had only ever really seen one beard, and it was the best one in the world (see table in Chapter 1).

'How dare you?' roared Mr Twit, who for some reason was very proud of his horrible beard. He launched himself furiously at the angel, knocking the entire Christmas tree to the floor. Mrs Twit, wondering what all the commotion was, slid down the chimney herself and arrived in the fireplace just in time to see her husband tearing the angel's wings off, shouting, 'Take that, you treetop-perching little flouncer!'

'Why are you tearing that angel to pieces?' asked Mrs Twit.

'It insulted my beard!' roared Mr Twit angrily, pummelling the angel with his fists.

'No, it didn't,' said a small voice from the mantelpiece. 'That was me.' Mr Twit got to his feet and squinted across the room. Mrs Twit, too, looked to see where the voice had come from. She jumped back from the fireplace in alarm.

'It's an **ELF!'** shrieked Mrs Twit.

'Yes, I am,' said Astrid. 'And what's more, I've had quite enough of you two twits. You like carrots so much? Well here, try these on for size.' And with a pop (all elf magic makes a popping noise; we don't know why, but it does) she turned both the Twits' noses into large orange carrots.

CHAPTER 6
A Visit from Saint Nicholas

At that moment, FATHER CHRISTMAS came sliding down the chimney. He'd been having an extremely busy night delivering presents to all the children in the world, and this was his very last stop. He was rather tired and not in a particularly good mood. Normally he would have looked forward to a refreshing glass of milk in each house, and a carrot for his reindeer. But in this town, the last on his flight plan, there had been nothing left except an empty glass and a vague smell of unwashed beard. He was very much looking forward to making this last delivery quickly before getting back on his sleigh and returning to the North Pole for a nice cup of tea and a sit-down.

Considering all of this, it's not especially surprising that Father Christmas was rather annoyed by the sight that met his eyes in the final front room of his long night's work. The tree had fallen to the floor, spreading needles and baubles everywhere. Astrid the Elf was standing on the mantelpiece, cackling like a hyena. And in the middle of the floor were two dirty, mean-looking people with carrots for noses, one of them grasping a partially dismembered Christmas angel.

'What the eggnog is going on in here?' said Father Christmas. (We know, it's not his normal opening line. Usually he goes with the traditional 'Ho ho ho', but these were exceptional circumstances.) 'Wait a minute, I know you,' he went on, narrowing his usually very kindly eyes. **'You're the Twits!'**

'Ooh, he knows who we are!' cooed Mrs Twit. (It's always fun to meet a celebrity, especially if they actually know who you are. It even distracted her briefly from the fact that her nose was now a carrot.)

'You're on my Twit List!' exclaimed Father Christmas.

At this point an explanation is probably in order.

As you may know, Father Christmas has a Nice List, for people who receive presents, and a Naughty List, for people who do not. What you might not have heard before is that Father Christmas actually has a third list, for people who are so foul, so horrible and so utterly useless, that the world would be better off without them. It is called the Twit List, and it doesn't have many names on it. (We could tell you some of them, but we'd probably get sued.) But, of course, the top two names on the list, bold and underlined, are Mr Twit and Mrs Twit.

Mr Twit saw a dangerous twinkle in Father Christmas's eyes and decided to seize the initiative. 'Get him!' he roared, leaping over the fallen tree and rugby-tackling the red-clad old man to the ground. 'Grab the tinsel, Mrs Twit!' he shouted. 'Tie him up!' Out of the corner of his eye he saw Astrid preparing for some more elf magic, so Mr Twit grabbed her and stuffed her into the sack full of carrots. Meanwhile, Mrs Twit unwound long strands of tinsel from the tree and securely tied Father Christmas's wrists and ankles together. It was very lucky that the people who lived in this house were deep sleepers. You would have thought all this would have woken them up. But it didn't.

Before long, Father Christmas was securely tied up with tinsel and Mr and Mrs Twit pushed and shoved him up the chimney. There, a gleaming red sleigh stood on the pristine white snow, and nine reindeer stamped and snorted, their breath misting in the cold early morning air. 'Dump him in!' screeched Mrs Twit in triumph. They pushed Father Christmas into the back of the sleigh, which earlier in the night had been filled with presents, putting the sack of carrots and elf beside him. Then they leaped onto the driving seat at the front and pressed a large red button that said: LAUNCH. And, with a neigh and a CLIPPITY CLOP and a jingling of bells, the reindeer galloped up into the dark starry sky, on autopilot for the North Pole.

Once there, Mr and Mrs Twit took over from Father Christmas, and nobody ever got any presents ever again and Christmas was cancelled for all time.

THE END

CARROTS

CHAPTER 7
The Great Battle in the Sky

Oh, all right then. That isn't what really happened, we were just joking. Calm down.

With a neigh and a CLIPPITY CLOP and a jingling of bells, the reindeer galloped up into the dark starry sky, on autopilot for the North Pole. In the driving seat, the Twits whooped and roared with horrible triumph. 'Dash away, dash away, dash away all, you horny-headed horrors!' yelled Mr Twit, grabbing a whip and flicking it at the nearest reindeer bottom. Mrs Twit, once she had spent a good few minutes cackling like the nasty crone that she was, even broke into song:

'Jingle bells, Mr Twit smells,

Jingle all the way,

Father C is rather cross

Because we've pinched his sleigh.'

'What do you think you're doing, you nincompoops?' shouted Father Christmas from the present compartment at the back. (This was the rudest word he had ever used.)

'We've tied you up, and now we've stolen your flying sledge,' replied Mr Twit with an evil leer. 'And once we reach the North Pole we're going to take over, steal all your carrots and cancel Christmas forever!'

'What is it with you and carrots, you strange, smelly little man?' grunted Father Christmas. He struggled to untie himself, but the tinsel was **STRONG** and well-knotted. Just then, there was a small pop and Astrid the Elf appeared beside him. She had been biding her time in the sack of carrots until the Twits had forgotten all about her, and had decided that now was the moment to stage a great rescue. 'Astrid!' whispered Father Christmas. 'What a relief! Can you untie me?'

'Of course I can,' Astrid replied. 'Elves are awesome.

Elves can do anything.' And, with another magical POP, the tinsel disappeared from around his wrists and ankles.

By now, the sleigh had been flying out across the sea for quite some time. Below, a rocky coastline was visible, with gigantic fjords and crashing waves. They were passing above a series of small islands, which looked like a splendid place to take a boat for swimming and picnics in the summertime. But in the early light of this cloudy Christmas morning the islands looked rather chilly and forbidding, with patches of snow here and there. The Twits were just peering down at them when something unexpected happened. With a blood-curdling war cry, Father Christmas leaped on the Twits from behind and started attacking them ferociously, using a large, knobbly carrot. (Now that's not a sentence you read every day, is it?)

It's a tough job, being Father Christmas. He needs to be an expert at toy manufacturing, of course, as well as navigation, chimney manoeuvring, moving stealthily and cheery HO-HO-HO'ing. What you might not know is that he is also an expert in the little-known skills of Elf Defence, a festive martial art. This comes in useful if he needs to defend himself against security guards, fierce dogs or – as on this occasion – a pair of idiots who've tied him up and nicked his sleigh.

'HI-YAAAAA!' screeched Father Christmas, knocking Mr Twit flying with the carrot and turning a backward somersault to face Mrs Twit, who was coming at him with her walking stick. They both leaped dramatically up onto the side rail of the sleigh and staged a very impressive sword fight – only with a stick and a carrot instead of swords. This being the case, it didn't make that cool ker-ching noise that sword fights make; it just sounded like a carrot being hit with a stick. But it looked extremely impressive.

'Take that, you carrot-nosed bat!' yelled Father Christmas, fetching Mrs Twit a terrific whack on the head with his carrot. The 'bat' part was quite rude of him, but the 'carrot' section was perfectly accurate.

'Have at you, you bushy-bearded, cookie-grasping chimney-botherer!' retorted Mrs Twit, cracking him painfully across the shins with her stick. She was an expert at hitting things with the stick, having practised on a daily basis for many decades. But in the end, even her skills were no match for the finely honed Elf Defence abilities of Father Christmas. Wielding his carrot expertly, he drove the Twits towards the back of the sleigh, which was now flying above a snowy forest, the dark pine trees looking as if they had been dusted with a thick layer of icing sugar.

Mr and Mrs Twit were balanced precariously on the very rear of the sleigh. And, like all true twits, it was only when they realized they could not win that they decided to apologize.

'We're sorry!' sputtered Mr Twit. 'We didn't mean to do it! I'll put all the carrots back, I promise!'

'Please take us home!' whined Mrs Twit. 'We'll be good forever and ever, I promise!'

'Yes, yes!' agreed Mr Twit frantically. 'We will celebrate Christmas every day of the year! We will honour Christmas past, present and future, and all of that!'

'Please have mercy!' pleaded Mrs Twit. 'After all, it is Christmas.'

You might be thinking that it sounds rather out of character for the Twits to be apologizing like this. And you'd be right. But in fact they weren't sorry at all. They were merely trying to distract Father Christmas so they could attack him all over again. This, though, was their downfall.

In preparation for leaping across the sleigh, Mr Twit took a small step backwards. His foot slipped on a small patch of ice, and with a wail he vanished over the back, pulling Mrs Twit with him as he flailed his arms in panic.

'Oh dear,' said Astrid the Elf. 'Do you think we should fly down and rescue them?'

Father Christmas thought about this for a moment. He thought about the kettle waiting for him at home. And he thought about the deep snow beneath them which, surely, would give the Twits a soft landing. 'Nah,' he said, and away he flew. After all, they were top of his Twit List.

CHAPTER 8
Frozen Two

All was quiet in the frozen pine forests of the far north. A blanket of snow lay across the ground and weighed down the bushy branches. The animals were fast asleep on this cold, cold morning, and flashes of bright colour danced in the sky as the Northern Lights ushered in another Christmas Day.

Suddenly, there was a strange sound from above. It was the sound of the Twits falling from the sleigh.

'We're walking in the AIIEEEEEEEEEEERRRR-RRRGGGGHHH!' screamed Mrs Twit, her black skirt ballooning out like a parachute as she plummeted towards the silent forest.

'We're falling from the flippin' **SKYYYYYYYY-YYYYY!'** added Mr Twit, clinging on to her ankle in an attempt to slow down his descent. It didn't work very well. With a loud flump, both Twits landed on a small tussock in a lonely clearing, their feet thumping so hard into the snow that they stuck fast, their carrot noses quivering.

'It's c-c-c-cold,' said Mr Twit after a few moments.

'Of c-c-c-course it's c-c-c-cold, you c-c-c-clam-witted old c-c-c-custard head,' replied Mrs Twit. 'We were halfway to the North Pole!'

'I c-c-c-can't feel my feet,' protested Mr Twit.

'Why's that?' she asked.

'C-c-c-cos my arms have frozen,' he replied. And, sure enough, Mr Twit's arms were now two blocks of solid ice, clamped tightly against his side. Mrs Twit tried to look sideways so she could laugh at his predicament, but discovered that her neck had also frozen and she could no longer turn her head.

'I think we're bec-c-c-c-coming frozen, Mr Twit,' she said with difficulty, as it was getting harder and harder to move her lips.

'Eeeeeeeeeeeeeeeech,' he replied. His tongue had frozen in his mouth, and he could no longer move it. It's very difficult to say anything without moving your tongue: try it sometime.

Before long, both Twits were completely motionless, frozen solid and wedged firmly into the ground. Presently it began to snow again. Giant white flakes drifted down from the clouds, coating the whole forest in a fresh blanket of purest white. And the Twits, too, were covered by the falling snow. Within an hour or two they were almost completely hidden, and all that could be seen were two silent snowpeople standing on the hill with their carrot noses sticking out.

And we know it's Christmas and it's supposed to be the season of forgiveness and all that, but we reckon it serves them right. So let's leave them there and have a chocolate, shall we?

MERRY CHRISTMAS!

GRAN AND THE MAGIC FINGER

Sally Rippin

What do you picture when I say the word 'grandmother'?

I'll bet I can guess. I'll bet you are thinking of a sweet, white-haired old lady in a floral dress and pearls, like the ones in children's books. Perhaps she is sitting in a rocking chair, knitting? Or baking cakes and preserving jams. Or perhaps you have a cool, pink-haired grandmother who takes you skiing or to rock concerts, or maybe even hang-gliding. Whatever type of grandmother you have, I guarantee you don't have a grandmother like mine. My grandmother is magic.

So, that day, when the Terrible Thing happened, I knew exactly who to turn to for help.

Gran was just where I'd expected her to be: in our backyard, snoozing on a sun lounge in the shade of the fig tree. It was three weeks before Christmas, two weeks until school broke up, and already it was stinking hot. You might celebrate Christmas in the winter, with turkey and puddings and snow, but here, in Walgum Springs, in Australia, our Christmases are smack bang in the middle of summer. And this one was gearing up to be a scorcher.

'Gran! Gran!' I yelled, as I ran across the dried-out lawn, my school bag bumping up and down on my back. 'I need your help! A TERRIBLE THING has happened!' I collapsed next to the sun lounge on the itchy yellow grass, panting and trying to catch my breath.

Gran was lying on her stomach in a floral bikini and floppy straw hat. She pushed her **HUGE** sunglasses down her nose and peered over the top of them to get a better look at me. 'Sugarbun,' she sighed in her raspy voice, a smile **TWITCHING** at the corners of her lips. 'What on earth are you doing rushing around in this heat? Take a breath, petal. Tell me everything. I'm sure it can't be as bad as all that.'

I wiped the sweat from my forehead with a corner of my school dress. Then I took a deep breath and the words came tumbling out. 'Well, it all started because Mrs Richards was away today, and we had a replacement teacher . . .'

'Oh, how's Carly Richards' hubbie doing, sweet pea?' Gran asked. 'He hurt his back a few weeks ago, didn't he?'

'Gran!' I said, frowning. Gran knew everyone in town, and she was always interrupting my stories with gossip.

'Sorry.' Gran nodded, a smile twitching the corner of her lips.

'So, we had swimming today and usually Mrs Richards just lets Shona help out with the little ones in the shallow end because Shona really doesn't like swimming. Anyway, the replacement teacher said Shona had to learn some time, and made her go in the deep end with the rest of us . . .'

'Well, she does have a point . . .' Gran shrugged.

'Gran, please!' I sighed, starting to get irritated. 'Can you let me tell the story?'

'Oops!' Gran said, chuckling and pretending to zip her lips. 'Go on, sweetie-pie.'

'Anyway, Mandy . . .'

'Mayor Martin's girl?' Gran asked.

'Yes,' I said. 'Anyway, Mandy kept calling Shona a chicken because Shona didn't want to put her head under the water. Shona is not a chicken. She just hates swimming, that's all. But Mandy is always teasing people, Gran, and I'm sick of it. Everyone is sick of it. But no one ever stands up to her just because she's the Mayor's daughter. She gets away with murder!'

Gran's forehead wrinkled with concentration as she tried to follow my story. 'Didn't you two used to be friends?'

I sighed. 'In kindergarten. I told you this already.'

Gran nodded, so I barrelled on: 'Anyway, Mandy just kept going on and on at Shona. You know, making **CLUCKING** sounds when the teacher couldn't hear, and all her mean friends were giggling, and I could see Shona was getting upset. Shona's my best friend, and you always told me we have to stand up for our friends and . . . look, I'm really sorry, Gran, but I let my temper get the better of me . . .'

Gran swung her legs around the side of the sun lounge. She sat up and leaned forward, giving me all her attention now. 'Yes, go on, go on . . .' she encouraged. I could see she was starting to put the pieces together.

'I know you always say how important it is not to

lose our tempers,' I explained, 'but I just couldn't help it. Mandy was being so horrible. And then, before I knew what was going on, this happened!'

I took a deep breath and held out my right index finger. 'Look!' It was still sparking and glowing pink. I winced, waiting for Gran's response, and feeling my cheeks burn hot with shame.

Gran grabbed my finger and stared at it. Then she cackled with **LAUGHTER**. 'I knew it! Oh, my darling little cheezlepuff, you've got the Finger! You've got the Magic Finger!' She pulled me into a tight hug, her arms slippery with sunscreen. 'I had started to think it may have died out when your dad never inherited it . . . But, you know, perhaps it's just passed down through the women in our family?'

You remember when I told you at the beginning of the story about Gran being **MAGIC?** Well, I should say, it's not all of Gran that's magic. Just her index finger on her right hand. The one with the bluish tip. It had been our family's secret for decades. But now it seemed the secret was out!

'Gran,' I interrupted. 'You might be excited I've inherited your magic, but there's a girl in my class who is now covered in feathers and squawking like a chicken!'

'Feathers, huh?' Gran looked down at her own index finger proudly and gave it a little flex. 'I wonder if it only turns people into birds?' She chuckled. 'Oh, I miss those days, when sometimes – just occasionally – I'd let my feelings get the better of me.' She sighed. 'It can be so boring being a responsible grown-up . . .'

'Gran,' I said. 'Please. You have to help me. I don't want the **MAGIC FINGER** if it's going to make things like this happen!' I yelled. 'Mandy might be a bully, but that doesn't mean she deserves to be a chicken for the rest of her life!'

Gran sniffed. 'Well. Some people would give their right finger for magic like that . . .' She slid her sunglasses over her eyes and lay back on the sun lounge, stretching out her LONG brown legs. 'Oh, it will sort itself out eventually, dear. Then the spell will disappear of its own accord. Just like it did for my neighbours, the Greggs. You remember that story? I lost my temper at that terrible hunting family when I was a child, back in England, and turned them all into ducks?'

I rolled my eyes. 'How could I forget? You've only told me about a million times.'

Gran glared at me over her sunnies. 'Cheeky.'

'Come on, Gran. You need to help me,' I pleaded. 'I don't know what to do! I couldn't live with myself if

Mandy ended up being like a chicken for the rest of her life. That's just horrible! No one deserves that. Not even a bully.'

But Gran just rolled over on to her tummy. 'If you are smart enough to get yourself into this situation, my dear, you are smart enough to get yourself out of it. I've already told you everything you need to know. The rest you need to figure out for yourself. I'd suggest that you start by returning to the scene of the crime. You'll find more answers there than with me. Now, would you mind moving a little? You're blocking my sun.'

I sighed and left Gran on her sun lounge. My mind was a ***WHIRR***. I had inherited her Magic Finger – which was a pretty amazing thing, when you think about it – but I had absolutely no idea how to control it. I thought about all those years Gran had warned me about losing my temper and what could happen. And now that something had happened, she was going to be about as helpful as a refrigerator in Antarctica!

Apparently, Gran had been hot-headed when she was younger. But these days, she meditated every day to keep the Magic Finger under control. At least when she wanted to. I wondered if I would need to take up meditation now? Drawing lotus flowers in my mind? Counting backwards from fifty? But it was already too late. Now there was a girl in my class I had accidentally turned into a chicken, and all because I had let my anger get the better of me.

What Mandy had said to Shona was mean. But not as mean as putting a magic spell on someone.

I looked down at my index finger, which had now lost its SPARK. And I sighed at the **HUGENESS** of it all. I just wanted to be settling in to eat snacks and watch TV in our air-conditioned loungeroom right about now. But it seemed this day had other plans for me!

Our main street in Walgum Springs was quiet. Everyone was inside, avoiding the heat. I skulked along the sidewalk, under the eaves, trying to stay in the shade as much as possible, peering in all the shop windows. Many of them were decorated with **TINSEL** and cardboard cut-outs of Santa and his reindeer, and some even had fake snow sprayed in the corners of the dusty glass. This looked pretty silly, if you asked me. It was close to forty degrees out! Even in the middle of winter, nowhere in Walgum Springs would ever get cold enough for snow.

In the main square, the **ENORMOUS** Christmas tree was drooping in the heat and a thick pile of dried-up pine needles circled the base. Around the trunk was a tangled wreath of barbed wire. In the past, mayors had encouraged residents to leave gifts for homeless people under the tree. But Mayor Martin said it made the square look cluttered and untidy, and he'd banned it. We all knew the real reason was that he hated anyone doing anything kind or generous. So, when people wouldn't stop leaving out gifts, he had barbed wire wrapped around the tree trunk, to keep them out. That's the sort of person Mayor Martin was.

Just thinking about Mayor Martin made me angry. And as soon as the feeling came up in me, my face got hot and my finger **TINGLED.** I looked down and saw the tip begin to turn red. Tiny sparks started to shoot out from under my fingernail. For the first time, a little thrill of excitement ran through me at the thought of the magic I had inherited from my grandmother. So much power, just in my index finger! I began to wonder what I could do with it . . .

Standing with my back against the newsagent's, in the shade of the awning, I pointed my finger at the horrible barbed wire around the Christmas tree. Then I let my anger towards Mayor Martin get BIGGER and **BIGGER** inside me until I was full of rage.

'Take that, horrible barbed wire!' I hissed, not knowing if there was anything in particular I should be saying, and squeezed my eyes shut. When I opened them again, I felt hot and angry. But the barbed wire was still there. I frowned and sucked more anger into my chest. 'Barbed wire – GO!' I yelled. **'ABRACADABRA!'**

Mrs Daley popped her head out of the newsagent's door. 'You all right, love?' she asked.

I quickly dropped my arm. 'Yes, fine,' I mumbled, my cheeks burning hot with embarrassment.

'Well, don't hang around in the sun too long, will you?' she said kindly. 'It's not good for you. Coddles your brain, my Langton always says.'

'Yes, Mrs Daley,' I said.

'Give my regards to your nan, won't you?'

'I will, Mrs Daley,' I said, then watched her retreat into the cool of her shop again before carrying on my way.

So, it seemed the Magic Finger wasn't something I could just turn on. This was disappointing. Come to think of it, though, if the **MAGIC** had been that easy to use, I'm sure Gran would have already turned half the country's politicians and TV presenters into poultry!

As I continued walking, I thought back to what had happened earlier that day to try and work out what I'd done differently. To tell you the truth, it was all a bit of a blur. It had happened so quickly, and there had been so much chaos and EXCITEMENT that all I had been able to think of doing at the time was to run and tell Gran. It had been easy for me to grab my school bag, throw my uniform on over my bathers, and slip away without anyone noticing.

But as I ran away, I caught a glimpse of Mandy from the corner of my eye, still sprouting feathers and clucking, and all the kids shouting and laughing, and I didn't feel proud of what I'd made happen. The poor substitute teacher was beside herself, not knowing whether to call a doctor or a vet!

Soon I arrived at the entrance to Mandy's street. Greenacre Bend was a **LONG** cul-de-sac with big fat houses sitting smugly on thick green lawns, watered day and night by sprinklers. No one else was allowed to run their sprinklers because it hadn't rained in Walgum Springs for months and we were all meant to be saving water. But Mayor Martin said it was important to keep Greenacre Bend looking lush in case any important politicians came to visit from abroad. Although, as far as I know, this has never happened in my lifetime, and probably not in Gran's either.

As Gran liked to say, Walgum Springs wasn't exactly a top tourist destination, and the only reason she'd ended up here was because she had fallen in love with our dear Pop when he was travelling through England as a young man. They ended up getting married, and Gran had followed him to Walgum Springs. Pop had since passed on, and now Gran was stuck here with Dad and me. But even though she complained about every single thing (except the heat, funnily enough!), I think she had secretly grown fond of the place. Sometimes I would overhear her on the phone to people back in England: 'You know, I have to say, Walgum Springs really grows on you. Like mould!' Then she would throw her head back and cackle.

Everyone in Greenacre Bend was deep inside their houses, curtains drawn to block out the afternoon sun, and air conditioners running full blast. So it was easy for me to slip off my shoes and school dress and wander over the lush green lawns in my bathers, under the heavenly spray of sprinklers. But after a while it hurt my heart to see the cool fresh water running down the wide concrete driveways and into the gutters. Especially when Dad had said there was so little to go around.

When we were still in kindergarten, Mandy and I used to dare each other to run down our driveways in bare feet, to see how long we could stand the blistering concrete. But then her dad became mayor and they moved to a bigger house on the other side of Walgum Springs. From then on, Mandy only hung out with the girls who thought they were too good for us. And she quickly became the meanest of them all, teasing Shona and me and anyone else she could find something to laugh about – from what we had in our lunchboxes to whether we were wearing the 'right' shoes. Remembering this made my stomach **TIGHTEN** and my head spin.

I arrived at Mandy's house and stood on their front lawn. Like all the other houses, it was closed up tight. I looked at their fancy white roses frothing down the sides of the house, big as saucers, and perfect green lawn, and felt a bubble of anger in the pit of my stomach. I thought about all the cold cups of tea Gran had tossed into her garden beds, trying to keep her flowers alive. My finger began to **TINGLE.** Picture a lotus, I told myself, hearing my grandmother's warning in my head. But they all made me so mad: Mandy, her dad, and the people in this street who thought it was OK to have their sprinklers on all summer.

As I walked around the side of Mandy's house, my cheeks grew hot and my head began to fizz. I peered into a window but couldn't see anyone inside, so I walked around the back. By now, my vision was starting to become blurry and red. My heart pounded in my ears. I remembered Mandy's teasing sing-song voice and a big ball of anger started to build up inside me. I felt my finger TWITCH and *FIZZ* and my ears started to crackle and hiss. I was ready for whatever might happen. And this time, I wasn't going to hold back!

But then, over the humming of the air conditioners and the swishing of the sprinklers, I heard another sound. A small squawking kind of sound coming from Mandy's back porch.

I rounded the corner, and there, on the back step, sat a small, brown chicken. A very sad-looking chicken.

'Mandy?' I said.

'Buk?' said the chicken.

Suddenly all the anger rushed out of me like the air from a balloon. I just felt very sad and very silly.

'I'm sorry,' I said, approaching the little bird sitting forlornly on the back steps of the big white house. I crouched down next to her in the shade of the porch and gave her soft freckled feathers a pat.

It's true her garden was greener than all of ours, and it was true that her dad was horrible and it was true that she had been really mean to Shona today in swimming lessons. But, to tell you the truth, seeing Mandy there looking so SMALL and helpless made me feel awful. Nobody deserved this. Especially not someone I'd once thought of as a friend.

'I'm sorry, Mandy,' I said. 'This is all my fault.'

'Buk buk?' said the chicken.

I wasn't sure if she was able to understand me, but I kept talking all the same. 'I don't really know how to fix this,' I admitted, 'but I guess I probably need to learn how to manage my temper better. And, Mandy, perhaps you could quit being so mean to me and Shona? And everyone, really!'

The little brown chicken cocked her head and looked up at me with a beady black eye. For a minute I thought she was going to peck me. But then she rested her soft little head in my lap, and I felt that great big ball of heat in my belly melt away.

Just then I heard Mayor Martin's voice coming from inside the house, yelling out angrily for his daughter.

The chicken looked alarmed. 'Buk buk!' she yelped, flapping her speckled wings at me. 'Buk buk!'

'Mandy!' came the booming voice again. 'Where are you, girl? Why isn't my roast dinner on the stove? Why haven't you started your homework? Mandy? Mandy!'

I stood up. It was one thing to admit to Mandy how I had been responsible for the Terrible Thing that had happened. It was quite another thing facing her father. I ducked around the side of the house. The chicken **FLAPPED** and SQUAWKED at the back door, desperately wanting to be let in. What would Mayor Martin do when he saw a small, brown chicken on his back doorstep?

I was so scared Mayor Martin might see me there, but I also couldn't leave Mandy like this! Suddenly cool blue sparks appeared, shimmering like water. I watched them encircle the little brown chicken, making her feathers turn blue and sparkly. Then I turned away, just as the back door opened.

From the corner of my eye I saw the little blue chicken slowly change from bird to girl, feathers slipping

back into her skin, beak turning back to lips, and her small yellow claws stretching out into legs, long and straight again. You should have seen Mayor Martin's face.

Now that is something I'll remember for a long time.

Later that night, when Gran and I were waiting for Dad at our local Chinese restaurant, I told her everything that had happened that afternoon with Mandy. And I told her about the feeling that had come over me at the end. Which was still with me, to be honest. It was a good feeling; the best feeling I'd had all day.

Gran smiled and put her arm around me. 'I knew you'd work it out, sugarcakes,' she said. 'Because one thing I know for sure is that you certainly can't make people be kind by being unkind to them.'

'Do you think she might stop being a bully now?' I asked, remembering the horrible voice of Mayor Martin from inside their house.

'Whether or not this is enough to change Mandy's behaviour – or her father's, for that matter – isn't up to you,' Gran said. 'You just have to do the right thing.'

I shrugged, still not completely sure whether I had done the right thing. There was a part of me that would have really loved to turn Mayor Martin into a chicken, even though I knew this probably wouldn't have solved the problem. But to be fair, I was still a bit shaken up by that long strange day. Looking back, I realize all this was an awful lot to process at just twelve years old, in the last weeks of school during a very hot summer.

Gran must have seen what was going on in my mind because she smiled and pushed my fringe back from my forehead to plant a big, lipsticky kiss there. 'I'm proud of you,' she said, pulling me in **TIGHTLY** for a hug. 'It's one thing to have inherited the magic, but it's another thing to have experienced its strange ways. Believe me, this isn't always easy. But didn't I always warn you: "With great power comes great responsibility"?'

'Gran!' I said, rolling my eyes. 'That was from Spider-Man.'

Gran huffed. 'Well, I'm sure I would have said something equally wise.'

'Obviously!' I assured her. We both burst out laughing.

Dad had been caught up at work and was running late, so Gran and I happily sipped on tea, munched on spring rolls and people-watched while we waited for him to join us. A love of people-watching was another thing we had in common. Sometimes we would invent stories about the people we watched, the sillier the better.

On the table next to us, I watched a woman, a man and a small boy eat their dinner without talking. The little boy accidentally dropped some food on the carpet and his father began to shout at him. A waiter rushed over to clean up the mess and the boy shrank into his seat as his father raged on.

Inside my belly, I felt a heat grow and my finger began to **TINGLE . . .**

Ben Bailey Smith

The skies above New York City seemed to be promising something.

It was a crisp, bright afternoon on 23 December, and ten-year-old Jesse Henry Trotter stared up at the wisps of cloud above, hoping that they might produce the most **MAGICAL** of things: a white Christmas.

Jesse loved the journey into New York from his home (a two-hour train ride away in the state of Connecticut). He'd been doing it almost every other weekend, alongside his mum, Wendy, since he was seven, and this was the best time of all to visit.

As they approached New York, the city outside felt to Jesse as if it were in festive fancy dress. Every home, every shop, every office block they passed was dripping with colourful lights, Santa and reindeer statues, fake snow and icicles. On almost every corner there were trees trimmed to the hilt and folks rushing back and forth, laden with gifts, the breath from their huffing and puffing visible from afar.

Despite the relative quiet of the crowded carriage, Jesse began humming merrily, swinging his trusty catapult back and forth like an orchestra conductor's baton and improvised his own carol:

'Joy to world, I'm in the mood

To eat all Grandpa's food!'

I wonder if you've heard of Jesse's grandfather? His name was **JAMES HENRY TROTTER.** You will have certainly heard of his house – it was known across the globe – for his was no normal house and he was no ordinary man.

Believe it or not, James Trotter lived in a *giant peach stone,* roughly the size of a small cottage, by a huge lake in the middle of Central Park. Everyone in New York – and many around the world – knew of the legend. Over sixty years ago, a magical gigantic peach flew above the city tethered to a *thousand seagulls*, piloted by a crew of *oversized talking insects* . . . and *one little boy*: James Henry Trotter.

Jesse felt a familiar tingle of anticipation as he rapped on the Peach Stone's front door, round and perfectly carved in the outline of a peach, with a bronze door knocker sculpted to resemble a ladybird's shell. The door was framed by a beautiful, curved wooden awning above, made from braided willow branches, from which a handmade sign hung:

WELCOME TO PEACH STONE MUSEUM

Underneath, a small note was pinned, which read

CLOSED FOR THE HOLIDAYS

The door was barely open before Jesse barged in and embraced his grandfather without saying a word, who laughed, then shared a knowing smile with Wendy at the doorstep.

'Well, merry Christmas to you too!'

'I missed you, Grandpa!'

'Come on, it's freezing out there – there's some warm milk on the stove.'

'Hot chocs!' Jesse squealed.

'Oh, you betcha.'

Wendy looked on from the threshold.

'You boys behave, OK? I'll be back tonight.' The three waved goodbye and Wendy turned to face the bright lights beyond the peace of the park, excited to visit some old friends in the city.

'Two ticks,' said James as he headed out through a little hatch at the other end of the stone, leaving Jesse to reunite with a home unlike any other in the world.

Jesse breathed in the unique smell – like cut grass and burnt oak – and took a moment to appreciate the time and effort his grandad had put into this marvellous place.

If you've ever eaten a peach, you'll know that there's a reason the seed is known more commonly as a 'stone' – it's as hard as a rock! And multiplied about a hundred times in size, it meant that James had plenty of material to work with.

Though incredibly robust, the stone had the texture of wood, so James had spent years creating columns and beams to support a second floor with two cosy little bedrooms – like wooden igloos. These were connected to the ground floor by a swirling spiral staircase.

The ground floor itself was like a log cabin, badger's den and fairy's dwelling all rolled into one. The living room doubled as the mini museum, and James had carved alcoves into the walls with shelves for various exhibits and photographs, charting the unbelievable adventures of the Giant Flying Peach and its former crew.

The only element Jesse didn't like was that the kitchen, toilet and shower were all in a separate little hut, next door under a big oak tree, which meant that going for a winter wee or a late-night snack was always a bit too chilly for his liking!

Christmas cards lined the walls, many from children who had visited the museum. Tinsel twisted around the spiral staircase, and instead of a tree, James had tacked fairy lights in a Christmas-tree shape on to the far wall. Jesse traced the cable to a switch, flicked it and the wall came to life. He stood back with a smile, just as his grandad came in from the kitchen with two steaming mugs of hot chocolate.

'This should warm your cockles!'

'What are *cockles*?' Jesse said, frowning.

'Good question!' James chuckled and nudged his grandson playfully. 'When yours warm up, let me know!'

Jesse blew on his drink and took a sip.

'How come I can never make my hot chocolate taste as good as yours?'

'Ah, that's a secret ingredient me and your dad came up with.' James smiled mischievously. 'Half a teaspoon of cinnamon and a little pinch of nutmeg! It's what makes it taste **CHRISTMASSY**.'

'Did he love it too?'

'Love it? He used to wolf his down and then finish mine the second I turned my back!'

Since Jacob Trotter had died after a short illness nearly three years before, James and Jesse had become incredibly close. Sometimes a shared experience can have that effect. When Jesse's friends – and even his own mother – didn't know what to say, his grandpa did. He could tell stories about Jacob that somehow managed not to make Jesse feel sad.

'"*It was the strangest thing, Dad –*"' he said to me when I looked at my empty mug – "*a sly fox wandered in and lapped up all your cocoa, then he just . . . disappeared!*"'

Jesse chuckled.

'Is that what he said?!'

'Word for word.'

'You've got a good memory,' said Jesse. 'Sometimes I forget his face a little bit. I have to look at photos.'

'That's the beauty of stories,' James said gently. 'Stories keep the people we've loved and lost alive forever.'

Jesse lingered on one of his favourite photographs in the tiny exhibit – James and his insect friends parading in an open-top **LIMOUSINE** down Fifth Avenue in front of thousands of cheering New Yorkers.

'But if you have stories, why do you need so many pictures and objects?'

'Well, it's because every now and then you need something that doesn't live in your brain to remind you of something that does!'

James pulled a small photograph from his wallet – a weathered snap of himself, his late wife and a ten-year-old Jacob, mischievously aiming a catapult at the camera as his parents smiled down at him – the very same catapult Jesse now had in his pocket.

'Right, enough lazing about,' James said, smiling. 'I've got a job for you.'

And that was their friendship in a nutshell (or a peach stone). A grandad and grandson finding joy in sadness, the present in the past and tending to a tiny museum in perfect tandem.

But in the Christmas holidays of this year, everything was about to change.

❄

Despite a few clouds, the early afternoon sky was bright and clear. James held a ladder steady and Jesse climbed above the awning, a long fairy-light cable running from inside coiled over his shoulder.

'Clear out any debris from the gutters while you're up there,' James called.

'What's debris?'

'Bits of things you don't need in places you don't want them.'

'Hmm. Do I get money for this?'

'I've got a bag of chocolate-covered raisins with your name on it!'

'OK, deal.'

Jesse started scooping out leaves and mud from the gutters. He even found a few rogue stones in there, which he stuffed in his back pocket – they were good catapulting size. Then he worked his way from the roof downwards, stringing fairy lights over the awning outside the front door.

Then – though it was not long after midday – the sky, very suddenly, and very spookily, turned **BLACK.**

'Grandpa?'

Above them, the clouds had formed an unbroken, gloomy sheet – the sun was nowhere to be seen and the city was plunged into darkness. Well, semi-darkness, as Manhattan had so many lights (more than usual with all the added Christmas decorations). But the park in which the Peach Stone sat really was dark. And Jesse was scared.

James kept his stare fixed on the strange cloud formation, then his eyes widened as he saw a second odd phenomenon. Tiny silver *FLASHES,* lasting no more than a split second each, began dotting themselves across this black blanket.

'What on earth are they?!' James exclaimed.

'I don't know!' Jesse offered. 'But they're definitely not *from* Earth!'

'The way they **TWINKLE**,' James chuckled, 'it's actually kinda Christmassy!'

The next thing he knew, a SHARP silver shard left the blackness at rocket speed and he and James watched it hurtle down to Earth, before disappearing from view.

'Crikey!' James shouted.

'What was th–' Jesse began.

'Jesse! Get down, quick! We're under attack!'

Jesse shuffled down the ladder. Just as he reached the final rung, he actually had to JUMP under the awning as two of these strange airborne daggers crashed like javelins into the ground on either side of the peach stone.

The pair hurried inside and ran to the small front window. Hundreds of the things were falling now. James and Jesse focused on one that jutted from the ground just yards away.

'Definitely looks shiny . . .' James strained to see in the dark.

'Hold on!' Jesse flicked the switch on the fairy lights he'd just hung, then returned to the window.

'It looks like . . . *ice*! They're a bit too big for hailstones, aren't they, Grandpa? Grandpa?'

But James was lost in thought.

'I need to make a phone call.'

He rushed to the Peach Stone phone – with an old-fashioned rotary dial, which James had encased in wood.

'Grasshopper? It's me,' said James, then paused. 'Yep, I was thinking the exact same thing. *They're back.* I think we should –'

CRACK! A huge noise from above rocked the Stone – a direct hit! Jesse and James exchanged a look of pure panic.

'Grasshopper? Grasshopper!' James dropped the receiver and gave his grandson the gravest of looks. 'The line's gone dead.'

WHAM!

SMASH!

BOOM!

Frozen missiles were raining down all around them.

Jesse thought for a second.

'Grandpa, what did you mean when you said you were thinking exactly the same thing as the Old-Green-Grasshopper? Who's back?'

But before James could answer, there was a very

urgent-sounding knock on the door.

Jesse and James exchanged a glance. Who could possibly still be outside in such a storm?

'Quick,' said Jesse, 'whoever it is will need shelter!'

He opened the door to find one of his grandfather's oldest and dearest friends: Ladybird.

'Jesse!' Ladybird exclaimed. 'Season's greetings.'

SMASH!

Another bolt from the black crashed into the ground a few feet behind her.

'I think I'd better come inside!'

'How did you manage to make it through the storm?' James asked.

'And *why*?' Jesse added.

Always one for looking on the bright side, Ladybird laughed, reached over her shoulder and rapped on her shell with her fist.

'It'd take more than ice to break me, James – I'm tough as old boots. And *why*, you ask?' She turned to Jesse, 'I have a message from the NYFD.'

NYFD stood for the New York Fire Department.

Ladybird had married the chief in the joyous aftermath of the Peach's final voyage. Although he was long retired now, the couple kept many firefighting friends.

'The fire chief, the army general and the mayor all came together at the fire station, two blocks from here, before we lost power. They were headless chickens until I told them what was happening up there.'

'The Cloud-People are back.'

Ladybird nodded and Jesse gasped.

He was reminded of when he was five or six, when he sometimes couldn't get to sleep in the peach stone for fear of the mysterious Cloud-People his grandad had told him about in various tales of his airborne adventures. '*You're safe and sound on the ground,*' James used to whisper in a gentle rhyme to calm him. Now he wondered just how true that was.

'Why now?' James asked.

'Beats me,' Ladybird said, shrugging. 'But they've already caused terrible damage to a lot of buildings and cars. Everyone's been told to stay inside and the mayor has asked for you personally, James. We're all to meet at the station.'

'She asked for me?' James frowned. 'Why?'

Ladybird gave James a knowing look and shrugged.

'We need a plan.'

At the door, James frowned and put a hand on his grandson's shoulder.

'Maybe you should stay here. I'll call your mum from the fire station and let her know –'

'No way!' Jesse interrupted. 'I can help!'

'Jesse, it's dangerous out there. Every child in the city will be at home right now.'

Ladybird raised an eyebrow.

'And how old were you the last time we saw the Cloud-People?'

'Exactly!' Jesse chimed in.

'I'll keep him safe, don't you worry.' Ladybird smiled.

James sighed and gave Ladybird a small nod. With that, they opened the door and looked out into the darkness – deadly shards plummeted left and right.

Ladybird stepped out first and extended her magnificent shell into a pair of giant wings, the left sheltering James, the right sheltering Jesse. She stared ahead.

'Now all you have to do . . . *is keep up*!'

And with that, she pelted forward and both grandad and grandson did their best to match her pace.

WHOOSH! **WHAM! SMACK!**

It was like some nightmarish obstacle course. With Ladybird weaving this way and that, and James and Jesse constantly trying to anticipate her next move, there were more than a few close calls.

As they approached the East Park Fire Station, a team of helmeted soldiers appeared, pulling the huge red shutters open.

Suddenly, an enormous icicle bounced off an army tank, and flew horizontally towards Ladybird's unguarded head!

'Ladybird, watch out!' James yelled – but even Ladybird's reflexes were too slow this time. Fortunately, young Jesse's weren't. In one swift motion he pulled his catapult from his right-hand pocket, a rock he'd found in the Peach Stone's gutter from his left, and fired off a shot right at the incoming icicle, shattering it into a thousand pieces.

'Bullseye!' Jesse cheered.

'That was close!' Ladybird exclaimed.

'Too close,' James added, puffing out his cheeks.

The soldiers looked on in awe as Ladybird, Jesse and a thoroughly exhausted James hurried inside.

❄

'Good to see you again, James, although I would have preferred it were in better circumstances,' the Mayor offered, as she, the fire chief and army general greeted the Trotters. 'And this must be your grandson!'

'Jesse Trotter, ma'am.' Jesse nodded back. 'Reporting for duty!'

The Mayor laughed and nodded to James. 'He's a Trotter all right!'

'Seems so, ma'am,' said James.

'Mind your backs!' a private called, as a tank slowly

rolled into the cavernous station and came to a halt. A hush fell over the group as the small round door atop the vehicle flipped open.

Jesse watched in awe as a wrinkly green head appeared, complete with a glint in his ageing eyes – it was the Old-Green-Grasshopper!

'Afternoon all,' he said with a wry smile. 'Or is it evening? Quite hard to tell in this weather!'

The Grasshopper climbed out and two soldiers helped him down from the tank, as another voice called out from inside it. 'Even harder for me!'

Jesse beamed as he saw a floppy safari hat, then the unmistakable dark glasses of the Earthworm.

'I can't see much at the best of times!'

'Darling, you can't see anything at any time,' said Miss Spider, following close behind, cradling the sleeping Glow-worm in two of her legs and passing him to a soldier.

Next Jesse watched a fine, shiny cord shoot out over the side of the tank, followed by the Silkworm, gracefully abseiling down her ready-made climbing rope, her little cape flapping behind her.

'What have I missed?' she asked playfully.

The Mayor took in the assembled group.

'Right then, shall we get started?'

'Not quite yet, ma'am, still one to go.'

Everyone looked at the tank.

'Just start without me, for heaven's sake!' a voice echoed from within. 'I don't even know why I'm here! I mean, I was having the nap of my life back there. Next thing I know, some hoodlum is yanking me out of bed, claiming to be a soldier of the US Army. I said I don't care if you're the king of England, how dare you wake a centipede from his precious slumber! The bare-faced *cheek* of it!'

Jesse chuckled, Miss Spider rolled her eyes and called out, 'Centipede, this is an emergency meeting, maybe the most important you'll ever attend! Now get out here!'

'Fine,' the Centipede huffed, and after much banging and clanging from inside, eventually poked his head up into view.

'Will there be snacks?'

'Here's the rub of it,' the General said in his matter-of-fact, Generally way. 'We can't send planes up there. The risk of icicles getting in the turbines is too great. We'd lose the fleet for sure. And we can't shoot 'em down, there's just too many of 'em.'

'What we're faced with here is the equivalent of an asteroid storm,' said the Mayor. 'Somehow we've gotta get behind it and speak to these Cloud fellows – and who knows them better than you?'

'But even if we could confront them, there's no way to get there in the first place,' Earthworm countered.

The General cleared his throat. 'Well, what we were thinking was – the impenetrable nature of that Peach Stone of yours . . . it's tougher than our tanks. It could withstand any asteroid storm.'

The Centipede gave a dry laugh through a mouthful of biscuits. 'You're not serious! And where would we find a thousand seagulls right now? Are they just wandering down Fifth Avenue? Perhaps they're all doing their Christmas shopping.'

The Mayor pointed to James. 'That's why you're here.'

'Me?'

'Uh-huh. The brains of this outfit. You gotta work out a way to get up there and stop these Cloudfolk before they destroy my city!'

The room fell silent for a moment.

'Think, James, *think*,' Ladybird begged her old friend.

James shook his head and sighed. 'I'm all out of ideas.' He turned to Jesse. 'I'm gonna call your mum, let her know you're safe.' A firefighter took him over to an emergency phone.

Jesse flopped uncomfortably on to a nearby bench – he'd forgotten his back pockets still contained stones and a catapult. He pulled them out and let them fall to the floor, then sat, elbows on his knees, chin in the palms of his hands, staring helplessly at the pile. Suddenly, his eyes widened, and he jumped up like a jack-in-the-box.

'Wait!'

Everyone turned to him.

'I've got it!'

❄

Two hours had passed and stage one of Jesse's plan was in full swing.

'This is madness. Sheer madness,' blubbered the Earthworm.

The Centipede baulked at him. 'It's worse than madness, you peabrain – it's a death wish!'

'If it is,' said Ladybird, shrugging, 'at least I wouldn't have to listen to you two any more.'

'It's **GENIUS,'** said James, winking at his grandson. 'And true genius is always a little bit bonkers, isn't it?'

Centipede shook his head. 'Fools! I'm surrounded by fools.'

'Oh, Centipede, you moaning Minnie!' Ladybird scolded. 'Why don't you and Grasshopper sing us a good old-fashioned working song? Do something you're actually good at.'

Centipede sighed and turned to the Old-Green-Grasshopper. '*Fine*.'

The Grasshopper rubbed his upper legs together,

making a sound like a bow on a violin string, and struck up a jaunty melody.

'B-sharp, please, old boy, you're out of my range,' said Centipede, then cleared his throat.

'*Oh, what a truly lovely day it is for you and I,*
What a sunny disposition, I feel so alive!
Oh, what fun we're having, such a bubbly little time,
I couldn't pick a better moment to go out and die!'

'Centipede!'

'What? I sing from the heart.'

'How long until the stone gets here?' James asked the General.

'Patrol should be back any minute, sir,' the General replied.

Sure enough, a moment later two armoured tanks pulled up, with the giant stone strapped on to a rolling platform between them.

A pair of fire officers slid the two huge red doors open and everyone gasped at the jaw-dropping sight outside – Jesse *really* did have a plan.

❄

Miss Spider had spun a **HUGE** horizontal web, spanning the width of the street outside, tethered up high between opposite buildings, like a **GIANT** hammock. She then trailed one strong cord from underneath the centre, which James now attached to the empty hose-reel of a fire engine. The firemen spun the wheel, pulling the web down to the ground and tying it off so it sat like a tightly coiled spring.

Or a catapult ready to fire.

Jesse smiled with satisfaction.

'Right. Time for Stage Two: Lift-off.'

'Er – I have a question.'

'What is it, Earthworm?' Jesse asked.

'Well, if – and let's face it, it's a big if – but *if* we make it up there, how in blazes do you suggest we stay up there long enough to converse with those Cloud-People?'

Jesse nodded towards Silkworm as she climbed to the top of the Stone, attaching a thick cord of silk with a loop on the end to the stalk, like a giant lasso.

'That's Stage Three,' Jesse said, grinning. 'Leave that to me.'

The soldiers then used a forklift to hoist the stone into the centre of the web.

'A-a-a-and,' Earthworm stammered, 'how do we get . . . *back*?'

Jesse looked sheepish. 'Stage Four. Not sure yet.'

'We'll figure that out,' the General offered. 'You just focus on getting up there!'

'*And* . . . how are you so sure we'll hit the target?' Earthworm wailed. 'Surely it's a lottery! You may as well leave the navigation to me!'

'You may be wrong there, buddy,' a soldier piped up. 'Why, we saw the kid hit an icicle with a slingshot from twenty yards, didn't we?'

'*Yessiree!*'

'Uh-huh!'

'The boy's hawk-eyed!'

Jesse looked up at James, who noticed a glimmer of fear in his grandson's face for the first time.

'I hope they're right,' Jesse whispered.

'You know what my grandad used to say?' James winked and grinned. '"*Trust a Trotter.*"'

❄

'Welcome aboard Giant Peach Stone Flight Zero Zero Two.' Jesse stood at the threshold, adopting a captain's voice as the team gingerly boarded the Stone. 'Please follow the safety instructions. We hope you have a pleasant flight.'

Centipede sat and folded his top eight legs in the way a disgruntled human might fold their arms.

'Very funny.'

As James boarded, he stopped and crouched down to Jesse.

'You don't have to do this, you know. I've told your mum you're here, safe and sound at the fire station.'

Jesse smiled his cheekiest smile. 'Then that's all she needs to know! I'm coming, Grandpa. You're gonna need me!'

Outside, a fire officer stood by the hose-reel with an axe poised above Miss Spider's taut cord.

'Launching in T-minus *TEN*!' the General called.

'*NINE!*'

The team huddled together on a wooden bench in a carved alcove while Silkworm strapped a worm-made silk seatbelt across them all.

'Well, this is it,' said Centipede. 'I wish I could say it's been nice knowing you.' The General's countdown echoed from outside the stone.

'*EIGHT! SEVEN!*'

'Tell my wife I love her,' wailed Earthworm.

'You never married, Earthworm,' said Grasshopper.

'A worm can dream, can't he?'

'*SIX! FIVE!*'

Jesse shuddered, suddenly nervous.

'Hold my hand, Jesse – don't be afraid,' offered Ladybird.

'*FOUR!* ***THREE!***'

'I've got eight more if you need!' added Miss Spider. Jesse took one of hers in his other hand and squeezed his eyes shut.

'TWO!'

'Here goes nothing!'

'ONE!!!'

TWANG!

If you've ever been on a rollercoaster, you'll know that feeling of going from a standstill to superspeed – it's like you've left your stomach behind.

And that's very much how the cabin crew of Giant Peach Stone Flight 002 felt when the axe came down on Miss Spider's cord.

WHOOSH!

Just as Jesse had planned, the web served as a giant slingshot, rocketing the Peach Stone directly up into the skies. What a sight that must have been for any brave New Yorker peering through their windows at that moment: the stone of an old peach, the size of a house, flying through a barrage of icy silver missiles.

The General was right: the Cloud-People's missiles were no match for the stone's rock-hard exterior. From the outside it had the look of a giant bowling ball, taking out tens of shiny skittles, strike after strike after strike.

Then, before they knew it, their speed began to slow.

'This is it! Time for Stage Three,' Jesse said.

'You mean we're not dead yet?' Earthworm wailed. 'There are more horrors to endure?'

'Miss Spider, are you feeling brave?' Jesse asked.

'I hope so!'

'You've got the stickiest feet – come with me!'

'What's he doing? What's he doing?' The Earthworm flailed about in terror.

'He's opening the door!' Ladybird shouted.

'He'll kill us all!'

James shivered, imagining what Wendy would have to say about all this.

Jesse pulled open the door and a huge gust of ice-cold wind blew in, making everyone gasp. He climbed on to Miss Spider's back and the two edged their way out and up to the stone's stalk, hundreds of miles from the safety of Earth.

Jesse and Miss Spider looked down. They were above the clouds! Below them, just to their left, lay the sprawling Cloud City, laid out on a mile-wide, metres-thick sheet of ice, itself resting improbably on top of a strange, voluminous cloud that sparkled like a gigantic sequined pillowcase. The city's towering ice-sculpted buildings shimmered in a magical moonlight – it was a magnificent sight that took Jesse's breath away.

'Here goes nothing!'

Using every ounce of his strength, he swung and swung, until he'd whipped the silk rope into a loop above his head.

SWISH!

Off flew the loop, just as the stone stopped rising and began heading downwards.

'Bullseye!'

The silk loop snared a particularly tall building.

'OK. Hold on!' Jesse yelled and the pair clung to the stalk as tightly as they could. They flew down past the surface of the Cloud City, and for a millisecond Jesse caught the faces of a hundred very shocked Cloud-People.

TWANG!

Silkworm's lasso held and the stone shuddered, bounced, bobbed and finally stilled. Jesse puffed out his cheeks.

'What now, Captain?' Miss Spider asked.

Jesse looked up.

'I guess we go say hello.'

❄

'The Cloud-People are very suspicious. We don't want them thinking this is an attack or a trap of any kind,' James said as the gang struggled up the lasso's cord towards the Cloud City surface, where they saw a crowd amassing.

'That's right,' Jesse agreed from above. 'In fact . . . Hey, Silkworm, can I borrow your cape?'

Silkworm pulled off her dainty white shawl and passed it to Centipede, who passed it up the line to where Jesse stood. Jesse took the shawl and, nearing the city's edge, waved it towards a group of Cloud-Guards – a universal signal of surrender or peace. He hoped it had the same meaning up here as it did back home.

'Hello, there!'

'Please don't kill us!' Earthworm screamed from further below.

The gang clambered one by one on to the city surface. Up close, the Cloud-People were most curious-looking.

Firstly, they were big - almost twice as big as you or I. Their limbs poked out from bodies that seemed coated in fine lambs wool, with wispy, candy floss-like hair on top of their angular heads. But one thing was certain. Every one of their otherworldly faces looked very angry indeed.

James held up his hands and smiled warmly. He adopted the gentlest tone he could muster.

'We'd just like to talk. If we may?'

Without reply, the guards grabbed each of their unwelcome guests and frogmarched them through the city's streets.

Despite their fear, the gang marvelled as they looked up at the sparkling architecture – tall, JAGGED homes sculpted quite beautifully from ice. Jesse even saw what looked like a playground, with young Cloud-People sliding around an ice rink in the centre. Soon there was a collective intake of breath as they approached a grand but ominous building, the biggest they'd seen so far. It was surrounded by a moat of solid ice with a huge glistening portcullis, turrets on every corner and more Cloud-Guards patrolling walkways around the sparkling roof. *Someone important lives here*, Jesse thought. Centipede wriggled furiously, resisting his guard's grip.

'Unhand me, you swine!'

'Centipede, be patient,' whispered James. 'Aggression won't work here.'

'*Nothing* will work,' gulped Earthworm. 'You don't expect to reason with these beastly fellows? They'll kill us all!'

'You don't know that,' Jesse assured him, as the huge portcullis swung down.

'It looks like a palace!' Miss Spider marvelled.

'Or a prison,' Earthworm whimpered. 'Or worse!'

'I feel a song coming on,' Centipede said. 'Grasshopper? A funeral march, please.'

❄

The gang shuffled into the GRAND hall of the magnificent ice palace. It had beautiful, intricate carvings on the walls, shimmering like diamonds, which seemed to show Cloud-People of the past in various victorious poses. In the centre of the hall sat what looked like a giant water fountain, except the plumes raining down into the pool were streaks of ice, frozen in time.

Ahead of them was a set of shiny steps leading to a huge stage, on top of which sat a giant throne occupied by an ominous figure: a Cloud-Woman sporting a huge crown of ice. Her face was long and pointy, like an upside-down triangle, her cheekbones, chin and brow all sharpened like pencil tips. Her hair, rolling underneath the crown, had the appearance of white candyfloss. She stood and all the guards knelt. The gang followed suit, Centipede hauling the gormless Earthworm down with him.

The Cloud-Woman looked upon them from the stage and when she finally spoke, her tone had the piercing quality of an operatic soprano.

'Who dares enter Queen Zephra's city without permission?'

James cleared his throat.

'Er, Your . . . Majesty?' he began tentatively. 'My name is James Henry Trotter. These are my friends. I know we're uninvited, but we have a bit of an urgent request.'

The Queen's eyes widened. '*You* are making demands of *me*?'

'Not at all, ma'am,' James offered quickly. 'More a, uh, humble plea. I'm not sure if you're aware, but your icicles are raining down on our city, causing damage and distress.'

'Aware?' The Queen gave a mirthless laugh. 'I ordered the strikes!'

'May I ask why?'

The Queen slowly descended the steps until she was so close to James that he could feel her icy breath on his face. The gang all seemed to shiver in unison.

'Mr Trotter. We Cloud-People do not bother Earthlings. We follow the winds, settling wherever the season is frosty enough for our city to survive. We settled above your human city and found ourselves under attack! How would you expect me to respond?'

'Attack? What tosh!' Centipede called out and a guard poked him with the handle of his spear.

'Centipede!' Jesse hissed.

'I think what my friend is asking, Your Majesty,' James continued, 'is what exactly you mean by an attack?'

'You attack our peace, Mr Trotter. By flying your huge, winged tin cans through our clouds. By choking us with the acrid, poisonous fumes of your wheeled vehicles rising from the streets below. The noise alone is enough to keep our children awake all night!'

'I see,' said James calmly. 'I have to say, I don't think anyone below purposefully tried to upset you and your people.'

'It's a little late for that, I'm afraid,' the Queen replied sternly.

'It doesn't have to be,' James offered. 'We have some pretty important friends down there. What if I were to promise that, for the rest of the winter, there'll be no planes in your path, less fumes from below and as little noise as we can muster?'

The Queen eyed James suspiciously.

'*A promise*. Why should I trust you?'

James looked at Jesse, who returned his questioning eyes with a look that said *keep going*!

James took a deep breath.

'I've been here once before.'

'You?' the Queen scoffed and called out to her subjects. 'Anyone here remember an old man coming to visit?'

'I wasn't old then. In fact, it was sixty years ago – I was a boy. And I was scared then, just as I am now. But then I saw other little children. Your Cloud-Children. And I remember thinking we weren't that different. We all have feelings and hopes and fears. Looking back, I think your people were just as scared as we were. We can all get frightened of things we don't know.'

The Queen raised a single frosty eyebrow. Her guards tensed behind her, tightening the grips on their weapons, and James's speech sped up a little.

'But now you know me, Your Majesty, and I know you know that nobody, no matter who they are or where they're from, ever wishes to live in fear or risk losing people they love. I remember the first time I felt it. I was no older than your little ones when I lost my mum and dad. For a moment I thought I might be alone, in fear, *forever*.'

James went quiet and Jesse looked up at his grandfather. The sheer, bright whiteness of the icy world around them bounced back off James's gentle eyes and seemed to make them **GLISTEN.** Something made the boy pipe up.

'I've felt it too. It's the worst feeling in the world – it really is!'

Jesse paused, his face scrunching up as if he was trying to push the right words out. 'Until . . .'

He took in the many faces turned his way, which seemed to be willing him on. 'Until it isn't any more.'

Jesse exhaled deeply and felt a reassuring pat on his shoulder from James. Grandfather and grandson turned back to face the Queen.

James waited until his eyes locked with hers and said, 'Every life is at risk of loss – of some kind – at some stage. But sometimes there's a chance – a brilliantly lucky chance – to stop the loss from happening in the first place. Maybe this is one of those chances!'

The Queen raised her other eyebrow to join the first, softening the harsher points of her angular face.

James bowed his head slightly and, speaking a little slower, a little quieter, but with greater assurance said, 'All we ask is that you give us that chance. A chance to go back home and let everyone know that your people may look cold, but they have hearts every bit as warm as ours.'

The royal eyebrows returned from their journey and Queen Zephra stared at James for a moment in silence, as one might stare at a tricky crossword puzzle. Jesse looked up at his grandad with pride and reached out to take hold of his hand. At that moment, two young Cloud-Children, both sporting crowns, popped out from behind the throne and joined the Queen.

'I'm guessing these are Their Majesties, the Prince and Princess,' Jesse asked.

The Queen nodded.

Jesse took a step towards the royal children. The siblings exchanged a look. He reached into his back pocket and pulled out his catapult.

'This is the most **VALUABLE** thing I own,' said Jesse. He held it out to the Prince and Princess. 'I want you to have it. A gift. To show you we'll keep our promise.'

The children took it gleefully and Jesse showed them how it worked.

The Queen smiled, shared a look with James and held his stare as she called out.

'Guards! Release them! And cease fire!' She turned to the Trotters. 'Now. Perhaps we should discuss just how you're going to get home.'

❄

At the city's edge, right above where the stone dangled, Centipede looked on doubtfully as a group of Cloud-Guards blew huge amounts of snow down on to Central Park below.

'You're certain that'll cushion our fall?'

'Like leaving one cloud and landing on another,' the Queen said, smiling.

'Goodbye, Your Highness. And thank you.' James bowed.

Jesse waved to the royal children. 'See ya!'

The Princess playfully threw a snowball at him and everyone laughed as Jesse dramatically collapsed, pretending he'd been hit by a boulder. Then they all exchanged farewells and the group headed back down the lasso.

Last inside, Jesse stayed by the door as the rest of the gang sat back under Silkworm's seatbelt. The Stone swayed gently back and forth.

'Jesse,' said James. 'Hey, Jesse. Come and get strapped in.'

'I'm gonna tell 'em when to cut the cord. Just waiting for the Stone to steady itself.'

'He's right,' said Ladybird. 'We need to fall straight and true, then we'll hit that lovely big pile of snow down there.'

Silkworm looked uncertain. 'And if we don't fall straight . . .?'

'We're worm-meat!' Earthworm cried.

'Yuck,' said Centipede. 'Speak for yourself.'

'OK,' said Jesse. He opened the door and called up. 'Countdown from five!'

He closed the door and walked over to the bench, strapping himself in with the others. From outside they heard:

'FIVE!'

'Here we go again!' Grasshopper said, squeezing his old eyes shut in hope.

'FOUR! ***THREE!'***

'We've made it this far,' said Jesse as cheerily as he could.

'TWO!'

'I think we're gonna be –'

'ONE!'

❄

'We lurched!' Centipede screamed. 'I felt a lurch! That was a lurch there! We definitely lurched!'

Jesse tried to control his panic. 'Hopefully not by too much. Miss Spider, can you climb to the window?'

Miss Spider, though terrified herself, nodded vigorously and, slipping from the seatbelt, crept along the wall to the window.

'We're definitely off course! Heading for the park but . . .'

'What?' Centipede shouted, 'But what?!'

Miss Spider turned to face the gang.

'Not towards anything soft.'

She was right. The Stone was hurtling towards – of all

areas – a formation of large rocks, on which children would normally climb and play in the summer. Centipede wailed.

'We'll be smashed to smithereens!'

'We're done for!' Earthworm cried.

'This really is the end!' Ladybird squealed.

'Oh, Grandad,' groaned Jesse, 'you were right, I never should have come!'

'We would have all perished already without you, Jesse. You're the bravest person I've ever met.'

'I love you, Grandpa!'

'I love you too, Jess.'

The pair hugged.

'That said,' said James. 'If we make it out alive, your mum's gonna kill me!'

Somehow the pair managed a chuckle. James put his arm round Jesse and pulled him in close. Then the whole gang moved closer to each other, creating as much comfort as they could.

'This is it,' said Miss Spider.

They all exchanged the most solemn of glances, then everyone squeezed their eyes shut.

BOING!!!

Just when they thought it was all over, the Stone was suddenly, inexplicably . . . flying back UPWARDS.

Jesse opened one eye.

'Guys. Guys! We're alive!' The gang all looked at Jesse in shock. 'And I think we're going . . . *up*!'

'Not again!' Earthworm cried.

The Stone met a sudden, weightless stillness.

'Wait . . .' said James.

Then it began to plummet again!

Centipede closed his eyes. 'Oh, I can't take this!'

Up they went again!

'What is going on?' James asked, as – sooner than before – the Stone began another descent.

BOING!!!

On this third boing, the Stone began to bounce up and down in quicker, smaller spurts, shaking the gang like an old bottle of ketchup.

'I think I'm going to be sick,' Centipede moaned.

But the bouncing became more gentle and, as a huge cheer echoed from outside, Jesse smiled.

'We're gonna be OK!'

❄

Jesse opened the door. His eyes widened as the gang gathered behind him.

They were in the middle of Central Park, right above the rocks, but rather than being smashed to smithereens, the Stone was nestled in the centre of Miss Spider's giant web!

A huge crowd surrounded them, cheering and waving. The Cloud-People's mini snowstorm had given the park a dusting that made it look like a winter wonderland. The Mayor stepped forward with a megaphone.

'Ladies and gentlemen of New York! Welcome back the heroes who saved your city!'

The General and his soldiers helped the crew down from the web. From the safety of the ground, Jesse looked back at the Stone, resting just metres above the rock formation in the web, which had been fastened to the tops of nearby trees.

'But how . . .?'

'We tracked your trajectory all the way down,' the General said. 'Soon as we'd calculated where you might land, we brought Miss Spider's web over from the fire station. Hey, kid, don't leave me hangin'!'

The General held up a palm and Jesse jumped up to give him a high-five.

Whoops and hollers rang in the gang's ears. Grasshopper waved. Miss Spider and Ladybird even did a little curtsy. A photographer gathered the group for a picture.

'It was nothing, really!' Centipede smiled. 'All in a day's work, I assure you!'

James and Jesse hugged each other, then Jesse looked out into the crowd as he heard a familiar voice.

'Jesse! Jesse! Oh, thank God!'

It was Jesse's mum, Wendy, pushing through the crowd. James smiled and the three of them embraced warmly.

'We made it, Mum, we did it!'

James shrugged. 'Your son's a hero.'

Wendy smiled and nudged her father-in-law playfully. 'And you are the worst babysitter in history!'

Meanwhile, Grasshopper had struck up a tune and Centipede led the crowd in song.

'Well, there's no better time of the year
Than when you know Christmas is near
And also especially fun when you know
You've not died like you previously feared.
We almost missed all of the fun
For that crash could have killed everyone!
We'd have got splattered
And you'd have got flattened
By a stone of one hundred tons!
So roll out the festive festivities
And thank the dear lord that we're living, please.
Let's dance in this wintery weather together
Be you human, cloud-folk or centipede!'

James nudged Jesse.

'I'm sorry if I ever doubted you, Jess.'

'You should be,' said Jesse, laughing. 'I never doubted you! *Trust a Trotter*, right?'

James smiled and ruffled the boy's hair. 'Right!'

People from all over the city danced and sang together in the park with the snow shimmering around them. Jesse looked up to the sky and nodded in silent thanks. Tomorrow would be Christmas Eve and families across New York would be able to prepare for the big day in peace and happiness.

And perhaps this would be a Christmas when they realized that fear – no matter how scary it may seem – could always be overcome.

❄

In many ways it was a **CHRISTMAS DAY** like any other. Jesse with his mother and grandfather, opening presents and sharing memories.

In other ways, it was totally different. For a start, New York was quieter than it had ever been. For this winter season and every winter to come, the Mayor had ordered a no-fly zone over the city, and only quiet electric cars, trains and buses were allowed on the streets – a promise kept to their Cloud cousins.

James carefully framed the photograph of the gang greeting the crowd in the park and hung it proudly alongside the others in the centre of the exhibit. He and Jesse stood back and admired it.

'There's still one more gift,' Wendy said, approaching the pair with a wrapped parcel. Jesse grinned with excitement and ripped open the paper. Inside was a beautiful pen and leather-bound notebook. Both bore the initials *JHT*.

'They were your dad's. Just like the catapult. I figured you've probably grown out of shooting things by now.' His mother shrugged. 'But you might wanna write about it all someday.'

And he did.

He wrote it all down and left the story right there in the museum for visitors to read. Eventually they made copies, sending the story around the world . . . and guess what?

You've just finished reading it.

Hannah Gold

One winter's day, down in the valley, three children were playing a game.

It was not a very nice game – but this was hardly surprising given who these children were. They were the sons of Boggis, Bunce and Bean: three farmers with an unenviable reputation.

The **TALLEST** and THINNEST of the three boys was called Beansprout. There was nothing especially remarkable about him, other than the fact he hated baths and had a tendency to smell of stinky feet (and the occasional cowpat).

The second boy was Boggis Junior. There was nothing special about him either, except for the fact that even though he was perfectly capable of speaking, he much preferred to grunt instead.

The final member of this trio was Bunce Junior. The shortest of the three boys, he was often accompanied by his boxer dog. It was hard to say who looked the more intimidating.

The game the three boys were playing involved taking turns in whacking a large metal bucket against a tree.

This tree was a beautiful tender sapling that had sprouted from the ancient oak tree that once marked this spot. As they rained blows, the three of them sang a song.

BOGGIS and **BUNCE** and **BEAN**
So **SMART**, so CLEVER, so CLEAN[1].
STRIKING in looks
And **BRILLIANT** crooks
As HANDSOME as ever you've seen.

With each hateful thwack, the three boys let out a guffaw of laughter.

Unbeknown to the three Young Farmers, they were being observed by a pair of watchful, amber-coloured eyes. These belonged to Frankie, the second youngest cub of Mr and Mrs Fox, who at this moment was hidden just out of sight in the entrance to the family den.

How dare they? thought Frankie, her paws curled in anger. To a thoughtful fox like Frankie, all life was sacred – even trees. *Why do they always have to be so horrible?*

---

1 The boys were not, in fact, clean.

Just as Beansprout swung the bucket again, a loud voice bellowed out from one of the three nearby farmhouses. The farmhouses were owned by Boggis, Bunce and Bean, and not that long ago they had been stationed much further away from the den entrance. But after Mr Fox, Frankie's father, was caught stealing their livestock, the three farmers tried their hardest to dig out the family of foxes from their den. When that failed, they filled in the gigantic crater they'd dug and rebuilt each of their farmhouses next to the den entrance. This way, they could ensure no foxes would ever escape.

'LUNCHTIME, BOYS!' Farmer Bunce called again. 'GOOSE LIVER AND DUCK FAT PIE!'

Beansprout, Bunce and Boggis screeched in delight. The three of them trampled through the snow, towards the farmhouse.

Frankie let out a sigh of relief.

She hadn't *intended* to spy on them. After that terrifying time when the Fox family had almost been dug out and killed, Mr Fox came up with a brilliant plan. This involved the creation of an underground haven, which ensured that none of the animals ever needed to step outside again to find their food.

The outside world was too dangerous.

But it was also **BEAUTIFUL.** The snow sparkled like diamonds under the winter sun, like something precious and alive – something hallowed that beckoned Frankie with every fibre of her being.

'Oh! I wish I could step outside!' she murmured wistfully. 'Just once – to feel the crunch of the snow under my paws.'

She inched forward, her black nose quivering in the clean open air.

'But I can't,' she sighed. 'Dad has worked so hard at creating our home.'

And it was true that over the past few years the underground den had become remarkable. There were rugs woven out of spider silk, beds as soft as cotton wool, tables and chairs carved out of the old oak tree, even paintings on the wall (including numerous portraits of the dapper Mr Fox). Each of the animal families, including the Badgers, the Weasels, the Rabbits and the

Moles, had their own private chambers. There were also a handful of communal areas such as the Library, the Storeroom and the Feast Room.

'Really, it is the best of homes!' said Frankie, reprimanding herself. 'And it is quite wrong of me to want to explore the outside world . . .'

But no matter how often she said this – and she would say it at least once a day – her words never felt entirely true. Not on the inside anyway, where all secrets matter.

'*Frankie!*' It was her brother Freddie. 'There you are! I've been looking for you everywhere. Dad wants us all in his study for an . . . an –' he sneezed loudly – 'an Important Announcement!'

Frankie took one last longing gaze at the outdoors before another thunderous sneeze took hold of Freddie. Her youngest brother, who sneezed at almost everything, appeared to be having an allergic reaction to the fresh air.

She grasped his paw, and the pair of them scampered deep into the den, until they arrived at a door that had a shiny gold plaque saying:

FANTASTIC

Underneath this sign was another, which said:

MR FOX'S STUDY

And underneath this, in tiny gold lettering, was yet another, which said: **ENTER IF YOU DARE!**

Frankie knocked – she was a polite fox after all – and then entered.

The study was one of her favourite places. Not just because it was where she would often find her beloved father thinking quietly about his latest master plan, but also because it was crammed full of books. These books weren't just lines of ink on paper. They were doorways to the outside world. A world full of wonder and adventure. If she couldn't actually see the outside world, a book was the next best thing. Though preferably, if Frankie was being honest with herself, a book with pictures.

Mr Fox stood behind his desk, and there was a spark of excitement dancing in his eyes.

'Ah, there you are! My two Smallest Foxes. Please do join the others and take a seat.'

Already in the study were Frankie's two elder brothers, Felix and Fraser, currently squabbling over whose turn it was to sit in the one comfortable armchair. The two Smallest Foxes, used to their brothers' constant bickering, sat quietly on the rug in front of the desk.

'As you know, our annual Winter Feast is the day after tomorrow!' proclaimed Mr Fox, gazing proudly at his fox cubs. 'A time of celebration and thanksgiving for everything we have created in our most magnificent den. A feast of kings, where all the underground families are invited!'

At the word 'family', Mr Fox surveyed the room. There was, of course, one Fox missing. Frankie's nose twitched in the air. As if on cue, her mother came into the room. She had been in the middle of baking some breakfast buns (Mr and Mrs Fox took it in turns to do the cooking) and there was a faint whiff of cinnamon.

'Sorry I'm late,' Mrs Fox said, taking her place by Mr Fox's side and squeezing his paw.

Freddie sneezed. Cinnamon was another thing he was allergic to.

'Bless you, my Smallest Fox,' said Mr Fox. 'Now the reason for gathering you here today is because I have come up with a cunning plan for us this year. *And what is most cunning about this plan?* I hear you cry. Because once again it makes fools of those three farmers, Boggis, Bunce and Bean!'

Mrs Fox placed a proud arm round her husband. 'Can you believe they are still waiting at the entrance hole for us to come out, when all this time we have been taking their food from right under their noses?!'

Mr Fox preened his whiskers modestly before continuing. He was not one for showing off too much.

'In previous years it has always been I who has selected the best produce for the Winter Feast,' said Mr Fox. 'But this year –' he twitched his ears mischievously – 'this year, I have decided upon a change. *Why?* I hear you ask – especially when I have done such a fantastic job so far of procuring our food.' Mr Fox cupped a paw to his ear.

'Why?' asked the four Small Foxes obediently.

'A good question! Why indeed? Because as from tomorrow, Boggis, Bunce and Bean have decided to go on holiday!'

'A holiday!' gasped Freddie, as if he had never heard of such a thing. 'But who are they putting in place to guard their farms?'

'Who do you think?' said Mr Fox, drawing out his words in anticipation. 'Why, none other than those three Turnip Brains that they call their children.'

Frankie clapped her paw over her muzzle in astonishment.

'So this year, instead of me acquiring the food for the Winter Feast –' Mr Fox paused dramatically – 'it shall be you! Yes, you. My four Small Foxes.'

Felix and Fraser guffawed and high-fived each other, Freddie sneezed three times in happiness while Frankie's insides did a somersault.

'Felix and Fraser,' said Mr Fox, turning to the two Eldest Foxes, 'you have the job of finding us the plumpest chickens from Boggis's farm, and the most succulent hams from Bunce's storeroom.'

As the pair of them bickered over who was going to get what, Mr Fox turned his attention to Freddie and softened his gaze. 'Now, Freddie, due to your, er, sneezing incident with the feathers, I do not think it is a sensible idea to send you anywhere near a bird coop. Sneezing and stealing are not the best companions. Instead,' he said, tilting his head to one side as if he had only just come up with the idea (and not been planning this very moment for weeks) – 'you shall be in charge of acquiring the cider. We don't want mere thimbles of the stuff, mind. We want flagons! Enough to bathe in. All good feasts are washed down with cider, as you know.'

Freddie nodded with relief. Cider he could do.

Mr Fox's eyes finally settled on Frankie.

'My sole vixen cub,' Mr Fox said. 'You have the grandest, most important job of all. You, my darling girl, are in charge of acquiring a turkey! And not just any turkey either. We want the **PLUMPEST,** juiciest prize turkey in the whole of Bean's turkey coop.'

Frankie gulped.

'You can do this, Frankie,' encouraged Mrs Fox.

Of course she could do it. She was, after all, a fox. And not just any fox. She was the daughter of the Fantastic Mr Fox.

Stealing wasn't the issue.

No. That wasn't the issue at all.

Nor was taking the prize turkey.

The issue was taking *any* turkey.

It wasn't because she had any particular qualms about stealing from Boggis, Bunce and Bean. Especially when the alternative was her family starving to death – or even having her tail shot off. Frankie shuddered as she glanced at the glass frame on the wall behind her father's desk. In it was the last, solitary strand of his once bushy fox tail – the only piece he had managed to salvage. The three farmers had shot the rest of it off when Mr Fox had tried to leave the den.

Yes, he had gone on to outwit them, cunningly digging a series of underground tunnels that took the foxes direct to the farmers' produce, without even having to step outside.

And yes, he'd had the last strand of his tail framed proudly on the wall, swearing it gave him good luck.

And yes, the thought of losing her own beautiful brush was horrible.

But that wasn't the problem.

The problem was that Frankie was the unfoxiest of things.

She was a vegetarian.

It had started back in spring, on a day when the bleating of lambs echoed **CHEERFULLY** down the tunnel – the kind of sound that makes you smile inside your heart. But the next day the bleating had stopped. Instead, there was a horrible silence, punctured only by the cries of mother sheep. The mournful noise of the ewes had rattled and rolled in Frankie's eardrums for weeks. Up until that point, she was ashamed to admit that she had never really stopped to think about her food, other than it was quite tasty. But from that point on, she swore never to eat animals again.

It wasn't as if she could admit to being vegetarian, either. Her father thought only rabbits ate vegetables – and that's the way it should stay. So, for the past six months, she'd had to pretend to eat her meat, while all the time saving her portions and giving them to Bella Badger, her closest friend in the den. Bella, an accomplished artist and sculptor, had in return painted a picture for Frankie of the Great Outside.

'Frankie?' asked her dad. 'What say you to this most cunning of plans?'

Frankie felt the gaze of the entire Fox family on her sharp face. She swallowed once. And then nodded, nervously.

'Fantastic!' said Mr Fox and clapped his paws together in glee.

❋

The next day at dawn, the four Small Foxes headed off on their respective missions.

Felix and Fraser made their way through the tunnels that took them to Boggis's chicken coop and Bunce's storeroom, still arguing over who was going to do what. Freddie scurried down another tunnel straight to Bean's cider cellar while Frankie made her way through a fourth tunnel to Bean's turkey farm.

Originally the turkey farm had been located in an orchard. But Bean had realized he could farm far more turkeys if he did so inside (and make lots more money in the process), so these days the turkeys were all housed in one giant barn.

The tunnel to the turkey barn had been added in more recent years by Mr Fox, the entrance to the hole craftily concealed by one of the feed pens.

Frankie raced through the tunnel, knowing each of its twists and turns off by heart. She made it to the entrance to the barn and poked out her snout. She sniffed once. Even though this was her first solo adventure, Dad had taken the Small Foxes with him on many previous missions, so she knew exactly what to do. The first thing was to make sure Beansprout wasn't about. She moved an inch or two forward and sniffed again.

No. She couldn't smell any hint of stinky feet or cowpats.

The coast was clear.

With her right shoulder, she shifted the feed pen to one side so she could get a clearer look around her. With a quick gaze, she swiftly took in the flat metal roof, the scattering of straw and seed on the ground and the one tiny solitary window that gave a glimpse out on to a brand-new field of carrots. She filed the information away in case it would be useful later.

The barn itself was crammed full of turkeys. So many turkeys they could barely even move, let alone notice her. The sight of them all bunched up together made Frankie feel a little bit sick and a lot more horrified. *Poor things.*

Some might say turkeys are peculiar creatures, with those red saggy pouches hanging from their chins and dark beady eyes. Frankie almost agreed. *Almost,* but not quite. Because she saw how their feathers fanned out at the tail, the way they hung together protectively. She looked at how they pecked almost balletically at the ground when eating their seed.

She saw –

What in Fox's name was that?!

Over in the far corner of the barn, standing upon a raised platform – almost like a stage – was the BIGGEST, **PLUMPEST,** most glorious of turkeys.

The prize turkey.

Although 'prize', Frankie knew, was the wrong way to describe him. He was not a prize. He was a magnificent and regal animal. Not just a thing to be sliced up and served with bread sauce.

Unlike the other turkeys, this particular one was not pecking seed. Instead, he was sitting in front of a dinner plate, a fancy blue chintz one that a human might use, and was feeding on fluffy roasted potatoes and a mountain of Brussels sprouts, all topped with thick, warm gravy.

'The thing is,' the turkey said in a surprisingly refined voice, 'although others might *sniff* at the odd sprout and turn their beak up at them, I for one am quite fond of the green marvels.'

'Oh, Gobble!' the other turkeys murmured in agreement. 'How right you are!'

Gobble acknowledged the other turkeys, then picked up a sprout in his beak, tossed it high in the air and swallowed it whole. Then, before Frankie could even take a breath, the turkey let out an almighty fart.

'Oh! Excuse me!' he said. It was hard to tell if he was actually blushing – but he did seem a bit bashful.

Holding her nose, Frankie eyed him warily.

Despite his size, she could easily dart out from her hole, grab him by the neck and be back in the tunnel before any of the other turkeys could say 'Squawk'.

It was what her father expected from her. It was what *all* the Foxes and the other animals expected from her. Even if she took the turkey, she told herself, it didn't mean *she* had to eat him.

But despite knowing all of that, Frankie couldn't move a single inch.

Gobble threw another sprout into his mouth before using the talons of his left foot to offer his plate to the other turkeys, who swarmed around it hungrily. 'We must remember to say thanks to the kind and gentle Farmer Bean, who once again has left us so much food.'

Kind and gentle? Frankie pricked her ears in alarm.

'How **GENEROUS** of him to feed us so handsomely,' Gobble continued. 'Just look how strong I have become!'

Gobble flexed one of his wings in demonstration. Admittedly, he did have rather large muscles for a turkey.

Frankie shook her head. *Gobble and the other turkeys had it all wrong!* They had no idea. No idea at all. There was only one reason why farmers kept turkeys close to Christmastime, and it wasn't for their company.

'After winter, once the snow thaws, I can be on my

way to find somewhere warm,' Gobble said. Using his beak, he pulled out a magazine – the kind of glossy magazine that had beautiful photos of faraway places. He opened it at a well-clawed page. 'Look at the white of those beaches! The turquoise of that sea!' Gobble let out a sigh of longing – a sigh Frankie understood all too well as she thought of her own yearning for the Great Outside. Turkeys and foxes had more in common than she thought . . .

If Frankie hadn't wanted to take Gobble before, she definitely didn't want to now.

How could she lead Gobble to his fate, knowing he had hopes and dreams just like her? There was no way she could let him be served up at the Winter Feast.

She scratched her whiskers thoughtfully. There had to be another way. All she needed was to come up with a plan.

A plan *so* cunning it would not only out-fox Beansprout and co, but out-fox her own father.

❄

'So, my Small Foxes, show me your goodies!'

Mr Fox had gathered the four of them in his study before breakfast, to see how each had fared in preparation for tomorrow's feast.

Felix held up a clutch of chickens and told an elaborate story of how he had to fight off an angry gang of squirrels to steal them.

Fraser told an even more elaborate story of single-handedly facing down a rabid stag, and then held up ten geese in one paw and, in the other, ten smoked hams.

Mr Fox nodded approvingly. 'And you, Freddie?'

Freddie held up a single flask of cider. Felix sniggered, and Freddie sneezed loudly. But then in came Mrs Fox, wheeling a trolley bursting with cider bottles.

Mr Fox performed a little jig on the spot. 'Bravo, my Smallest! **BRAVO.**'

Now it was Frankie's turn.

'And Frankie?'

'Erm. Er.' Frankie hated lying – especially to her

father. 'The thing is . . . Beansprout was there. It was just too risky.'

'Too *risky*?' Mr Fox said as if he had never heard of such a thing. He was about to continue when Mrs Fox nudged him softly in the ribs. 'Aha. Of course. A cunning fox must know the dangers of *too much* risk.'

'I will go back tomorrow morning,' said Frankie. 'I'll go before the feast and I will take Gob– um, I mean the turkey, then.'

Mr Fox gave a big paws up.

❄

'I need your help,' Frankie whispered to Bella Badger over breakfast. 'I want to get my dad a present for the Winter Feast to say thank you for everything he's done for us over the past few years.'

'Why, Frankie. That is so **KIND** of you!' said Bella, touching a striped paw to Frankie's shoulder. 'But how can I help?'

'I'd love you to make me something.'

'Another portrait, you mean?' Bella replied. 'Because I did one of him at the last feast!'

'Actually –' said Frankie, handing Bella a bag of feathers – 'I'd like you to make him a turkey. A turkey that looks as real as possible. So real that if you looked at this turkey and an actual turkey you wouldn't be able to tell the difference. You're good with your paws, Bella – if anyone can do it, you can.'

The Small Badger scratched her chin thoughtfully. 'That would be a challenge,' she said. 'But I'm sure I could do it. Anything for Mr Fox.'

'By tomorrow morning?'

Bella gulped. 'Of course.'

❄

'Rabbits?' Frankie said, cautiously pushing her head into the rabbits' chamber.

'Who goes there?'

'Frankie.'

'Frankie?' they answered. 'Frankie who?'

Frankie sighed. It wasn't the rabbits' fault they could be a bit forgetful.

'I bring news,' she said after explaining who she was. 'Good news.'

A hundred pairs of rabbit ears perked up.

'I have seen evidence of an enormous new carrot field,' said Frankie. 'And I thought you might like to go there . . .'

'Carrots? Did I just hear *carrots*?' one of them asked. The rabbits all began to chatter at once. 'Boiled carrots. Steamed carrots. Carrots fried gently in butter. Raw carrots . . .'

'YES! LOTS OF CARROTS!' yelled Frankie to make herself heard. 'As many carrots as you can eat!'

'*Where?* Where is this carrot paradise you speak of?'

'It is just beyond Bean's turkey barn where the old orchard used to be. It would mean you'd need to dig a new tunnel to link the two,' Frankie said slyly. 'But I know if anyone can dig a tunnel, it is you.'

There was just one last thing to do. The trickiest task of all. And it wasn't as if Frankie needed it for her plan to be successful. It was just a Fox's instinct.

But first she had to come up with a reason to entice Dad away from his study. Surprisingly, telling him that Mr Badger had just made a fresh batch of his legendary pork pies didn't seem to hit the mark.

'That's fine, dear,' Mr Fox said, waving her away. 'I'll eat four later.'

The next time she entered his study, she tempted him with a tankard of fresh cider. Mr Fox simply replied that he was saving himself for the feast so he could enjoy his drink all the better.

Frankie frowned. She needed to be bolder in her cunning. Out-foxing her father was proving harder than she thought. There was only one thing for it. For the third time in less than an hour, she knocked on the study door.

'*Dad?*'

'Hmmmm?' he answered, his nose buried in the Winter Feast seating plan.

'Could you tell me The Story again?' she asked. 'The story of how you outwitted the farmers with your bravery, your daring and your cleverness?'

Frankie held her breath. *Please let this work!*

She let out a sigh of relief as Mr Fox took off his spectacles and leaned back in his chair with his hind paws propped up on his desk.

'Well, if you insist, Frankie. As you remember, it all began a few years ago . . .'

As he became engrossed in the tale (and it was rather a long tale) Mr Fox eventually shifted from his desk and padded across the study to gaze at the portrait of himself hanging on the wall. It was the portrait Bella had painted of Mr Fox to commemorate the fantastic brilliance of his plan – showing him at his most dapper.

'Of course,' continued Mr Fox, 'not just any old Fox could have pulled off such a feat . . .'

And as he shared his story (again), he completely failed to notice Frankie sneaking behind his desk, carefully prising open the glass frame and stealing her father's last remaining tail strand from right under his nose.

❄

That night, Frankie hardly slept a wink.

Up before the crack of dawn, she guided the group of excited rabbits to the turkey barn.

DIG,

DIG,

DIG, they went, until they emerged into the field full of carrots that Frankie had spotted out of the barn window on her previous visit.

The new tunnel now ready, Frankie headed back to the turkeys. In her mouth, she carried the item Bella had worked on all night, while in her paw she tightly grasped her dad's tail strand. (In truth, she hoped she might not need the latter, but she knew that a clever fox had to be prepared for all eventualities.)

As she darted into the barn, the turkeys squawked in terror.

'I'm not here to hurt you!' she panted.

Gobble pursed his beak. 'Please understand that under the circumstances we might find this hard to believe.'

Frankie dropped the fake turkey from her mouth. 'Look,' she said breathlessly. 'Farmer Bean is not what you think! He's not feeding you to keep you strong. He's feeding you . . . he's feeding you because he wants to *eat* you!'

The entire barn of turkeys gasped.

'Why should we believe you?' one of them shrieked while the rest squawked in agreement. 'Foxes are the ones who kill us!'

'Remember your manners, everyone!' Gobble hushed the flock. 'Let the Small Fox speak.'

'That is what Foxes do because that is what Foxes have always done,' Frankie said. 'They eat turkeys. But I am different. I . . .'

Just as Frankie was about to say more, there was a horrible creaking noise. It was the sound of the barn door being opened. Suddenly, her nostrils were assaulted by the stench of cowpats and sweaty feet.

It was Beansprout.

Then she heard something even worse:

BOGGIS and **BUNCE** and **BEAN**
So **SMART**, so CLEVER, so CLEAN.
STRIKING in looks
And **BRILLIANT** crooks
As HANDSOME as ever you've seen.

Each of the Young Farmers was swinging a loop of thick, menacing rope between their hands. Bunce kicked a turkey out of the way and laughed loudly as it catapulted across the barn.

'Hello, turkeys,' shouted Beansprout. 'It's time for tea! *Our tea!*'

The turkeys cowered together in terror. 'Try to stay calm!' shouted Gobble before turning to Frankie. 'You were r-r-r-right.'

While the three boys were still on the far side of the barn and only focused on the turkeys right in front of their noses, she hurriedly placed the fake Gobble on the stage, burying his beak in a plate of sprouts. 'You have to come with me,' Frankie urged the real Gobble. 'It's you they want.'

With a gasp of terror, Gobble followed Frankie to the safety of the tunnel entrance, arriving in a flutter of feathers and fur.

'I didn't think they would want to eat you so soon,' Frankie said. 'It must be because their fathers are on holiday, and they think they can get away with it.'

'But once they realize I've gone, they'll take one of the other turkeys!' whispered Gobble. 'What shall we do now?'

'It's OK,' reassured Frankie. 'A fox always has a back-up plan. Gobble, how **BRAVE** do you feel?'

Gobble puffed himself up to his full majestic height.

Grinning, Frankie told him the plan. 'We just need to wait until Bunce passes by the tunnel entrance. Here he comes! On my count . . . *Now!*'

Gobble burst out of the hole with his feathers waggling. Then he leaped into the air and pecked the hat right off Bunce's head, before dropping it in a trough of dirty drinking water.

Bunce let out a grunt of alarm, dropped his rope and started scrabbling in the trough water to retrieve it. As quick as a fox, Frankie grabbed the rope and tied it round the young farmer from head to toe.

'What the . . .?'

She shoved some soggy straw in his mouth.

'One down.'

Meanwhile, Beansprout and Boggis were so focused

on reaching the stage and the fake Gobble, they hadn't noticed Bunce was now indisposed.

'Shall we do it again?' asked Gobble hopefully. 'I rather enjoyed that.'

Frankie shook her head. 'No. A trick like that only works once. We need something new. Something unexpected.'

Behind her in the tunnel, there came a loud sneeze.

'ACHOO!'

'Ah!' grinned Frankie. 'Right on time. I hope you don't mind, Gobble, but I asked my brother to help us.'

To his credit, Gobble only took a moment to adjust to the sight of another fox. Though, admittedly, it was hard to be alarmed by a fox who was sneezing.

On hearing the noise, Beansprout paused and snapped his gaze to where they were all hiding. '*Who's there?*'

'It was just one of the turkeys,' Boggis muttered impatiently. 'Come on, we have work to do. I'm starving!'

'Freddie! Here's what I need you to do,' Frankie said, whispering the plan in her brother's ear. His eyes lit up and he slithered, belly down and unseen, into the far corner of the barn.

'ACHOO!'

'There *is* somebody in here!' yelled Beansprout, spinning round to where the sneeze came from. 'Deal with it, Boggis.'

Boggis stumbled over to the corner and kicked the straw with his boots. 'Nothing here,' he muttered, before leaning down and giving the straw a few punches just to be sure. It was a mistake to lean over. Because Freddie had snuck up behind him, and with great relish, he now took a large bite out of the hapless Boggis's bum.

'Aargh!' yowled Boggis. Before he could make any more noise, Freddie tied him up, and stopped any words of protest with some soggy straw.

'Now just Beansprout to deal with,' said Frankie, rubbing her paws together. 'Any minute now . . .'

Beansprout, who had finally made it to the stage, picked up the fake turkey with a triumphant leer and then his face dropped.

'WHAT IS THIS?'

'Hey! Beansprout!' Frankie whistled. 'Over here!'

Beansprout whipped his gaze towards her, and his

face turned bright red.

For, at the entrance to the tunnel, sitting in plain sight, was Gobble, preening his feathers.

'MY TURKEY!' screeched Beansprout, and he started to run across the barn at full speed on his two gangly legs. Furiously intent on his prize, he didn't even bother to look down. Which was a very silly thing to do because he failed to spot the single strand of Mr Fox's tail that Frankie had stretched between two feeding pens to use as a tripwire.

SPLAT!

Beansprout went flying and landed with his face in a very large pile of turkey poo.

'I'm so glad I trusted my instincts and brought Dad's tail!' grinned Frankie.

Working quickly, Gobble, Freddie and Frankie tied Beansprout up with the rope.

'I think my work is done!' Frankie said and broke into a jig of joy.

It was finally time for the Winter Feast and the big Feast Room was full of animals. The table was covered with chickens and ducks, geese and hams. There were jars overflowing with cider for the grown-ups, and apple juice for the little ones plus a large mountain of carrots for the rabbits, alongside a generous portion of sprouts.

'There you are!' cried Mr Fox, leaping to his feet.

Frankie hovered in the doorway and suddenly found she couldn't speak.

'Darling,' Mr Fox's gaze softened. 'I know about you . . . not eating meat.'

'You do?'

Bella gave Frankie a guilty look.

Mr Fox sighed. 'I've been such a foolish Fox, haven't I? Insisting that you have to do things *my* way. When any Fantastic Fox knows that there is no one right way to do things.'

'Do you really mean that?' Frankie said, her heart lighting up.

Mr Fox nodded. 'Freddie told me how you made

fools of those three Turnip Brains. You have earned the right to eat vegetables for as long as you live!'

Frankie cleared her throat. 'Actually, Dad . . . I brought a guest.'

'A guest!' exclaimed Mr Fox. 'Why of course – they are most welcome!'

Gobble poked his head into the dining room. 'Bonjour!'

Mr Fox's eyes almost bulged out of their sockets. He swallowed and his Adam's apple bobbed up and down. 'A *turkey*? At our Winter Feast?' he protested. 'But . . . but not one to eat?'

'He's my friend,' said Frankie protectively. 'And foxes don't eat their friends, do they?'

The other animals around the table murmured in agreement.

'Well,' Mr Fox exclaimed, for once lost for words. 'I don't quite know what to say.'

'Luckily I do,' said Mrs Fox, offering out her paw to Gobble. 'Naturally, you must stay. A friend of Frankie's is a friend of ours. Isn't that right, Mr Fox?'

Mrs Fox nudged Mr Fox sharply in the ribs.

'Yes!' he exclaimed loudly. 'That is right . . . Please do come in.'

'Gobble,' said Gobble, entering the room.

Mr Fox pulled out his own seat at the head of the table. 'In fact, you can be our guest of honour!'

'Don't mind if I do,' said Gobble, hurrying to the offered chair. He reached out one wing and picked up a sprout. 'Don't mind if I do at all.'

Mrs Fox beamed, and the rabbits, hidden behind their mountain of carrots, cried out, 'Speech! Speech! Speech!'

Mr Fox rose to his feet and opened his mouth. But before any words came out, he paused. He glanced across at Gobble and smiled as he motioned for the turkey to do the honours.

Gobble blushed (a little), then rose to his feet and said, 'I am not one for talking much. But I just want to say one thing and it is this.' He turned to Mr and Mrs Fox. **'YOUR DAUGHTER IS A FANTASTIC FOX.'**

Everyone clapped and cheered for several minutes.

But no one clapped, or cheered, as loudly as Mr Fox. Then they all sat down to eat, and for a while there was only the sound of crunching, chewing, the occasional belch and, every so often, a fart from an embarrassed Gobble.

Halfway through the meal, Frankie stood up tentatively. 'There is *one* more thing.' She cleared her throat. 'My father – a very clever and wise fox – once said that if we leave our den we risk being killed. And it is true. We animals have many enemies and the biggest enemies of all live right outside our door.'

'Right outside the door!' shouted the rabbits in unison.

'But *also* right outside this door is a whole new world,' Frankie continued, her voice slightly louder now. 'A world of **WONDER!** A world of **ADVENTURE!** A world not without risks, admittedly. But . . . I also know my father would be the first to say, that you "enter if you dare". And Dad –' she turned to her father – 'I *do* dare.'

Mr Fox watched his daughter pensively. For deep down he was a very clever fox, and he knew exactly what she was about to say next.

'I'd like to leave the den,' Frankie said in a rush of excitement. 'I'd like to go outside and explore the world!'

All the animals fell into a hush. A couple of the moles even gasped. Mrs Fox watched her husband with a worried frown.

Mr Fox blinked nervously a couple of times. 'This is all rather a lot to deal with in one evening,' he murmured.

Frankie held her breath.

'But . . .' Mr Fox continued slowly. 'who am I to stop you from following your **DREAMS?'**

For a moment, Frankie hardly dared speak. 'You mean I can go?!'

Mr Fox had the largest of lumps in his throat and found he could only nod.

'Oh, Dad!' Frankie threw her arms round her father and hugged him tight. And then tighter still. Then she shyly held out the tail strand. 'I . . . borrowed this.'

Mr Fox smiled. 'It is yours to keep,' he said with a twinkle in his eye. 'After all, it is not every day a fox gets outwitted. Especially not a fox like me! Take it with you on your travels, and may it bring good luck.'

There were many more hugs and kisses and nose rubs. But finally, it was time to leave. Goodbyes were best done quickly, Frankie soon discovered, so rather than hang about too long, she took Gobble by the wing and the pair of them headed back to the barn.

After filling in the tunnel that led to the turkey shed so all Fox tracks were covered, there was just one last job to do.

The three Young Farmers were still tied up on the floor where they had been left for their fathers to find when they returned home from their holidays.

'We'll get you back for this!' Beansprout said, spitting out some dirty straw. 'Just you see!'

But there was nothing any of them could do.

Frankie guided the way through the newly dug escape tunnel. They emerged just outside the orchard, and for a minute not a single squawk was uttered. The turkeys simply gazed at the **GINORMOUS** blue sky that glistened overhead. It was a sight none of them had ever seen before.

After the last turkey was finally free, Frankie closed up the tunnel. Then Gobble, using all his strength, blocked the barn door with a large block of wood.

'That should do it,' he said. And then, with his travel magazine tucked under one wing, he turned to Frankie. 'Shall we?'

Frankie took a deep, glorious breath of the open air. It was everything she'd ever wanted – and more. Together, they went into the world to explore all its wonder and beauty.

And so far as I know, they are still **EXPLORING.**

Books by Roald Dahl

THE BFG

BILLY AND THE MINPINS

BOY: TALES OF CHILDHOOD

BOY and GOING SOLO

CHARLIE AND THE CHOCOLATE FACTORY

CHARLIE AND THE GREAT GLASS ELEVATOR

THE COMPLETE ADVENTURES OF CHARLIE AND MR WILLY WONKA

DANNY THE CHAMPION OF THE WORLD

THE ENORMOUS CROCODILE

ESIO TROT

FANTASTIC MR FOX

GEORGE'S MARVELLOUS MEDICINE

THE GIRAFFE AND THE PELLY AND ME

GOING SOLO

JAMES AND THE GIANT PEACH

THE MAGIC FINGER

MATILDA

THE TWITS

THE WITCHES

To discover more books, and find out more about Roald Dahl, please visit the website at **www.roalddahl.com**